LILAC MILLS

The Tanglewood Tea Shop

CANELO

First published in the United Kingdom in 2019 by Canelo

This edition published in the United Kingdom in 2019 by

Canelo Digital Publishing Limited
57 Shepherds Lane
Beaconsfield, Bucks HP9 2DU
United Kingdom

A CIP catalogue record for this book is available from the British Library.

Print ISBN 978 1 788 63534 9
Ebook ISBN 978 1 788 63437 3

Look for more great books at www.canelo.co

Printed and bound in Great Britain by Clays Ltd, Elcograf S.p.A.

Chapter 1

Stevie didn't do black. It didn't suit her. She was far more comfortable in white – chef's whites to be exact – but she could hardly have worn *those* to a funeral, could she? Although she suspected Great Aunt Peg would have seen the funny side if Stevie had worn them.

Tears threatened, and she tried to push them away as Peg's last words drifted into her head.

'Don't be sad, my dear,' Peggy had said. 'I'm ready to go. I've had a long life and a good one. Life is for living *and* for dying, Stevie – you don't get one without the other.'

'Shh,' Stevie replied. 'You're not going to die, I won't let you.'

Her aunt had wheezed out a feeble laugh. 'You're not going to get any choice in it, my lovely. Now, don't mope and do me a favour?'

Stevie, with tears streaming down her face, said, 'Anything.'

'You only get one chance at it, so live it your way, otherwise I'll come back and haunt you.'

After that, Peg seemed to sink into herself and slowly faded away.

How could I not be sad? Stevie wondered, for the twentieth time since that awful night. Peg had been like a grandmother to her, much more than her own had ever been. It was a pity her mother didn't see it the same way though, she thought, stealing a glance out of the corner of her eye at the woman standing next to her. No one could accuse her mother of being sad, more like bored if she were honest. Hazel regarded Peggy's funeral as a duty, nothing more, something which had to be got through and then moved on from.

For a moment, she quite disliked her mother. And right now, she wasn't too keen on her sister, either. None of her relatives wanted to be here (not that anyone ever actually *wanted* to be at a funeral) but those two, in particular, hadn't felt any real need to pay their respects, and she suspected they were only doing so for the sake of appearances. After all, neither of them had bothered with Aunt Peg while she was alive, so why Stevie expected them to behave any differently now the old lady was dead, was beyond her.

Karen leaned into her side and Stevie gave her a watery smile. At least her friend had cared for Peg, and she hadn't even been related to the old lady.

Karen whispered, 'It's a beautiful service. You've done your Aunt Peg proud.'

This time a tear did fall. She *had* done her aunt proud, hadn't she? The nursing home where Peg had lived for the final six months of her life had recommended holding the service at the chapel next door to them. Stevie had wondered more than once if the care home had been built next to the chapel for the express purpose of providing the reverend with a steady stream of clients. But Stevie had chosen the little church near her aunt's old house. The old building tended to get lost among the blocks of flats and offices, but she knew Peggy used to go there once in a while, and always at Christmas. Besides, there were still one or two people who remembered the old lady and had wanted to attend her funeral without having to trek halfway across London to do so.

All her mother had done was to gripe about the cost of the funeral cars, which Stevie found hard to understand – they weren't exactly being charged by the mile, and Hazel wasn't paying for them out of her own pocket. Peg had left enough money to cover the cost of her funeral. Her mother was at least being consistent, Stevie conceded, because she had grizzled about the cost of everything, especially the flowers. Even now, Stevie swore her mother was giving the simple, yet effective withering look. But Stevie had been adamant – Peggy had loved flowers, and so she was determined not to skimp. It was the only thing she could do for her aunt, except for scattering her ashes. But she didn't want to think about that right now...

'Here.' Her mother thrust a hankie into her hand. 'Try to stop snivelling.'

Stevie took it with a scowl, and Karen slipped her arm around Stevie's shoulders as the service drew to a close and the final hymn was sung. Lord, but Stevie was going to miss the curmudgeonly old lady dreadfully. What else was she going to do on a Saturday morning? Ever since Peg had been forced to live in the nursing home due to her increasingly poor health and frailty, Stevie had visited on Saturdays. She always took the old lady a treat or two, and renewed her library book (she only had one out at a time, because with her eyesight failing Peg had been forced to rely on others to read to her), and Stevie had always given her a bunch of flowers.

At least I don't have her house to worry about, Stevie thought. It had been bad enough having to sort out the few possessions which Peg had taken with her to the nursing home. To be fair to the old woman, when Peg understood she could no longer care for herself (Stevie had offered to move in with her, but Peggy was adamant she didn't want Stevie nursing her), she had sorted out her own affairs with remarkable efficiency.

It was one of the things Stevie had loved about Peggy – her independence. If the old woman could do it herself, then she did. 'I don't want to be a burden,' was her favourite expression, and it used to exasperate Stevie no end. As if Aunt Peg could ever be a burden!

It was just a pity the rest of her family hadn't viewed Peg in the same way. Neither her mother nor her sister seemed to have had any time for the old woman. Admittedly, her mother used to invite her round for lunch at Christmas and Easter, but that was about it – token gestures, nothing more. And since Peggy had moved to the nursing home, her mother had only visited once and Fern hadn't visited at all as far as Stevie was aware. In fact, her sister seemed to have completely forgotten their great-aunt existed.

There – it was over. Stevie had been dreading this day ever since the nursing manager had called to say Aunt Peg was slipping away and if she wanted to say goodbye she needed to get there quickly. And Stevie had been glad to have been there at the end, holding her aunt's hand and telling her she loved her as the old woman took her last breath.

The only regret she had, was that she hadn't been able to do more. What with working the unreasonable hours chefs were expected to put in, and the restaurant being on the other side of London, it had been hard to get to see Peg more often than each Saturday.

At least Peggy knew how much Stevie loved her, and she took comfort from that.

Chapter 2

'How much?' It came out as a strangled yell as Stevie spluttered tea down her chin. She dropped the cup back into its saucer with a loud clatter. 'You can't be serious!' Her eyes widened in shock. 'Can you?'

The rather elderly gentleman staring at her over his equally elderly desk nodded once, his eyes twinkling. Was it because he was having her on, or because he enjoyed imparting good news? She desperately hoped it was the latter. Please let it be true!

'You're sure you've got the name right? Peggy Langtree?' Stevie asked.

Another nod.

'But she didn't have any money – only enough to bury her. She used to keep her "funeral funds", as she called them, in a vase on the windowsill.' Stevie smiled fondly.

'She clearly had more than you thought,' the solicitor pointed out, dryly.

'What about Mum and Fern? Don't tell me she left the same amount to them, too?' Stevie gulped at the thought. 'She must have been loaded.'

Mr Gantly shuffled forward in his chair and steepled his hands together, elbows on his desk, a faint whiff of mothballs emanating from his direction.

'No,' he said solemnly, after a dignified silence.

Stevie waited for him to elaborate, but he made no move to speak again.

After tapping her fingers on the desk and swinging her crossed leg, she asked, '*No*, she didn't leave the same amount to Mum and Fern, or *no* she wasn't loaded?'

'The first option. She left differing amounts to your mother and your sister.'

'Oh, I see,' Stevie thought, still in shock, but thankful Aunt Peg had left them something, too. Whoever would have thought the old lady was worth so much?

The solicitor cleared his throat and the loose skin on his neck draped even further down over his knotted tie. Just how old *was* he? He reminded Stevie of a tortoise she'd had as a child. The reptile's extendable neck had been an endless source of interest as she poked at his head each time the wizened creature had risked emerging from his shell, only for him to pull it in again with as much speed as he could muster. Her mother had told her that Ralph, as Stevie had oddly called him, had run away. Crawled slowly was more like it, Stevie had thought at the time, but she got the picture. She didn't blame him. She'd have crawled away too, if she'd been in his shoes. Or shell.

A semi-hysterical giggle bubbled to the surface. She pushed it back down, resisting the urge to poke Mr Gantly on the nose to see what *his* head would do. She had visions of him retracting it down inside his shirt collar and popping it back out again.

Aware her mind was wandering (it must be the shock) she wrenched her attention back to the ancient solicitor, to find him patiently waiting, his chin still resting on the tips of his fingers, a faint smile on his face. She flushed, staring at him like a naughty schoolgirl facing the headmaster; a feeling she had once known very well indeed. The silence continued for a while until she realised he was waiting for her to ask a question. Not any old question – *the* question.

Stevie asked it. 'How much did she leave Mum and Fern?'

The solicitor shook his head sadly. 'Not nearly as much as you. One thousand pounds. Each.'

'Bloody hell!' Stevie's hand flew to her mouth. 'Er, sorry,' she added, wondering how soon her family would demand their share of her not-inconsiderable booty. She hadn't meant to swear, but he had said "each" as if it would make things any better. Her mother and sister would go ballistic. She'd have to split her inheritance precisely three ways else she'd never hear the end of it. Damn and blast. Not that she was greedy or anything, but in the current circumstances she could do with the money.

'It's so much to take in,' she said, trying to excuse her bad manners.

'No doubt,' Mr Gantly agreed calmly, picking up his glasses and wiggling the arms behind his large hairy ears. He flicked a page or two.

'Let me reiterate, in the interest of clarity,' he said. 'Peggy Langtree left you two hundred and sixty-three thousand and twenty-one pounds, and fifty-seven pence. Give or take,' he added. 'Mrs Taylor and Mrs Chalk were both left one thousand pounds. And if you try to give any of your inheritance to Mrs Taylor or to Mrs Chalk, then the cats' home gets it,' the solicitor added succinctly.

'But, but… there'll be hell to pay,' Stevie wailed. 'Why did Aunt Peggy do this to Mum and Fern?'

Mr Gantly reached across the desk and patted her hand. 'I'm not privy to the late Peggy Langtree's reasons, but perhaps she thought you deserve it more than they do. Or maybe she thought you might benefit from it more.'

'She's not wrong,' Stevie said. 'I've just lost my job.'

'I'm so sorry. Your inheritance has come at an auspicious time, then,' Mr Gantly said.

'I was knocked down by a London double-decker bus. A red one.'

The old man's lips twitched.

'Yeah, yeah, I've heard all the jokes about getting run over by a bus,' Stevie said.

'Were you hurt?'

'I broke my leg.'

'That was lucky.'

'Lucky? Huh! I don't call being run over "lucky". There was nothing "lucky" about it.' Stevie knew she was ranting but couldn't seem to stop herself. It must be the shock still.

'I mean, it could have been much worse,' Mr Gantly added. He looked at his watch.

'No, it couldn't! I lost my job.' Her eyes filled with tears and she scrabbled around in her enormous handbag for a tissue, her fingers grasping a roll of toilet paper in lieu of a packet of the proper stuff. It would have to do.

Mr Gantly frowned when she broke a length off, and silently held out the box of tissues sitting on his desk. She took a couple – softer on the nose than loo roll. Although, with over two hundred and fifty thousand pounds in the bank, she could now afford to treat herself to a box or two of tissues.

She blew her nose. 'Corky said he had to let me go.'

'Corky?'

'Corky Middleton. You must have heard of him?'

Mr Gantly shook his head. The soft folds of flesh under his chin wobbled and shook.

'Corky Middleton, owns The Melon, always on the telly?' Stevie persisted, ignoring the solicitor's second, more obvious look at the time.

'I'm afraid not,' he said, rising creakily from his chair. With considerable effort, he got to his feet, wobbling unsteadily for a few seconds.

'It's only the most famous Michelin star restaurant in London,' she said, twisting in her seat to watch the old man walk to the door. 'When I landed the job, I was stupid enough to think I'd finally got it made. Oh, that must have made the gods laugh,' she added bitterly. 'I'm a pastry chef and a damned good one too, but bloody Corky sacked me just because I broke my leg!' Stevie made no move to leave.

'I'm sorry, but I have another appointment.' The solicitor opened the door, then tutted. 'Forgive me, but I nearly forgot.' He trundled back to his desk and rifled through the various items lying on it, peeking under envelopes and lifting up flyers advertising pizza delivery. Stevie wasn't sure whether it was his skin making the dry, rustling noise or the assorted papers.

'I really miss her,' Stevie said, blowing her nose again on the now-sodden clump of tissues. 'I'm sorry, I don't mean to cry, but I just can't help it. It creeps up on you, you know?' She paused, screwing up her nose, and peered at him over the tissue. 'Are you sure she left it to me?'

'Quite sure. Here.' He found what he was looking for and handed it to her.

She stared at the pristine cream envelope in her palm. 'Is this her last will and testament?' she asked, baffled. Surely he needed to hold on to that?

'It's a letter from your aunt.'

'Ah. Of course. It would be.' Stevie was unsurprised. 'Did she write it before or after she died?' For a minute there, Stevie had the insane thought her aunt might have kept her threat to haunt her.

Mr Gantly raised his tufty eyebrows.

'Sorry,' Stevie muttered, coming to her senses. 'Thank you for your help.'

'I'll have the documents ready for you to sign in a few days and we can transfer the money to your account,' he said.

All at once the solicitor was pure business and Stevie was dismissed. Clutching the letter to her chest she got to her feet, but before she left, she turned back to look at the elderly man in his dusty old office and hesitated.

'Yes,' he confirmed, knowing what she was about to ask. 'Two hundred and sixty-three thousand and twenty-one pounds, and fifty-seven pence. Enjoy.'

Chapter 3

My dear Stevie, the letter began. *I'm dead.*

I know, Stevie thought sadly. I went to your funeral.

You're getting nearly all my money.

I know that, too. The solicitor told me, but what he didn't say was why, she mused.

You're wondering why.

Got it in one, Aunt Peg. You always were a canny old lady. Stevie smiled, recalling her favourite image of her – long white hair, purple lace-up boots, bright pink denim jacket (where on earth had she managed to get that from?) and pushing a supermarket trolley with a stuffed cat in the child's seat. Bless her, but she had been rather eccentric. Or mad, depending on one's point of view.

It's because you deserve it, and you need it, too. Now, I know what you're thinking, that money won't make you happy, but at least it might just make things easier for you. All I ask is that you spend it wisely and don't fritter it away on baubles and geegaws.

Geegaws? What the hell are geegaws? And who said money can't make you happy? People with loads of it, that's who.

Do something with it you would never have the chance to do otherwise.

Yeah, like backpacking around Australia, or spending three months in the Caribbean, or buying a BMW convertible, or… the possibilities were endless. For the first time since the funeral, excitement rolled in her stomach, sending little flutters up through her chest.

Oi! I know exactly what is going through your mind and I call that sort of thing frittering. You'll have nothing to show for the money once you've spent it.

Stevie looked up from the letter with a sigh. Riiiight… as if a whole load of drunken memories, a new car, a great tan and a designer wardrobe were nothing. Hey, perhaps Steve will be interested in me again, she thought, now she didn't have a reason to be miserable anymore. Steve and Stevie – she'd always thought they'd sounded like a drag act.

She returned to the letter with a mixture of reluctance and a sense of comfort. Reading it made her feel as though her dead aunt was in her head and could read her thoughts.

And don't think about courting that Stephen boy again, either. He's in your past and that's where he should stay.

Courting? What kind of a word was that? Unless it was an old-fashioned way of saying two people were getting friendly between the sheets.

Please, use the money to follow your heart. I know you'll spend it well. I have total faith in you. You always were my favourite. I know I shouldn't say it, but it's true. I loved you like a granddaughter and I always will, wherever I am now.

Your loving aunt – Peggy.

The last paragraph was Stevie's undoing. She put the letter down, leaned forward, folded her arms on the table and sobbed her heart out.

Despite feeling the old lady had one hand on her shoulder, she knew her aunt had truly gone.

Her sobs turning to sniffles and snuffles, Stevie sent her aunt silent thanks for her generosity and wondered how she was going to explain her inheritance to Hazel. She was going to have to tell her mother what Peg had done, and she wasn't looking forward to it one bit.

Hazel Taylor wasn't a bad woman, she just hadn't approved of her aunt. Peg had never married, had been as mad as a box of frogs and had lived in a houseful of cats right up until the day she'd been forced to relocate to Stanley Road Residential Home. Oh, and she'd had a really odd dress sense.

Stevie's mother had totally disapproved of her aunt's eccentricity, and she often took a black delight in recounting stories that Peg had variously been a madam in a strip-club; a cat-burglar when she worked in a posh hotel; a nude model for an under-the-counter magazine. Stevie had once asked her mother what that meant, and Hazel had wrinkled her nose in disgust and had hissed 'porn', before refusing to elaborate any further.

And Hazel had consistently compared the rather flighty Stevie to Peggy (not the porn bit, obviously, or the cat burglar part), which made Stevie think that if her mother had a favourite child, then it certainly wasn't her. In some ways, Stevie couldn't blame her. Fern, four years older, had always been a diva of a child, and had appeared to resent having to share their mother with the squalling, red-faced infant that was Stevie. Apparently, Fern had been a model baby, sleeping through the night from day one, never crying, and was so good that Hazel never even knew she was there.

Her mother had known *Stevie* was there, all right! Stevie, according to her mother, had hardly ever slept and had cried all the time for no discernible reason. She had driven her mother to her wit's end, as she had frequently told the young Stevie.

Fern was charmed, too. Very charmed. The kind of charmed which meant if her sister bought a raffle ticket, she'd win first prize. The kind of charmed that led Fern to have a small lottery win on the one and only time she'd played it; to get PPI cashback, although she'd never taken out a loan in her life; to receive a nice compensation claim for sexual discrimination when it transpired her male equivalent at work was being paid more than her. That kind of charmed.

It wasn't all about money, either. The two girls were total opposites. Fern had loved school, Stevie had hated it. Fern had played with dolls, Stevie had climbed trees and more often than not had fallen out of them and broken something. Fern was Mary in the reception class Nativity play, Stevie was one half of the donkey – the not-so-nice half with her nose up Nigel Hemming's farty bottom, and the donkey had to be quickly guided off the makeshift stage when Stevie persisted in blowing loud raspberries and waggling the donkey's tail. Fern had handed her homework in on time without fail, Stevie used to claim the dog had eaten hers ("but, you don't have a dog!"). The list went on.

As the two girls grew older, Stevie's sister was clear about what she wanted to do: get married and have babies. Fern very quickly found husband material in the form of Derrick Chalk ("all my friends called me Dezza" – purleeze!), had the traditional white wedding with Stevie doing a guest performance as a pink meringue, and proceeded to produce two daughters with the minimum amount of fuss. The eldest was named Jade, and the next little Chalk to put in an appearance was called Macey, and apparently both were just as perfect as their mother.

And there was Stevie – jobless, boyfriendless and homeless. Jobless because of that stupid bus, homeless because she was jobless and couldn't afford her share of the rent on the astronomically pricey flat which she had shared with four other people, and boyfriendless because Steve was an arse. So Stevie had temporarily moved back in with her mother until she found another job.

Actually, it was about time she started looking for a job, now her leg was almost mended because, let's face it, two hundred and fifty thousand pounds wasn't an amount one could live off for the rest of one's life, was it? And once she'd secured herself a job, then the next thing she needed to do was to find a place of her own to live.

Stevie, pleased with her sensible decision-making, set about job-hunting. It was only later, when she'd folded the precious letter to put it in her keepsake box where she kept her memory things, like the tiny fossil she had found one year on holiday in Cornwall, a stolen lock of Steve's hair, and her very first Valentine's card (no need to tell anyone she'd been twenty-three at the time), she noticed the PS on the back.

PS Don't be sad. I haven't left you, even though it may feel like it. And don't forget, there are more things in heaven and earth…

Now, what was the old bat rambling on about? Stevie wondered fondly, and put the letter carefully away, a sad smile lighting her face.

Chapter 4

Karen had been Stevie's best friend since even before infants' school. She was petite, dark-haired, pretty, great fun to be with and she told it like it was. No flattery or falsehoods from her. If Stevie looked like poo in a dress, Karen told her. If Stevie inherited two hundred and sixty-three thousand pounds and didn't know what to do with it, Karen would have an opinion on that, too.

'You lucky, lucky, lucky cow,' Karen said, taking a large slug of wine.

Stevie waited with bated breath for the advice which would change her life. Instead, all she got was another chorus of "lucky, lucky, cow", and an "I hate you" to finish it off.

'What am I going to do with it?' Stevie whined.

'Oh, come on! I can't believe you haven't got any ideas of your own. You're young, free, pretty – go spend! Enjoy!'

'That's what the solicitor told me,' Stevie said gloomily.

'If it's going to cause you this much grief, give it all to your mum. She probably doesn't deserve it, but she *has* had to put up with you living back at home.'

'It's not my fault I got run over by a bus, then lost my job and my boyfriend!' Stevie protested, her cheeks turning pink with indignation.

Stevie saw Karen bite her lip to prevent herself from laughing and she narrowed her eyes at her friend. Finishing her drink, Stevie fished in her jeans pocket.

'Fancy another?' she asked. 'I guess the drinks are on me.'

'Too right, they are.' Karen handed her glass to Stevie. 'Make mine a large one.'

While Stevie waited for her pint to be poured (no fancy wine for her), she stared at the contents of her purse, feeling like one of those businessmen who were rich on paper but didn't have a penny to his name. She scraped together the ten pounds fifty the barman was holding his hand out for, counting the change into his waiting palm. If she and Karen stayed for another round, she'd have to ask if he'd take a debit card. Then she'd have the anxious wait to see if her bank would accept the transaction because Peggy's funds hadn't gone in yet.

'You might want to get your hair done for starters,' Karen suggested when Stevie returned with the drinks.

'Why? What's wrong with it?'

'You haven't had it cut since you were about twelve.'

'I like it long.'

'You look like you've been dragged through a hedge backwards, as my mum says.'

Stevie bent down, rooted around in her gigantic bag and came up with a band and proceeded to comb her fingers through her hair until she'd brought it under some control. 'Better?' she asked, turning her head this way and that to showcase her ponytail.

Karen huffed. 'Haircut.'

'But—'

'No buts. You should get it cut to about there.' Karen poked Stevie in the chest, just above her boob.

'Ow!'

'And have some highlights or lowlights, or something, put in so it doesn't look so *carroty*.'

'*Carroty*,' Stevie repeated, deadpan. OK, so she'd been called "carrot-top" all through school, but the colour had toned down a bit since then. Hadn't it?

'And invest in some decent straighteners,' Karen added. 'You'd be surprised how much sexier you'd look without the fr— curls.'

'You were about to say "frizz", weren't you?' Stevie demanded, and Karen blushed.

'Look, chicken, I'm only saying this now because you have the money to do something about it. It costs a fortune to look this good.' Karen tossed her shiny dark tresses, and Stevie had an urge to find a pair of scissors. 'You couldn't afford it before. Hell, you could hardly afford to pay the rent with that good-for-nothing boyfriend sponging off you all the time. Treat yourself. You're worth it.'

Stevie knew Karen was only trying to help, but it did rankle a bit that she was only now telling her that her hair was a mess. She could have said something sooner and not let her waltz around thinking she looked OK.

'Anything else?' she asked, through gritted teeth.

'Now you come to mention it, how about some new clothes? You've got a gorgeous figure. You should show it off more.'

'There's never really been much opportunity,' Stevie protested. 'I'm usually in chef's whites.'

'Look at you – curves in all the right places, and plenty of them. It's criminal to keep them covered up.' Karen pointedly looked Stevie up and down.

Stevie glanced at her jeans and baggy sweatshirt. 'These were the only clean things I could find.'

'Precisely! Ergo, you need new clothes.'

'*Ergo?* Eh? Aunt Peg warned me not to fritter it away,' Stevie said.

'Spending some on yourself isn't frittering. It's an investment in your future.'

'What future?' She lived from day to day, just glad to get through the hours between breakfast and bed without any major mishap, and had little thought for the future, although she did have dreams to own her own restaurant one day and to be famous on TV, like Corky Middleton.

'Your—' Karen stopped and gasped. 'I've got an idea!'

Stevie looked anything but impressed.

'Don't you want to hear what it is?' Karen demanded.

'Go on, then. If you must,' came the ungracious reply.

Karen ignored Stevie's tone of voice. 'Why don't you get your own place?' she cried, with the air of someone who had just pulled a rabbit out of a hat and shouted, 'Ta da!'

'What? Move out of Mum's? I intend to, but not right now, not until I get another job, and anyway I get my washing and ironing done, sometimes; I don't have to pay much rent; I—'

'Shut up a minute,' Karen interrupted. 'I mean, run your own restaurant.'

'Oh yeah, and what mug is going to let me do that? You've got to work your way up the ladder and I'm only about halfway there. And it doesn't look like I'll get much further,' she added. Then she said brightly, 'There's always McDonald's. Do you want fries with that?' she chirped.

Karen shook her head in exasperation and leaned forward. 'That's. What. You. Use. The. Money. For,' she stated, very, very slowly as if talking to a small child.

The penny finally dropped.

'Oh? *Oh!* I see what you mean. Yes! Yes, I could, couldn't I? Oh. No. No, I couldn't. It would take much more than two hundred and sixty-three thousand to get a restaurant up and running, not to mention I've got no business experience, and I'd be dreadful at all that hiring and firing stuff, and where would it be? I couldn't afford a shed in London, and I would have to spend lots of time practising main courses and things, because for ages now I've mostly done pastry work and...'

'Shush,' Karen said, firmly.

Stevie did as she was told for once.

'Think smaller,' Karen instructed, then sat back expectantly.

'What do you mean "smaller"? Fish and chip shop? Mobile burger van? Café? Tea shop? Tea shop... *Tea shop!* That's it!' Stevie leapt to her feet, her eyes shining, and flung out her arms.

'Yes! Yes!' she cried, twirling around in sudden inspiration, unaware the whole pub was silent and motionless, staring at her curiously. Karen barely had the chance to respond to a comment from the table next to theirs ('Is she having some kind of fit?') before the inevitable happened and Stevie knocked a pint glass out of the hand of a man standing behind her, who had been happily minding his own business. She sent it sailing a good ten feet, arcing into

21

the air and spraying everyone beneath with pale golden liquid.

'Oh, goodness. Sorry, sorry.' Stevie fished around in her bag and pulled a length of loo roll out, oblivious to the irritated expression on the face of the man whose drink she had sent into low orbit. She dabbed ineffectually at his wet head with the, by now, extremely soggy bit of tissue.

'Come on. It's time we left.' Karen grabbed her by the upper arm and dragged her through the door, Stevie profusely apologising all the while, and deposited her out on to the street.

Stevie fell silent and stared at Karen. Karen stared impassively back.

'So, was it a good idea?' Karen asked eventually.

'It might be. I'm not sure,' Stevie replied, biting her lip, then she grinned impishly. 'Yeah. It's brilliant.'

Karen gave her a playful smack across the head. 'Come on. You've got some planning to do.' She strode off up the road.

Stevie followed behind, dancing along the pavement, full of excitement, and trying not to step on the cracks. Just in case. Because she still had the unfortunate task of telling her mother and her sister about her inheritance – and their lack of one. And she still wasn't looking forward to it one bit.

Chapter 5

'Mum?' Stevie sidled into the kitchen, aware of the nervous whine in her voice but unable to do anything about it.

'What, Stevie? I'm in a hurry.'

'You're going to meet the solicitor. I know.'

'I'm surprised he didn't want to see you too, considering he asked for me and Fern to be there.'

'Um… yeah… about that…'

'Of course, I don't blame your aunt. No one wants to see their hard-earned money being frittered away.'

There was that word again, *frittered*.

'Never mind, I won't see you starve,' her mother added, generously. 'Now, what is it you wanted, because I'm going to be late.'

Stevie debated not telling her mother at all and letting Mr Gantly do her dirty work for her, but she had a feeling she might seriously regret it if she allowed her mother to be blindsided, so she gathered what little courage she could find and blurted it out. 'She left it all to me.'

'Left what, dear? Where, oh where, did I put my keys?' Hazel scanned the kitchen worktops while patting at her raincoat pockets.

'The money. Aunt Peg. She left it to me.'

'What are you talking about, dear? Be a love and see if you can find my keys. I could have sworn I left them in here. I came home from my flower arranging class last night, took my coat off, put my— Ah! I know. The bathroom. I had to do a mad dash for the loo. I must have left them in there. Would you run and fetch them for me?'

'OK, but listen, Mum. I went to the solicitor, yesterday. He wanted to see me. Aunt Peg left me practically everything.' And with that, Stevie turned tail and made a dash for the stairs, racing into the bathroom and slamming the door behind her.

Her mother's keys were sitting on the side of the wash hand basin. Stevie scooped them up, cradling them to her chest as she listened for the fallout.

Silence.

After a minute or two, she risked opening the door and poked her head out.

Still silence.

All was quiet as she tiptoed across the landing, and the calm held as she crept down the stairs.

Her mother was waiting expectantly, exactly where Stevie had left her. 'I was just about to send a search party. I thought you must have fallen in. My keys?' Hazel held out her hand.

'Did you hear what I said, Mum?'

'Hmm?' Her mother was now digging through her bag, looking for something else.

'About Aunt Peg's will?' Stevie persisted.

'What about it?'

'That she left nearly all of it to me.'

'Very funny, dear.' Hazel clearly wasn't taking this seriously.

'Mum!' Stevie took a couple of steps forward until she stood directly in front of the older woman. 'It's true. Mr Gantly asked to see me yesterday.'

Hazel narrowed her eyes. 'You didn't say anything.'

'I assumed you'd be there too, and when you weren't and he told me Aunt Peg had left it all to me, except for a thousand pounds each for you and Fern, I sort of didn't know what to say.'

'I bet you didn't! I hope you told him Aunt Peg was being unfair and it should be split three ways.'

You've changed your tune, Stevie thought. A minute ago, when you assumed Aunt Peggy's inheritance was going to be divided between you and Fern, you didn't mention anything about a three-way split then, did you? she continued to herself.

'I did,' Stevie sighed. 'No dice.'

'What do you mean, "no dice"?'

'If I try to give any money to you or Fern, then it all goes to the cats' home, Mr Gantly said.'

'Oh, what does he know? It's *your* money, you can give it to who you like.'

'Apparently, not.'

Hazel put her hands on her hips, her mouth drawn in a straight line. 'Why you?' she demanded.

Stevie shrugged. There was no way she was going to divulge the contents of the letter she'd received from Aunt Peg or confide in her mother her own educated guess that it might be because Stevie had actually cared for the old lady, and her mother hadn't given two hoots.

'You get it all, then, do you?' Hazel demanded, eyeing her narrowly.

Stevie shrugged again, not wanting to get into an argument, but not seeing how she could avoid one, either.

'And your sister and I get a thousand each?' her mother continued, tapping her foot.

Stevie nodded once.

'The ungrateful old bat!' Hazel shook her head. 'After everything I did for her.'

Stevie was about to ask exactly what it was that her mother had done for Aunt Peg, but she wisely kept her mouth closed.

'I wonder what Fern will have to say about this,' Hazel continued. 'She wants an extension.'

Fern always wants something, Stevie thought. Never happy with what she had and forever searching for the next quick fix – if I have a top of the range hot tub, I'll be happy; if I could just get my hands on that new Smeg fridge which does practically everything, including the ironing, I'll be happy; and so on. But her new acquisitions never did make Fern happy. As soon as she got them, she immediately forgot about the whatever-it-was she had so desperately wanted and moved onto some new thing which she simply had to have. Over the last couple of months, she'd had the garden landscaped, and now she was talking about building an extension.

'Fern can say what she likes,' Stevie said. 'It won't change anything. She still only gets a thousand pounds.'

That'll buy her a couple of tons of bricks, Stevie thought, uncharitably.

'She won't be happy,' her mother predicted. 'I'm not happy about it, either. I'm glad you warned me before I saw this Gantly person. I'm going to contest it, you know.'

Stevie had guessed as much.

'I don't know why she left it all to you. It's not as if you'll do anything useful with it,' her mother continued.

It stung to think her mother had so little faith in her. 'You're wrong there,' she said. 'I'm going to open my own place.'

Hazel's eyes narrowed even further until they were nothing but slits. 'Exactly how much did Peg leave you? You never actually said.'

No, she hadn't, had she? Stevie was reluctant to say now, but she had little choice. Either Mr Gantly would tell her mother, or Hazel would find out by other means. It might be better to simply get this over with.

'Two hundred and sixty-three thousand pounds,' Stevie said, in a small voice.

Hazel slapped a hand to her chest and gasped, her eyes bulging out of their sockets. 'She never had that much!'

'She did,' Stevie said, mournfully, wishing she'd never heard of Mr Gantly or the money. It was going to cause more trouble than it was worth. Now that her mother was aware of the full extent of the inheritance, she'd never let it lie.

And Stevie was right, as she discovered later, when her mother returned from her less-than-satisfactory meeting with the solicitor with Fern in tow.

'I can't believe you've had all this land in your lap,' Fern announced, as soon as she spied Stevie. 'It's not as if you've had to work for it, is it?'

Stevie slammed a lump of dough down on the worktop and kneaded it furiously. Fern, having done hardly a scrap of work in her life, was a fine one to talk. At least Stevie had worked every day since she left school, often for a pittance, except when she'd broken her leg and had been

27

unable to. Fern had managed a couple of desultory years swanning from one temp job to another, before bagging Dezza and living the sort of life she'd always wanted. Once she'd had the children Fern had considered her job done, and was now a lady who lunched while the kids were in school (and shopped, and played tennis, and did lots of other things which involved enjoying herself). Fern had everything dropped in her lap and was now accusing Stevie of the very same thing.

I bet she's jealous, Stevie thought, pummelling the dough into oblivion. She always did like baking as a means of working out her frustration. She'd got the first batch of pastries started almost as soon as her mother had whisked out of the door. I bet Fern wished she was me, Stevie mused: I've got all the money and no boring Dezza to put up with. Or maybe not.

Two hundred and sixty-three thousand pounds wouldn't get you very far in London, and it certainly wouldn't buy a four-bedroomed, two reception-roomed house in a nice area like Fern lived in. Nor would it be enough to send two children to private schools. It wouldn't really be enough to give up work, unless she planned on doing nothing except eating toast for the next forty years and never stepping foot outside her front door ever again.

Her aunt's words came back to haunt her. *Don't waste it,* Peg had said. But was treating herself to the odd holiday, or upgrading her beaten-up, ancient hatchback, wasting it? Or was it simply making life that little bit more bearable?

Suddenly the dream of using the money to set up her own business seemed very far-fetched indeed. It was a tidy sum, but not enough to do anything constructive with.

Not unless the business was a van and she sold cupcakes out of it (that was a thought but one Stevie and Karen had only contemplated for a few moments).

Sadly, and with one final thump of the innocent bread dough, Stevie set her dreams to one side. Despite her enthusiasm about setting up a tea shop after her drink with Karen, she'd since decided, hadn't she, that the sensible thing would be to get a job, then take stock of her situation? At least she could afford to rent somewhere decent for a change, and not flat-share with twelve other people (OK, that was a slight exaggeration). Job first, then she'd have some idea where to rent, because she didn't want to spend three hours on the Tube every day, just to get to and from work.

Of course, this was assuming she could actually stand the recriminations and the guilt trip her mother would lay on her for the foreseeable future.

Decision made, Stevie put the bread in the airing cupboard to rise and returned to the kitchen to face the music.

Chapter 6

That was the trouble with all these 'top' London chefs, Stevie grumbled to herself: they all knew each other. She plonked the phone back in its cradle with a frown after hearing yet another version of the "I wonder why Corky felt he had to let you go" monologue. It was proving to be popular. 'There'll be a CD brought out with it on next,' she thought sarcastically.

Some of the chefs hadn't even given her a chance to explain about the broken leg, although a few others had listened, then made a non-committal 'hmmm' noise, or said, 'I'll have to think about it.' She had wanted to scream at them, 'I'll take that as a "no" then, shall I?', but was terrified of scuppering what tiny chance she might have of securing a job.

There was one notable exception who had said, in his usual forthright manner, 'If Corky don't want you, what the fuck makes you think I do?'

'Cheers. Thanks for that. They are all thinking the same thing, most likely,' Stevie muttered, her tone disconsolate as she had listened morosely to a dead line when the chef on the other end hung up on her.

Her newly-healed leg throbbed in silent sympathy and Stevie flexed it absent-mindedly, wondering who she could phone next, and if there was actually anyone

left who hadn't heard about her less-than-shining performance at The Melon, Corky's million-pound Michelin
star establishment which was rumoured to have been
named after his fascination for women with large breasts.

But that was the whole crux of the problem; she simply
couldn't think of anyone whose kitchen she wanted to be
in and who wouldn't have heard about her misfortune. It
was like she had leprosy or something. She'd become the
restaurant equivalent of a pariah, an outcast.

'No luck?' her mother enquired.

Stevie shook her head. 'Nope. I think I'll give Little
Chef or Burger King a ring. No, on second thoughts, they
have probably heard about me, too, and wouldn't want me,
either.' She dropped into an armchair and hugged a sadly
depleted cushion.

'You keep doing that and there won't be any stuffing
left in it,' Hazel pointed out.

'Don't care.'

'No, I doubt if you do, not with all the money you've
got.'

Stevie rolled her eyes. Not again! For the past few
weeks her mother had brought the subject up at every
opportunity, and she wasn't being nice about it, either.
Thanks, Mum.

'Don't start,' Stevie warned.

'Start what?' Hazel was all wide-eyed innocence. 'All
I said was—'

Stevie stuck her fingers in her ears and hummed loudly,
screwing her eyes up just in case she suddenly and inex-
plicably developed the ability to lip-read.

After a few minutes of this, she risked opening one
eye. Her mother was nowhere in sight. She gingerly

opened the other eye and looked around cautiously, before taking her fingers out of her ears. Banging noises from the kitchen told her where her mother was, and Stevie breathed deeply, slightly ashamed of her teenage reaction. She was twenty-six. That woman had the knack of reversing time, which made Stevie feel like, and behave like, a thirteen-year-old. Did all mothers have this ability, or was hers unique? Perhaps she could conduct a survey; after all, she had nothing else to do.

She shrugged and sighed loudly. It was time she trawled the Internet again. The last few weeks had seen Stevie hunched over the electronic taskmaster hunting for a job, at first with hopeful enthusiasm but which had gradually dwindled to a form of self-flagellation, when her lack of success became apparent as she made a series of pointless phone calls to all the restaurants in the known universe. Well, all those of any importance, anyway, then lots which were not so important, followed by several who were downright unheard of.

She had also, just for the dubious fun of it, searched any and all available properties within a twenty-mile radius, just in case there was something out there with her name on. But she simply couldn't find what she was looking for – too expensive, wrong location, building not right…

Stevie scowled in discontent as she made for the small study which had once been a bedroom and switched the laptop back on, mentally girding her loins to do battle with her emails.

Scrolling and deleting the usual rubbish (Viagra? *Really?*), she was about to press delete on another, when a tiny photo caught her eye. Curiously, she opened it and stared incredulously at the screen. A double fronted, three-storey building stared impassively back at her. She read the email twice, then squealed with excitement. It was a café, well below budget, in a village called Tanglewood (she had no idea where it was, but it sounded lovely). The tea shop itself looked perfect. Too perfect. There must be something wrong with it.

The building was a shop premises with a self-contained flat upstairs, which had previously been used as a coffee shop and was being sold with a well-equipped kitchen, but it could be used for alternative purposes, the blurb said (not that Stevie would want to use it for anything else).

OK, it still sounded perfect, but what about Tanglewood itself? She Google-mapped it and zoomed out. Set in a valley along the River Usk, on the tourist trail to the Beacons and the Black Mountains beyond, the village was further from London than she anticipated. But then, look at the price, she thought. You'd be lucky to get a pothole in Hemel Hempstead for that!

The name of the estate agent was emblazoned across the top of the email, and although Stevie couldn't recall registering with them (how could she, considering she'd registered with so many), she didn't have anything to lose by going to see the property.

She'd have to view it, and it would be a good idea to suss out any competition too, and maybe, if possible, discover why the current owners were selling. Perhaps there were too many eateries already in Tanglewood, or maybe it was so far off the beaten track people only visited the place if they were lost and had no other choice.

All those doubts swirled through her head, but try as she might, Stevie simply couldn't damp down the spark of excitement whenever she thought of Tanglewood.

She had a good feeling about this. A *really* good feeling.

Chapter 7

I wish I'd caught the train, Stevie thought, as she hauled her car around yet another bend, hoping there wouldn't be a tractor coming the other way (been there, done that, nearly had a head-on collision). Tanglewood really was out in the sticks and although most of the roads were two-lane, Stevie had the idea the person who had measured the width of the road down some of the stretches must have been under the impression cars were half the size they actually were.

She held her breath as she pulled in close to the hedge, hearing branches slap her little car in its proverbial face, then scrape down the paintwork. She winced every time it happened, and the wince became a grimace as the van she'd pulled in for carried on going at a fair old clip and whizzing past her without even a token touch of the brakes. Bloody white van drivers – they shouldn't be allowed on the roads and certainly not on roads as narrow as these.

A line of vehicles had built up behind her, and she noticed it was getting longer every time she slowed down for any oncoming traffic. She couldn't see the end of it, obscured as it was by the bends in the road and the overgrown hedges on either side.

And that was another thing! There was far too much vegetation for Stevie. She simply wasn't used to it and it made her feel rather uncomfortable, as if it might close in on her at any second and swallow her car whole.

But at least the locals appeared friendly enough, she decided, as yet another car took the opportunity to slip past her on one of the rare straight stretches of road. A toot and a wave – that was nice. Stevie waved back and got a flash of tail lights in return, then realised the "wave" was actually a rude gesture.

Finally, after what seemed like hours, the hedgerows and the trees fell away and the road opened up to reveal fields with fluffy white sheep grazing on them on the right, and purpled mountains on the left. She didn't mind the sheep (and she adored lamb with mint and rosemary) but those mountains looked a bit wild and a bit high. Trees and fields were spread halfway up their slopes, but above that they looked pretty desolate. They were a nice backdrop though, as long as she was never expected to go anywhere near them. She'd never actually been up a mountain, and she wasn't sure what you were supposed to do when you got to the top. Stevie preferred the flat – you knew what was what on the flat. She wasn't entirely sure about the countryside, either… it all looked so *green*.

A mile or so further on, she came to a crossroads with a sign pointing to a narrow stone bridge arching over a wide, serene river.

Tanglewood.

She had arrived, and from what she could see of it, the village looked chocolate-box pretty, with little stone-built cottages, grey slate roofs and planters filled with spring flowers.

She couldn't wait to get close enough for a proper look, but first she had the tiny, narrow bridge to negotiate. Continuing to peer at the houses on the other side of the river, she flicked on her indicator, turned the steering wheel sharply, and attempted to turn right, only to be blared at by oncoming traffic. She slammed on her brakes, her heart thumping. Oops. I'd better concentrate, or I might cause an accident. But despite her good intentions, her gaze kept returning to the hump of the bridge and the imagined delights of the buildings on the other side.

Another blast of a horn and she was jolted back into the here and now. What? Oh, traffic lights. How come she hadn't seen them before now? But at least it explained why the driver coming from the opposite direction had been so irate – it had been his right of way. But now it was hers, she realised, and she shoved the car into first gear before the traffic lights had a chance to change their mind. Aiming her car at the bridge, she trundled up the little hump, before cresting it, then pootled down the other side, grinning like an idiot at what she saw.

'Oh, but the village is so pretty!' she said aloud. The main street rose gradually from the river, and as she travelled slowly up its gentle slope, she glanced at a little row of five cottages which lined the riverbank, adoring their quaintness. On the right was a pub called The Duke's Arms, whose garden stretched almost to the water's edge, and further along the road she could see a variety of shops, and was that another pub at the crossroads at the top?

A double-fronted shop on the right caught her eye just as she was dawdling past, and she slowed even more, desperate to get a decent look while at the same time trying to keep an eye on where she was going.

She knew she'd recognised it! It was her shop. *Hers!* Looking all sweet and inviting in the early afternoon sun.

Drat! She slammed the brakes on, narrowly avoiding shunting the car in front, and muttered a string of swear words. It wasn't easy driving in this part of the country, she decided, what with car-eating verges, massive tractors and numbskulls who stopped dead in the middle of the high street.

Then she saw what had caused the car in front to stop, and her eyes nearly popped out of her head.

It was a man on a horse, trotting up the road as if he owned it. All the other vehicles in front of her were giving him a wide berth or waiting patiently for their turn to pull out around him, while the oncoming traffic had slowed to a crawl.

What on earth was the guy playing at?

Stevie didn't even know if it was legal to ride a horse on a road. She'd gone to Hyde Park a couple of times and watched the riders and their mounts, but that was in a park with grass, and trees and stuff. You'd expect to see a horse there. And of course, police horses could go anywhere they wanted because they were allowed. 'But as for the general public – shouldn't they be in a field somewhere? Not the people,' she hastened to add, chuckling to herself, 'the horses.'

And while all this was going through her head, she was examining the bum of the rider as it rose and fell. On the way up it was all taut muscle and firm thighs, and coming down it was about the same, apart from a brief squish when the man's backside connected with the saddle, and then it was up again, and—

More tooting and Stevie looked back at the road to see an impatient driver waving at her, indicating she should pull out around the beast. The beast in question hadn't much liked the car horn, because it danced a little, skittering further into the road, prancing and flicking out its hooves and swishing its tail.

As Stevie gingerly manoeuvred her car into the centre of the road, she feared for her new Beetle's paintwork.

The rider must have feared for his life, because he hauled on the reins, trying to edge the horse closer to the side of the road, and at the same time he turned to give her a disgusted glare as she eased around the excitable animal.

What? She gave him a glare in return. It wasn't her fault – she wasn't the one who'd beeped her horn.

Spotting a sign for a car park, she accelerated quickly to get past the horse, then pulled in again just as fast and made a swift, sharp turn to the left. As she pulled off the road, she could have sworn the rider had yelled at her, so she took her time in finding a space and getting out of the car. She wanted to make sure he was long gone before she ventured back onto the main road. Stupid man. He would be better off prancing about on one of those mountains. That's where animals belonged, not on roads.

She grabbed her bag off the passenger seat, got out of the car, and stretched. It had been a fair old drive from London – a bit further than she'd anticipated to be honest, and she felt as though she was in a different country. Which she was, if she thought about it, because once she'd crossed the massive bridge (it was a day for bridges, it seemed) separating England from Wales, then the signposts had suddenly become unintelligible (bits of them, anyway), and stopping for a rest break had revealed some decidedly non-London accents.

Stevie had to admit she felt a degree of trepidation in coming here, as she made her way out of the carpark. Tanglewood was a considerable distance from everything she was used to, and apparently the nearest city was Cardiff, or was it Bristol? (she couldn't remember which), and both of those were simply miles away. Tanglewood was in the Welsh Marches, which apparently referred to those counties running along the border between England and Wales (although what the term "March" meant she had absolutely no idea) and—

She halted, her eyes wide with pleasure. Oh, the village really *was* lovely, she realised as she came out onto the road she'd driven up and saw Tanglewood properly for the first time. Hardly a main road at all, the street she was standing in was more like a sleepy high street, and she decided to walk up the one side, then back down the other until she reached her shop – no matter how much she tried to hold her excitement in, she couldn't help but think of the tea shop as hers.

Tanglewood itself was built on a crossroads, with tiny old streets, some of them still cobbled, radiating outwards from the two main roads. The other shops were a perfect complement to a tea shop business, she noticed. On her left was an old-fashioned, traditional butcher shop, selling home-cured bacon and with rabbits hanging naked in the window, although she tried not to look too closely at those. A baker, with the mouth-watering smell of freshly baked bread wafting out through the open door was next to it, and Stevie was relieved to see it seemed to specialise in breads, rolls, and buns, and had little in the way of cakes and pastries – she didn't need any competition. There was a grocer, a florist, one or two hiking shops, a shop selling bicycles, and even an old-fashioned ironmonger.

But what swung it for her were the three pubs ('Only three – yippee!' and at least one of them didn't seem to serve food) and the handful of art and craft shops selling hand-made cards, carved Welsh coal, love spoons and everything else a tourist could possibly want to spend their money on. This meant that there was only one café in the village – hers!

Finally, after a good scout around and after scrutinising anyone and everyone she passed and taking a guess on what they were (tourist, tourist, local, hiker, local, tourist), she reached her tea shop and the estate agent who was waiting outside to show her around.

He looked a bit miffed, and Stevie realised she was a little late. Never mind, she was here now, and eager to see inside.

The shop itself was beautiful. Two large bay windows were situated either side of a central door which had a tinkling little bell that rang whenever someone came in or out, and the space itself was large enough to hold around fifteen tables. A counter with a display cabinet underneath ran almost the full width of the café at the back, with plenty of workspace behind it, plus a sink, a fridge, and a gleaming metal monster of a coffee machine. There was also a customer loo.

Behind the counter was a door leading to a surprisingly large and well-equipped kitchen, boasting an abundance of steel cabinets, worktops and two enormous double ovens. In the middle was a good-sized island with shelves underneath, suitable for storing pans and bakeware.

Stevie stared around in excitement. It was perfect, absolutely perfect. The business could be up-and-running in a matter of weeks, and her mind darted ahead as she envisioned herself standing behind the counter, serving a delicious selection of cakes and pastries to a patient queue of waiting customers.

Now all she needed was somewhere to live…

'The flat upstairs is part of the purchase price, isn't it?' she asked, and the estate agent pointed to a door to her right.

'You can get to it through here, but there is a separate entrance outside if you wanted to use it.'

Stevie poked her head out of the door marked "Fire Exit" and found herself staring at a tiny, walled courtyard with a tall, wooden gate and a metal spiral staircase to one side.

'If you want to rent it out, this can be the entrance to the flat,' he explained, as he closed the door and pointed her in the direction of the internal stairs instead. 'This door can be locked from down here, so you won't have your renters traipsing through the café every five minutes.'

She followed him up the stairs and he showed her into a two bedroomed flat, which was partly furnished and nicely decorated. Stevie was in complete agreement with the current owner's taste, which was lucky because it would save her having to fork out for redecorating. She especially loved the main bedroom, with its sanded floorboards and white walls.

Having two bedrooms meant her friends could come and stay, (she couldn't wait to show it to Karen) and a little kitchen meant she didn't have to fire up the eight-ring hob in the kitchen downstairs whenever she wanted to heat up a tin of soup. The living room looked out onto the street and had a view of the river – if she craned her neck a bit.

Perfect, she thought again. Simply perfect.

'I want it,' she declared.

'Good.' The estate agent smiled benevolently at her.

'Can I pay for it now? Will you take a card?' She thought of all the money sitting in her deposit account and her heart did a little flip of excitement. It had only been transferred to her a couple of weeks ago and she still couldn't believe it, checking her online balance with something bordering on obsession.

'Um…,' Mr Whitworth replied, watching as Stevie fiddled about in her bag. 'Um…' he repeated loudly.

Stevie lifted her head and smiled questioningly at him. 'Yes?'

'There's just one little problem,' he said, his brown eyes solemn and his moustache drooping with anticipated sympathy.

'Problem? What problem? Oh, no, don't tell me, let me guess. Rats.' She paused for a second, but not long enough for the estate agent to get a word in. 'Or what about flooding – the river is only a stone's throw away? Or perhaps the place is haunted, or you don't sell properties to women on a Friday?'

'No, to all of those,' he replied, calmly.

'So, what is it, then?' Stevie demanded impatiently, her eyes wide with anxiety. Nothing was going to stop her from buying this beautiful little business – nothing!

'It's for sale by auction,' he said.

Nothing except other people bidding against her, she realised, and Stevie's shoulders sagged. Just her luck. Someone else was bound to want it.

'Can't you take it out of the auction?' she asked, in a small voice.

Mr Whitworth shook his head sadly. 'I'm afraid not. However, I can tell you that you are the only person to have viewed it so far. The auction is on Monday so you may be lucky,' he added.

'Are you allowed to tell me that sort of thing?' Stevie wanted to know. 'I thought estate agents had a law or something which said they had to make people think the whole world wanted to buy it.'

Stevie watched the man's moustache droop even further as he replied by way of explanation, 'I always wanted to be a racing driver.'

'Ah.' Stevie could accept that as a perfectly good reason for him informing her she was the sole interested party. 'Would you have been any good, do you think?'

'No,' he replied, his voice mournful.

'Ah,' she said again. 'Are you any good at being an estate agent?'

'Yes. Very.' By now Mr Whitworth was sounding like a whipped dog and looking like one, too. 'But I tend to be too truthful for my own good.'

Stevie changed the subject back to the tea shop. 'I've got to have it,' she said again.

'See you on Monday,' Mr Whitworth replied firmly, locking up behind them and slipping the keys into his pocket.

Oh, how Stevie wished those keys were in *her* pocket right now. She couldn't wait to start baking in that glorious kitchen.

'By the way,' the estate agent said, as Stevie began to head to her car. 'The price listed is only a guide price, not necessarily the price you'll actually pay.'

Stevie sighed. Typical! She'd thought it had been too good to be true.

Chapter 8

Nick Saunders hated idiot drivers, especially those drivers who had never seen a horse in the flesh before and had no idea how to act around one. He was still grumbling and muttering under his breath when he trotted into the yard sometime later.

Thankfully, the gelding had calmed down, none the worse for his little outing. Nick was halfway through bomb-proofing the horse for its owner, and although it wasn't his usual job, he was happy to do it as a favour.

Slipping out of the saddle, he led the horse to a tether point and tied him to it.

'Good lad,' he murmured, loosening the girth and lifting the saddle off the animal's back. The horse flicked his tail, stamping a hoof at the sudden chill on his super-heated flesh. Even though it was a relatively warm late spring afternoon, steam curled into the air from the horse's damp coat.

After exchanging the bridle for a halter, Nick proceeded to brush the horse down. He loved nearly every aspect of his job and this bit was no exception. He found it soothing and therapeutic, the rhythmic strokes of the brush bringing a shine to the gelding's coat. He didn't necessarily like cleaning tack though, so when he spotted one of the grooms, he called the lad over.

'Can you do me a favour and give Domino's tack a clean?' he asked.

'OK, boss. Do you want me to put him away?'

'No, I'll do it. I want to check his tendons when he's cooled off a bit.'

'How was he?' All the stable hands took a very active interest in the animals in Nick's yard, and Jordan was no exception. Young and keen, the lad lived and breathed horses. Nick did too, but along the way he'd grown older and some of the keenness had withered a bit, experience taking its place.

'Not bad, until some silly girl in a bright yellow Beetle held up the traffic, and some other idiot in a Range Rover beeped his horn at her, giving Domino the heebie-jeebies. For a minute, I thought he was going to bolt. Then the stupid woman in the Beetle pulled out around him and straight back in, cutting us up. It's set him back a bit, I can tell you.'

'Poor lad.' Jordan gave the horse a pat on the neck. 'Do you want me to school Achilles after lunch?'

'Good idea. Put him on a long rein and put up some jumps set on the first hole. Walk him over those a couple of times, then raise it up a notch. Get him used to them.'

'Right, boss.'

'After that, you can ride Monte Carlo.'

'Right, boss.' Jordan's grin split his face in two.

Nick continued grooming Domino, with an answering smile on his face. Apart from his own jumping, he also enjoyed bringing on young talent, both horses and riders, and Jordan was a talented lad indeed. The boy had already won several competitions in his age group, and his name was starting to be bandied about as the newest up-and-coming rider in various show jumping circles.

Nick remembered when he'd been in that position, far too many years ago than he cared to think about. He consoled himself with the thought that at least show jumping was one sport where age didn't have too great a bearing. Take Peter Charles, for instance – he was nearly sixty and still competing. You couldn't say that about many other sports. Most of them had you on the scrap heap at thirty.

Not that Nick was anywhere near sixty, but at thirty-two his body felt the knocks more profoundly than it had done a decade ago. Thankfully it had been a while since he'd been thrown (although he'd come close to it today, thanks to that idiot driver), but a careless hoof stamped on an unwary foot, or a thump in the face from a horse's hard head hurt more than it used to. Only last week he'd been crushed against the side of a stall, and his ribs still ached even now. He really ought to be more careful – he, of all people, knew how easily accidents could happen, especially where horses were involved. He was also acutely aware of the aftermath.

No, he definitely wasn't as young as he used to be. Still, he didn't want to be anywhere else, or to be doing anything else. Horses were his life, the reason he got out of bed in the morning, and they had been good to him, giving him the lifestyle he loved, a certain degree of fame and a career he was darned good at. But he was forced to admit that he enjoyed the training more than the competing, these days.

He patted Domino on the rump to signal the grooming session was over, untied the horse's halter and led him into his stall, where Nick unclipped the lead-rope and set the animal loose. The horse went straight to his wall-mounted drinker and sucked up mouthfuls of cool, fresh water, lifting his muzzle every now and again to look at Nick. Water droplets coated the fuzzy hairs on the horse's nose and chin, and once he'd drunk his fill, Domino sauntered over to the door, hung his head over the top and wiped his face on Nick's jacket.

'Thanks,' Nick said wryly, pushing the large head away.

The horse snorted at him and turned to his feed, those mobile lips pulling strands of dried grass out of the hay net and soon the sounds of contented munching filled the stall.

Nick wished he could have a leisurely lunch, too, but he had paperwork to do and calls to make, so Nick's lunch would be a hastily made sandwich eaten at his desk. Sometimes he really wished he could swap places with his pampered equines.

'Nick Saunders,' he said, answering the phone around a mouthful of ham salad baguette. The baguette was a little stale, but better than the mould-spotted, sliced, white loaf in the bread box. He really needed to do a proper shop but couldn't seem to find the time. Tia usually saw to the groceries, but lately...

'Darling, it's Miranda. How are you?' A plummy voice drawled down the line and Nick rolled his eyes.

'Fine thanks, and you?'

'Much better for hearing your voice, sweetie. I've had a dreadful day.'

Nick guessed he was supposed to ask what was wrong, but he couldn't be bothered. There was always some crisis or another in Miranda's life, usually of the "my stylist is on holiday for two weeks – what am I supposed to do now?" variety. Miranda could be great fun, was certainly attractive, was well-bred, and had money (loads of it, courtesy of her father, Lord Tonbridge), but she was also rather narcissistic and shallow –although he had to admit, he'd once caught her crying over a TV advert for raising funds for children in Sudan. As he recalled, she'd sold one of her pieces of jewellery and had sent the proceeds to the charity. He'd admired her for putting her purse where her mouth was.

To be fair, the whole family were often involved in local causes, so Miranda often did her bit for the community. But she could be a bit dramatic sometimes.

'There's a reason for me calling,' she continued, after a pause which Nick refused to fill. 'We're having a bit of a do up at the house on Saturday evening and I wondered if you'd like to come. Please say yes, because if you don't, I'll be stuck listening to Daddy's old cronies drone on about the last hunt, or their stocks in some frightful company.'

'Won't there be anyone else there who you can talk to?' Nick was playing devil's advocate, but he just couldn't help himself. He enjoyed teasing Miranda – she was so easy to wind up. It was one of his little pleasures in life and she knew he didn't really mean it.

'Silly! Of course, there will be! Mummy is expected to entertain the wives of the cronies, but,' she lowered her voice to a conspiratorial whisper, 'listening to them is worse than talking to the cronies themselves. Please, please, come, and save me from a fate worse than death.'

'You could always invite Tia, have some girly time,' Nick suggested. 'She'd love a chance to dress up.' Actually, Tia probably wouldn't. Nick scoured his brain trying to remember the last time his sister wore anything other than jeans and trainers and failed. He couldn't recall the last time she had gone out, either.

'I'd love to, but Mummy said she had to keep the table even.'

'Eh?'

'You know, boy, girl, boy, girl. Tia would mess up Mummy's seating arrangement.'

Oh, for Pete's sake, Nick thought. Seating plan? Really?

'What's your mother serving for tea?' he asked instead, and opened a spreadsheet. He tried to read it, but multi-tasking wasn't his thing.

'It's called supper as you well know,' Miranda replied huffily. 'I'm not sure what Mrs Abbott is preparing, but whatever it is, it will be delicious, as usual.'

'In that case, I'll come,' Nick said. 'A man's gotta eat.' And it didn't do to refuse a dinner invitation from his wealthy neighbour, either...

'Oh, you! You're nothing but a tease, Nick.'

Mrs Abbott was one of the best cooks around and Nick had enjoyed many a meal at Tonbridge Manor. Supper indeed! Where he came from, the evening meal was called tea, the midday one was called dinner and supper was what you had if you were still hungry just before bed. He found he couldn't help reminding Miranda of his less-than-salubrious background. Not that it put her off – it didn't. Miranda was always seeking him out. In fact, Domino belonged to her, and although the horse did need a considerable amount of schooling to give him some manners and to calm him down, Nick had a sneaking suspicion Miranda had placed the horse in his yard purely as an excuse to see Nick. He had to admit there was some attraction between them (Miranda was a gorgeous girl) but not enough for Nick to act on, so he treated her with a certain amount of caution and reserve; he didn't want her to get the wrong idea…

'What time do you want me?' he asked, clicking on an email, and was rewarded with a low chuckle.

'Anytime, Nick, anytime.'

Nick waited her out. It was his own fault for not thinking about what he was saying.

'Seven, for seven-thirty,' she eventually said, with a sigh.

'I'll be there,' he promised, and ended the call.

The penance of having to eat surrounded by Lord and Lady Tonbridge's friends and acquaintances, was offset by the opportunity to network. They might not necessarily be horsey people but they moved in those circles, and training and riding show jumpers was an expensive business. Nick needed all the referrals and recommendations he could get, and word-of-mouth was an excellent way of getting those.

Turning back to the more immediate problem of which horse to enter for what competition, he enlarged the spreadsheet and stared at it. It was a hefty document, complex and thorough, and he studied it for several long minutes, before leaning back in his office chair.

Nick had fourteen jumpers in his stable, five of them his. The rest he trained for other owners, and sometimes he rode those horses in competition and sometimes they were ridden by other riders. In addition, he had a couple of problem animals (to Nick's surprise, he found he had an aptitude for turning "difficult" horses into steadier mounts), and one or two youngsters who were being gently broken in.

It was a lot to juggle. The stable hands saw to the day-to-day running of the yard and Nick would be lost without them (he had five, three of them lived on-site and the other two in Tanglewood itself), but it was still a great deal of work. Tia helped as best she could, despite her disability, and she was a whizz at organising the yard and the house, but recently some of her hard-won sparkle had deserted her, and she didn't seem to be as focused as usual. Take the grocery situation, for example…

He promised to sit down over their evening meal and try to get to the bottom of what was worrying her. But that was later, and this was now, and he had work to do, so he shoved his concerns about his sister to the back of his mind and tried to concentrate on the job in hand.

But one thing still rankled and wasn't pushed away so easily – the image of a red-headed girl driving a yellow Beetle, waving apologetically at him.

Bloody idiot drivers!

Chapter 9

The following Monday found Stevie perched nervously on a wooden chair in an auction room, along with a couple of dozen rather bored-looking potential buyers. She prayed they were there for any other property than hers. She also hoped they couldn't smell fresh blood, because she felt like a goat staked out and waiting for the tiger. Surely, they could see on her face just how much she wanted the café.

She leaned back, crossed her legs at the ankles and tried to look nonchalant, failing miserably, then she caught the stern look on Karen's face and struggled to control her giggles.

'You've gone puce,' Karen stated. 'It's not your best colour.'

'It's nerves,' she spluttered, clamping one hand over her mouth to keep the hysterical laughter inside.

Karen shifted slightly in her chair, turning her body away from her friend.

'Sorry,' Stevie said in a muffled voice, tears trickling down her cheeks. She took her hand away and waved it in front of her face.

'Three hundred and seventy-five thousand, I'm bid.' The auctioneer's voice cut through Stevie's antics. He pointed directly at her.

'What?' She gasped, her eyes wide open and she stared at the podium in horror. She looked around frantically, realising many of the people in the room were watching her.

'Any advance on three-seven-five?' the auctioneer demanded.

Stevie sucked in her breath and Karen turned to glare at her.

'See what you've done now?' her friend hissed. 'You've only gone and bid on something. I told you to keep still and be quiet.'

'I'm selling at three hundred and seventy-five thousand pounds to the lady at the back,' Stevie heard the auctioneer say, and she let out a low moan as he pointed at her again.

'No, I don't want it,' she groaned.

'Sold!' The hammer slammed down, making Stevie jump. 'Can I have your number please?' he asked her.

'No!' she cried. 'I didn't mean to bid on it. I don't want it!' She blushed furiously at the tittering around her and shrank down in her seat.

'Not you, madam. I was referring to the lady behind you,' the auctioneer explained.

Stevie sagged with relief. 'Thank God!' she said, rather more loudly than she intended. The slight tittering became outright sniggering. Karen glared at her again and shifted her seat a few inches to the right, trying to pretend she was nothing to do with the crazy girl sitting next to her. Stevie knew Karen often did that – she also knew her friend didn't really mean it.

Stevie had never been to an auction before and had spent the first half an hour sitting on her hands, fidgeting in her seat, and cracking naff jokes along the lines of 'don't sneeze, or they'll think you want to make a bid'. Now, it seemed, the joke had almost been on her.

Chastened for the moment, she sat quietly, her eyes downcast, wishing she was a chameleon. This got her to imagine what it would be like to actually be one, so, surreptitiously underneath her lashes, she tried to move each of her eyes independently of the other. The best she could manage was a cross-eyed grimace.

Karen elbowed her sharply in the ribs. 'I thought this was the one you wanted to bid on,' she hissed.

'Oh, yes. It is.' Stevie flicked the curls off her face and sat up straight. She raised her hand deliberately, smiling sweetly at the auctioneer.

'Yes?' he asked, utterly perplexed.

Stevie dropped her hand, her smile fading into uncertainty.

'Did you want something?' The auctioneer's voice could best be described as irritated.

'I want to bid on this one,' she said, quietly.

'Certainly, madam, but the bidding hasn't started yet.'

'Oh. Sorry.' Stevie bit her lip, did the seat shrinking trick again and thumped Karen on the thigh when she thought no one was looking.

'Oi! That hurt!' Karen whispered crossly.

'That was your fault,' Stevie hissed back. 'I thought I was supposed to bid.'

'Oh, just shut up and listen.' Karen shook her head in annoyance, her sheet of dark, gleaming hair swinging about her face. Stevie scowled into the distance, until the steady drone of the man describing the café's merits captured her attention.

She nodded determinedly as the auctioneer took the reins.

'Who'll start me off at one hundred and fifty thousand?' he asked, staring straight at Stevie.

She was about to put her hand up again, when Karen murmured out of the corner of her mouth, 'Don't say or do anything. Wait.'

Stevie, for once, took the advice and froze on the spot, her mouth half open. The only things to move were her eyes, as they darted from face to face.

'Come now. It's worth one hundred and fifty.' He paused, his attention focused on the rest of the room. 'One hundred, then? Thank you. One hundred thousand, I'm bid.'

Stevie craned her neck to see who her rival was.

'Any advance on one hundred thousand? Do I hear one hundred and ten? One ten, anybody?'

Karen nudged her, and Stevie's hand shot up.

'One hundred and ten thousand pounds? Are you sure?' The auctioneer was staring at her intently.

Stevie nodded, her hair bouncing on her shoulders.

'Right. One hundred and twenty thousand?' He nodded to a rival bidder in acknowledgement. 'One twenty, I've got. Who'll give me one thirty?' He shot back at Stevie, who waved her hand at him.

The bidding quickly rose to two hundred thousand and beyond. At two hundred and thirty-five thousand it stopped.

'It's against you, sir,' Stevie heard the auctioneer say to her unseen rival on the other side of the room.

'Two hundred and thirty-five, for the first time. Two hundred and thirty-five, for the second time. Going at two hundred and thirty-five...' A dramatic, too-long pause, then, 'Sold! For two hundred and thirty-five thousand pounds to the lady with the ginger hair.'

Chestnut, chestnut, Stevie thought, leaping to her feet and shouting, 'Yes! Yes!'

This time the smiles and laughter from her fellow bidders were indulgent. She held her number up for the auctioneer, waited until he had made a note of it, then she grabbed Karen's hand and dragged her outside.

'It's mine! It's mine! It's mine!' she sang, dancing around in a circle and swinging Karen with her. 'I need a drink,' she declared, breathlessly.

'So do I,' Karen agreed, and they teetered off to the nearest public house to celebrate.

Chapter 10

'No, no, that simply won't do,' Stevie cried crossly. 'You've put an *o* in – it should be an *e*.'

'Where?'

'There, see?' Stevie jabbed a finger at the recently painted sign outside her recently acquired tea shop.

The sign-writer scratched his grizzled head and peered upwards.

'You'll have to do it again,' she stated.

'No, I won't. I've done it exactly as you wrote it.' The elderly man fished around in his pocket and drew out a crumpled, grubby bit of paper. He smoothed it out against his chest, then stuck it under her nose. A dirty, paint-covered finger stabbed at the writing. 'There? See? *Poggy's Tea Shoppe*.'

'No, it's not. It doesn't say that at all. It says *Peggy's* Tea Shoppe. That's an *e*.'

'Well, it don't look like it to me, and I paints what I sees, don't I?' he pointed out, reasonably.

'But it's wrong. That's an *e*. Doesn't that say *e* to you?' Stevie grabbed the paper out of the old man's hand and thrust it in the face of a passer-by. The woman almost jumped out of her skin.

'See what?' she squeaked, holding her anorak close to her bosom with a shaking hand.

'The *e*,' Stevie almost shouted. 'As in "P*e*ggy's Tea Shoppe".'

'Oh. Yes. Tea. Yes, I think it's going to be a café and I'm sure they'll sell tea, dear,' the woman gabbled. 'Some young thing from over London way has bought it. I hope she'll do better than the last lot.'

'What do you mean?' Stevie demanded, the misspelt sign momentarily forgotten, but her informant shuffled quickly down the pavement and was soon out of reach.

'What was all that about?' Stevie asked no one in particular.

For the first time since she'd seen Tanglewood and made the most important and spontaneous decision of her life, Stevie felt a tad uneasy. She knew there was something she should have done and it had niggled at her ever since she set eyes on the tea shop, and now it hit her – she hadn't asked why the previous owners were selling up. It simply hadn't occurred to her. She'd been so caught up in the excitement of it, she hadn't once considered the reason why the café was on the market.

Stevie probably wouldn't have been allowed to look at the books anyway (not that she'd even thought about it) as the premises wasn't being sold as a going concern. The business itself hadn't been for sale, just the property. The fact that the fixtures and fittings were included, was just a lucky bonus.

'Don't know and don't care,' the sign writer stated, his singsong Welsh accent carolling the words, pulling her out of the faint worry which was now starting to cloud her mind, and she frowned at him as he bent to his paints, snapping the lids back on.

'You haven't finished yet,' she protested.

'Yes, I have.' The old man was adamant. 'Unless you want to pay me to do it again?'

'I haven't paid you at all yet,' she corrected.

At that, he held out a slightly trembling grubby hand.

Stevie ignored it. 'I'm not paying you until you put it right.'

'And I'll tell everyone as how you wouldn't pay an old man for an honest day's work. How you cheated him out of his wages and now he can't afford to turn on his gas fire,' the old man shot back at her.

'But it's the middle of May! You don't need the fire on.'

'Gets cold in the nights,' he retorted, then added, 'And I won't be able to have any luxuries, like food and a bit of tobacco.'

'Oh, for goodness' sake!' Stevie stomped inside the café and returned with her purse. She counted out the notes, then waited for him to pick up his things, which he did with annoying slowness. Finally, he hoisted his ladder over his shoulder, his back bent under its weight.

'Right then, Miss Poggy,' he said. 'I'll be off. Call me if you want any more work done.'

'It's Taylor! Miss Taylor,' she shouted at his retreating form, the ladder bobbing gently up and down as he staggered off under its weight. Miss Poggy indeed!

'If you say so,' she heard him call back.

'Balls,' she muttered under her breath and stomped off to get her own ladder.

She didn't have one, she discovered. She also discovered she didn't have any paint either, or a paintbrush.

Sighing in frustration, she picked up her purse again, locked the tea shop and headed for the ironmonger further up the street.

'Hiya, love, what can I get you?' a man in his fifties asked her. He wore a dark green apron which reached to mid-calf and looked as though he knew one end of a screwdriver from the other.

'I need a ladder,' Stevie began, then a rack of wooden prong things caught her eye. 'Er… what's that for?' It looked a bit like a coat rack but had been placed on its flat side with the two-foot-long straight prongs sticking into the air.

'A wellie rack. Would you like one?' he said, grabbing a wellie from a shelf behind him and plonking it upside down on one of the wooden prongs.

Actually, now he came to mention it, perhaps she did have a need for a wellie rack in her life, even though she didn't have a single pair of wellies to her name.

No, she'd come here for a ladder, and a ladder was exactly what she intended to return home with. *Home* – it felt strange to call the tea shop "home". She'd only moved in the day before yesterday, and she had yet to acclimatise.

'Just the ladder, please,' she replied firmly.

'What kind do you need? Single ladder, extension ladder, step ladder, platform ladder, dual-purpose ladder, roof ladder?'

'Um…' Gosh, who knew there were so many varieties? 'I want to paint a sign above my shop,' she said.

'How high?'

'I dunno, two to three feet?'

'I meant, how far off the ground is the sign?'

'Oh, I see. About the same height as yours,' Stevie said. 'I think.'

'A tall step ladder will probably do it,' the ironmonger said, and fetched a sturdy red-coloured one from the back. 'It extends into one, if you need a bit more height,' he added.

'That's brilliant,' she agreed. 'I'll need some paint, too.'

'What kind of paint? We've got emulsion, both silk and matte, gloss, satinwood, undercoat, damp corrector, masonry paint—'

'Whatever is used to paint a sign,' Stevie interrupted. She had an odd feeling of déjà vu, as if this sort of scene had played out before on a TV show... something to do with fork handles, or was it four candles?

Never mind. It didn't matter. What did matter was getting the sign right, otherwise Poggy, I mean, Peggy, will be coming back to haunt me, Stevie thought.

She paid for her purchases and was just about to pick the ladder up (how she was going to carry it down the street was a bit of a mystery at the moment) when she spotted something else. And this was something she most definitely had to have.

It was a wooden hat and coat stand and would look perfect just behind the door, for those rainy days she'd heard so much about. Apparently, Wales was renowned for them. The stand even had a kind of tray at the bottom to catch the drips as well as somewhere to stash wet umbrellas.

'Can I pay for this, take the ladder home, then come back for the coat stand?' she asked.

'Of course, you can, love, or we can deliver them both at the same time. Where do you live?'

'I've just bought the café down the road,' she said, unable to keep the pride out of her voice.

'That's you, is it? From London?'

'That's me.'

'Well, in that case, give me a minute and I'll pop them both down. Jack, here, can mind the shop.' Jack was a beanpole teenager who was glued to his phone. 'What am I thinking? Jack, stop playing with that thing and carry this ladder to the café down the street. You know, the empty one. Get a move on, lad, the lady hasn't got all day.'

'Thank you, that's really helpful,' Stevie said. 'How much do I owe you for delivery?'

'Nothing. It's on the house.'

Stevie was touched. 'At least let me buy you a cake and a coffee,' she offered. 'Come and see me when I'm open and I'll save a slice of something nice for you.'

A half an hour and a tin or two of enamel paint later, her sign now read:

Peggy's Tea Shoppe

Wiping her hands on a duster, Stevie admired her handiwork. It wasn't perfect, but it would have to do. Besides, she didn't have time to mess with it any more – she had a tea shop to open. Not right this very minute, of course, but in a week or so, and before she did, she wanted to give the place a really good scrub. It didn't appear to need it, to be fair, but she'd feel happier if she gave it a clean, almost like a dog scent-marking its patch.

She'd start with the front-of-house, the tea shop itself, because that was what passers-by could see through the windows, then work her way back to the kitchen. Upstairs would have to wait. She had unpacked some essentials, but that was as far as she'd got.

She set to her cleaning with gusto, wiping and mopping, disinfecting and scouring, until the tea shop was positively gleaming, and when she was satisfied, many hours later, she put her cleaning cloth to one side, took off her rubber gloves and stepped back to admire her work.

Perfect. Her own little empire; a blank canvas ready for her own stamp. The walls were a pale shade of old rose, and she had no intention of changing the colour, but she desperately needed tables, chairs, curtains for the gorgeous bay windows, not to mention plates, cutlery, serving dishes, napkins, tablecloths… the list seemed endless.

In fact, she'd made an actual list last night, and it was quite daunting. She'd managed to order a great deal over the Internet, things like the baking equipment, a state-of-the-art food processor, mixing bowls, spatulas, and the hundreds of other things she needed for the kitchen. She'd even managed to get a good deal and early delivery on catering-standard tables and chairs. But she still needed those all-important finishing touches, and a frantic scroll through eBay had shown her how hard it was going to be to ensure everything arrived on time.

There was nothing for it – she had to call in reinforcements.

Chapter 11

Nick caught a movement out of the corner of his eye as he turned the young horse. He had spent the last hour in the indoor arena with the animal on a long lead rein, walking, trotting, and cantering the filly around in circles, getting her used to his commands, making her aware of what was going to be asked of her. Another few minutes, he judged, and she would have had enough. Little and often was better for horses. He would reward her with a good rub down and a nice bucket of oats.

He took his attention off the horse, to see Tia lurking in the doorway. The floor of the arena was difficult, but not impossible, for her to manoeuvre her wheelchair on, but he couldn't remember the last time she had ventured inside.

He slowed the filly to a walk, then gradually brought her to a halt. When she was standing quietly, he strolled over to her, took hold of her halter and undid the clip on the lunge rein. Preparing to lead the horse out, he turned to the huge barn doors with a smile on his face and then his expression fell.

Tia was gone.

He found her in the house, staring out of the living room window with its views of the fields behind the stables and the horses grazing them. He didn't often want to admit it to himself, but he guessed the sight of the animals which had been responsible for Tia's accident might not be easy for his sister to cope with.

'Tia?' His voice was soft, hesitant. These days she tended to fly off the handle at the slightest thing.

'Hmm?' She didn't turn around to look at him but kept her attention on the view beyond the window.

He wanted to ask what was wrong, but he held his tongue. It was a silly question, as she had pointed out whenever he'd asked it in the past. What was wrong was imminently clear – the fact she was now confined to a wheelchair.

He guessed she would never truly accept her situation and might always feel resentment for having lost the use of her legs, but he had hoped she would come to terms with it. Every time Nick thought (hoped) Tia was settling down, she had a relapse.

Physically, she was as good as she was going to get, so her doctors said, but mentally, there was still some way to go.

'Did you want me for anything?' he asked, instead.

She shrugged.

He tried again. 'I saw you outside the arena. You should have joined us. Feisty Girl is coming on in leaps and bounds.'

'Stupid name for a horse,' she muttered, by way of response.

He wrinkled his nose. She was in one of those moods and it always floored him. He knew from past experience that no matter what he tried, he wouldn't be able to prise her out of it, but as always, he carried on trying.

'We've been invited to Tonbridge Manor for dinner tonight,' he said, knowing full well the invitation had been for him alone. If Tia agreed to come, he'd square it with Miranda and her mother somehow.

He saw Tia's shoulders hunch even further and suppressed a sigh. She used to be such a fun-loving girl and although she had slowly been showing signs of returning to her old sunny self, for the past few weeks she'd retreated back into her shell. Counsellors and doctors alike had warned both of them to expect this roller coaster of emotions, but knowing it was normal after such a life-changing event didn't make it any easier to deal with, either for him or for Tia.

'No,' she replied, after a long pause.

'Come on, Tia, you'll enjoy it,' Nick cajoled. If he could just get her out of the house and into the big, wide world, surely she'd see that life could be good again…?

'I said, no.'

This time, Nick let the sigh out. 'Why not?'

He knew he was being confrontational and argumen-tative, but he couldn't seem to help himself. He really did want to know what was holding her back. She'd been to Tonbridge Manor loads of times, and since her accident, too, so why wouldn't she come with him now? The idea she might be suffering from depression flitted across his mind, and he briefly closed his eyes in despair. Maybe it was time he recognised she needed more help and support than he could give her, but now probably wasn't the best time to broach the subject.

The heavy guilt he already felt, suddenly weighed a few pounds more and he looked up at the ceiling, blinking away the sting of tears. He hadn't cried much since her accident, but every now and again sorrow for his sister caught him unawares.

'Will Miranda be there?' Tia asked, cutting into his thoughts.

'I expect so.'

'Good.'

Despite himself, Nick smiled. 'Why "good"?'

'She likes you.' Tia turned her chair to face him.

Nick shrugged. 'I doubt it,' he said, although he knew Tia was right.

'She does,' his sister insisted.

'It makes no difference if she does or doesn't,' Nick pointed out, knowing where this particular conversation was heading, because they'd been there before.

'You need to start dating again. All work and no play...' she trailed off with a wry smile.

'I'm not interested in dating,' he said, firmly. It was true, he wasn't – he had his career and that took up most of his time. He studiously ignored the fact that he had dated frequently before Tia's accident, and his career hadn't prevented him from enjoying female company then.

'You should be,' Tia stated.

'No.' It was his turn to give one-word answers.

She shook her head, her mouth a thin line, and put her hands on the chair's wheels. Nick stepped aside to let her pass, seeing the closed expression on her face and wondering what he'd said to upset her. Surely, if he didn't want a girlfriend it was up to him?

He watched her leave, a frown creasing his brow. He had a feeling there was something more to his sister's mood and he intended to discover what it was.

Chapter 12

The car boot sale was huge. Stevie stood at the entrance to the field and gazed around with a mixture of excitement and dismay. She was bound to find what she wanted here, but she worried she might not get to see all of it and might miss something exquisite.

There was nothing for it, she and Karen would have to split up.

'You know the sort of thing I'm looking for?' Stevie asked again, probably for the twenty-sixth time, and Karen rolled her eyes.

'Anything cutesy, mismatched, old-fashioned – I've got it,' Karen said. 'You do realise none of it will be able to go in the dishwasher, don't you?'

Stevie sighed. 'I know, but I have this vision in my head of flowery tea-cups and tiny silver tongs for the sugar lumps, and real linen napkins, not those awful serviettes.' Suddenly, her eyes filled with unexpected tears and she brushed them away, angrily, fluttering her hands in front of her face. 'Sorry, I'm just a bit…' She wasn't exactly sure why she was crying, but for a moment everything felt a bit too much.

Karen moved closer and gathered her into a hug. 'Come here, silly. You'll be fine, you know you will. It's just pre-opening nerves.' She patted Stevie's back.

Stevie sniffed, 'But what if I'm not good enough, or there's no trade or…?'

She worried at the niggle the passer-by had put in her head the other day, in the same way a child poked at a loose tooth, and for the umpteenth time she considered giving the estate agent a call. She really should have asked a few more questions about the place before she bought it. Not that she was regretting buying Peggy's Tea Shoppe, because she wasn't, but it may have been prudent to have asked why the previous owners were selling, and maybe she should have made some enquiries of her own – like, what sort of footfall could she expect, what business was like during the winter, that kind of thing. Sensible questions, the sort of questions serious business people would have asked. Instead, she'd let her heart rule her head and fallen in love with both the shop and Tanglewood.

'No regrets, eh?' Karen said, pulling away slightly to look Stevie in the eye. 'You are going to make a go of it, I know you will. How can you not, with the pastries and cakes you make? You're a brilliant baker, your choux buns are the best I've ever tasted.'

'But that's just it,' Stevie wailed. 'I'm a baker, not a businesswoman; I belong in front of an oven, not behind a desk.'

Karen gave her a gentle shake and smiled. 'Have you even got a desk?'

'Nooo, but—'

'You *will* be in front of your oven. Both of them. Most of the time.'

'Yeah, it's that bit when I won't be which worries me. I have no idea how to do accounts, or how to balance the books, or even if I've got the right insurance.'

'Slow down. One thing at a time, yeah? Have you kept all your receipts?'

'I think so.'

'That's a good start. How about I cook us a meal tonight, then we'll settle down with a bottle of something chilled and open up a spreadsheet?'

'Blimey, Karen, you really do know how to party.' Stevie pulled a packet of tissues out of her bag and blew her nose. 'Anyway, you're not cooking – I am. You're my guest.'

'Nonsense! You've got enough to do.' Karen put her arm around Stevie and Stevie leaned into her.

'I'm so glad you're here,' Stevie said to her best friend. 'I'll be even more glad if you make your poached salmon with horseradish crème fraiche.'

'We'll see,' Karen said with a smile.

'And a watercress velouté?' Stevie gave her a pleading look.

'I swear you only invited me up here for my wonderful sauces,' Karen said but she was laughing as she did so, and Stevie did a mental fist pump.

Karen was one of the best sauciers Stevie knew and her mouth was watering already. 'Yep, I dragged you all this way just for your culinary skills,' Stevie teased. 'And the only reason you agreed to come was because I said we'd be going shopping.'

'You know me so well, although I must say, I hoped it might be for shoes, not teapots.' And with that, Karen sauntered off, clutching a purse full of money which Stevie had given her.

'No buying any shoes,' Stevie called after her and Karen waved a hand in the air without looking back.

Stevie felt better about things already, despite the momentary lapse in confidence. She was also having a momentary lapse of funds too, or would be shortly if she wasn't careful. She'd already spent an inordinate amount, and there was loads more she needed to buy, but hopefully she'd be able to get most of it at this flea market without shelling out too much.

Ooh, look, there is a stall selling lots of china. Stevie sauntered over to it, trying to look casual, but her eyes lit up when she spied a beautifully decorated bone-china cake-knife with a silver blade that was carved with an intricate pattern. This was exactly the kind of thing she was looking for, and she set about bartering for her first purchase of the day.

By the time she met up with Karen near the entrance, she was more than ready for doughnuts and coffee from a nearby stand.

Karen was beside herself with excitement, and laden down with assorted bags which she was handling with more care than if they contained the crown jewels.

'Shall we take this lot back to the car, then treat ourselves to a coffee?' Stevie suggested.

'I gotta show you these first. Please let me show you these. There is a woman selling her grandmother's things, boxes and boxes of stuff. The old lady died and the grand-daughter has been left to clear out the house.' Karen was practically hopping from foot to foot. 'Ooh, I really do like spending other people's money,' she declared with a huge grin.

Karen opened one of the bags to reveal bundle after bundle of newspaper-covered parcels. Carefully, she took one out and unwrapped it to reveal a pair of matching salt and pepper pots. They were in the shape of a dog.

'There were loads of them, all different, so I bought twenty sets, one for each table and a few spare, just in case. I've got tiny pots with lids and holes cut out for spoons, and little jugs, and— oomph!'

Stevie caught Karen in a hug and danced her around in a circle, their bulging carrier bags on the grass between them. 'I love you!' she cried.

'I know. I'm good, aren't I?' Karen replied. 'Let's go back to the car and have a good look at what we've got already and what else you need, then we'll have that coffee.'

'Good idea.'

Stevie was like a child on Christmas morning as Karen unwrapped each item, and Stevie checked it off her list. The two friends had already made a good start and after a quick pit-stop for refreshments, Karen led her through the rabbit-warren of parked cars and vans until they came to the one she wanted to show her.

'Teapots!' Stevie cried and rubbed her hands together in delight. There were delicate china ones, sturdy practical ones, novelty ones…

The china ones, she decided, and picked out several she thought would work in the shop. She had a vision of her typical customer in her head – middle-aged, a bit on the particular side, likes things just so – and she felt the teapots would do very well indeed.

A couple of stalls along and she was buying a mishmash of plates in a variety of sizes, while she sent Karen off to scout for cake stands. She simply had to have cake stands, loads of them. And tablecloths. Peggy used to insist on a tablecloth and although it would mean the washing machine might be on 24/7, Stevie saw the attraction.

She was aiming for a kind of Victorian-Edwardian feel (she wasn't quite sure which) but when she thought about what she wanted the tea shop to look like when it was fully kitted out, a vision of afternoon tea taken by ladies in high-necked, long, white dresses came to mind, where gentlemen always held chairs out and the women never failed to have a lace hankie about their person. Something which wouldn't be out of place in a production of *Pride and Prejudice* (although she suspected that might be the Regency era – or was it Georgian?). She wanted her customers to feel as though they had stepped back in time to a more genteel, civilised era, where pouring a cup of tea and eating a selection of cakes and pastries was an occasion to be enjoyed and lingered over – the exact opposite to a Gregg's sandwich. Not that she had anything against Gregg's sandwiches (she didn't, and she'd eaten plenty of them in her time) but she was aiming for a different end of the catering market.

'Are we done?' Karen appeared at her elbow with yet more bags and the two of them staggered back to the car for a final time.

The Beetle was stuffed from ceiling to floor with assorted bags, and after a bit of shuffling and squeezing, Karen managed to wedge herself into the passenger seat for the drive home.

By the time they'd unloaded the car, both girls were starting to flag.

'If I knew it was going to be this much work, I might have had second thoughts,' Stevie said. 'I want to open next weekend, but I'm nowhere near ready.'

'Yes, you are,' Karen replied firmly. 'Although if I knew I was going to be a pack horse for the day, I might have stayed in London.'

She nudged Stevie with her elbow to show she was joking, and Stevie nudged her back, suddenly tearful again. How was she going to manage all on her own, in the middle of nowhere, with no friends or family close by?

Although, by the time she'd unpacked, washed and found a place for everything, and had stood back to admire the tea shop, she was starting to feel a bit more optimistic. The place really did look great. It was still lacking a few bits and pieces, but she could get those done over the next few days.

'Dinner is ready,' Karen called from the kitchen and Stevie suddenly realised just how hungry she was.

'I envy you, I really do,' Karen said, as she plated up their food. 'You've made your dream come true. I wish I could do the same.'

Stevie blinked. 'I didn't know you wanted to run a café? You never said.'

'I don't. I want to run my own kitchen one day.' She sounded so wistful, Stevie's heart went out to her friend.

'You will,' she said, meaning it and wishing she could do something to help make it happen. Her friend was one of life's good people and she deserved a break.

'Right then, enough of me,' Karen declared, clapping her hands. 'The rest of today and most of tomorrow is all about the tea shop. We've got the accounts to sort out and some price lists to decide on. But before we start, I want to say one thing – Peggy would have been so proud of you.'

And, as Stevie surveyed her beautiful, quaint little shop, she knew Karen was right.

Chapter 13

Stevie took a deep breath and unlocked the door, the bell tinkling as she wedged it open, letting the late spring smells waft in. She breathed in the scents of the (very) early morning, savouring the aromas of recently mown grass, the river and the flowers in the hanging baskets and pots along the road. Then she sneezed hugely. Oh great, she thought, hay fever, and she hastily slammed the door shut.

She stood for a second, surveying her little kingdom, trying to see it through a customer's eyes, hoping it would go down well with the armies of walkers, hikers, campers, and that particular breed of elderly person who drove aimlessly because they were "out for a run in the car" and the only thing they wanted was a nice cup of tea and a slice of cake in the middle of it.

Stevie reversed the sign on the door from "Closed" to "Open" and checked the display cabinet and counter. Though she said so herself (and she may well be a teensy-weensy bit biased), it all looked very tempting. She took a deep breath and said a silent prayer of thanks that she'd managed to get it ready in the time she'd set herself. She couldn't believe it was only two weeks since she'd been handed the keys, and now here she was, ready to serve her first ever pot of tea and slice of cake in her very own place. She felt like pinching herself to make sure she wasn't dreaming!

She took another look around, making sure everything was perfect and nodded to herself.

In pride of place was a toasted marshmallow and ginger cake – four layers of moist ginger sponge, interspersed with buttercream and coated with meringue which had been lightly toasted, giving it a marshmallow flavour. Next to it sat a maple and pear cake, made with freshly bought fruit which had been caramelized in its own syrup. On the other side of the chiller was a rich chocolate cake, which oozed gooeyness and decadence. She was aiming to bake three large cakes a day, with a variety of different flavours and ingredients. She was even going to make notes about which ones sold the best, and any comments she received.

She'd also baked three varieties of muffins (apple, carrot and the more traditional blueberry), cupcakes, an apple and blackberry pie which she would serve with a dollop of thick cream, Danish pastries and croissants (although she'd not baked too many of those), for the anticipated morning trade, then she'd followed all this up with some brightly coloured macaroons, chocolate-iced eclairs, and madeleines.

In addition, she'd produced some savoury dishes for those customers with not so much of a sweet tooth, and she was keeping her fingers crossed the cheese scones (one of her favourites) would prove to be a hit.

She stocked twenty-one different teas (it *was* a tea shop, after all!) from the more traditional breakfast and after-noon teas and her favourite Earl Grey, to Lady Grey (it made her chuckle every time she saw the label as images of *Fifty Shades* came to mind), to Lapsang Souchong, and the less well-known white tea, as well as various flavours of herbal teas.

Coffee would be served in tiny cups, glasses, mugs, wide-mouth cups – whatever the type of coffee demanded – and she'd even bought a few cafetières. She was also the proud driver of that menacing machine which spat hot milk and even hotter water at her whenever it felt like it. For some reason, she'd decided to call it Bertie.

Everything about the tea shop was cute and sweet, and she had paid great attention to detail. She simply loved the bone-handled cake knives and forks with their intricate carvings, and the lidded china pots for cream or jam, complete with tiny spoons, and the tea-bag coasters. Then there were the miniature tongs for the lumps of rough brown and white sugar, all of them one of a kind and quite unusual.

The cake stands were gorgeous too, and they made an impressive display of yumminess inside the chilled cabinet. Single, two-tiered, and three-tiered stands, each of them sporting their own lovely cakes, and lying by the sides of every single one was a cake knife or a server. Her favourite was made of china with delicate pink roses all over it.

With a satisfied sigh, Stevie went back to her kitchen to put the finishing touches to the strawberry and kiwi meringues she was in the middle of preparing.

Sometime later, the bell's fairy chimes announced a customer, and Stevie wiped her hands on a towel and straightened her apron, her heart hammering in her chest. This is it, this is the true start of my business, my new life, she thought, and she put a welcoming smile on her face and stepped out to greet her very first customers.

Chapter 14

The Hen and Duck's presence could be felt from a hundred yards away, the aroma of beer and smoke drifting on the wind like an olfactory trail of breadcrumbs, leading the thirsty to its door.

Stevie gladly followed the siren call of the pub. Since she moved to Tanglewood she'd hardly managed to snatch a minute for herself. What with moving, then settling in and preparing the tea shop for opening, she had been on the go from breakfast until supper and well into the night.

But today was a day to remember. Today she had opened her doors for the first day's trading and she had been busy. Very busy indeed. All in all, it had been an encouraging start, and she had the rest of the summer stretching out before her, with its tourists and walkers, during which to establish her business. The only thing to make the day even better would be someone to share her celebration with.

She'd give Karen a call in the morning if she had a chance, otherwise she'd send a text. She checked her watch; it was gone nine o'clock and her friend would be up to her eyes in plating up meals for hungry customers right now, so she continued to make her weary, but happy, way to the nearest public house to celebrate on her own. Anyway, she was sick of the sight of baked goods, having cooked another batch this evening after she'd shut the shop, and she was hoping the pub sold food. Anything but cakes or pastries. A nice lasagne would do the trick, or a beef hotpot.

Screwing up her courage, she stepped inside, her eyes trying to adjust to the gloom. Crikey, it's quiet in here, she thought disappointedly, having sworn she'd heard voices when she was standing outside.

It took a moment for her to realise the voices she had thought she'd heard did, in fact, belong to real people; unfortunately, those people were all now silent and staring at her.

Stevie smiled ingratiatingly, her eyes darting from face to face, and then she bit her lip when the only responses she got back were blank looks. She took a deep breath, squared her shoulders, lifted her chin, and marched up to the bar. It was only when she placed her elbows on the polished surface she noticed all the faces were male. There was not one woman amongst them.

Stevie cleared her throat noisily. 'A pint of bitter, please,' she squeaked.

The barman put down the glass he had been polishing and gave her a hard look. Stevie stared defiantly back.

'Other door,' he eventually said, gruffly, jerking his head to the right.

'Sorry?'

'Next door.'

'That's what I thought you said.' Stevie risked a quick glance behind her. All eyes were still focused on her. 'Um, I asked for a pint of bitter. Please.'

'I know, and I said, "next door".'

The man was big, around six feet six, with a large, rotund belly which seemed to start at his neck and finish at his knees. He was in his late fifties, but for all his weight and age he gave the impression of someone who could take care of himself, and others too, if it became necessary. The almost-bald head, the florid face, and hands the colour and texture of slabs of marbled beef, helped the image along nicely.

Stevie almost turned tail and ran, but her pride kept her feet cemented to the floor. Anyway, there was something she needed to know.

'What about next door?' She simply had to ask.

'You'll get served in there.' The landlord placed both chunky hands on the bar and leaned forward.

'Why won't I get served in here? What's wrong with in here?' Stevie wanted to know.

'Men only, that's what.'

'*What?*'

Stevie caught the nods of agreement out of the corner of her eye.

The landlord leaned forward even further and Stevie shrank back by a corresponding amount.

'I said,' he repeated slowly, 'it's men only in this bar.'

'But, but, that's discrimination,' Stevie blustered, her cheeks red with embarrassment and indignation in equal measure.

'Aye.'

'You can't do that!'

'I can, and I do.'

'But—'

'Listen, love. No one asked you to come in here, but I'm asking you to leave this bar. It's my pub and I can do what I damn well like in it.'

There was a low murmur around her and Stevie swallowed nervously.

'The Ladies' Lounge is next door.' This came from a figure huddled at the end of the bar who was cuddling a pint of dark liquid like it was a small puppy. A wizened little face peered out at her from underneath a flat cap. 'We come in here to get away from the likes of you.'

'"The likes of me?"' Stevie was incensed. 'What do you mean, "*the likes of me*?"'

'Women.' The old man smiled, revealing a set of startlingly white dentures. They rattled gently in his mouth as he spoke.

'Aye, that's right. I see enough of my missus at home, without having a good pint spoiled by her nagging,' someone else added.

Stevie turned to the owner of the voice and encountered more disappointed faces.

'Leave the girl alone, lads,' someone else said.

Ah, someone who was on her side. Yay!

'Can I help?' the newcomer continued.

Stevie, startled out of her daydream, found the man who had just spoken standing inches away from her and she squeaked in surprise. Squeaking was quickly replaced by drooling and simpering. He was *gorgeous*: tall, well built with broad shoulders, and what appeared to be a flat stomach. He had dark hair curling over his ears, a chiselled jaw and deep blue, dreamy eyes fringed by long, black lashes. Eyes that a girl could just drown in but were at the moment staring quizzically at her. He was also somewhat familiar, but she couldn't for the life of her think where she had seen him before.

Stevie pulled herself together and tore her gaze away from a tiny scar dissecting his left eyebrow. He also had nice shaped lips, not too thin, or too fat like a double row of pork sausages. No, his lips were just perfect, and from what she could see of his teeth, they were just perfect, too. In fact, everything about him was just perfect…

She shook her head – the silence had gone on for some time. He was staring at her, the expression on his face making her realise her thoughts had been displayed for all to see. Especially him. Marvellous! She might as well have spoken them out loud, and she groaned in dismay.

'It's OK,' he continued. 'Mads doesn't bite.'

'Mads?' Stevie shook her head, puzzled, wondering if she had heard correctly.

'The landlord. His name is Maddox but Mads suits him better.'

Stevie was barely listening to this man's actual words. She was concentrating more on his accent, and the sexy, husky tone. There was a Welsh lilt to it, but it wasn't nearly as strong as most other people in Tanglewood. Anyway, whatever the accent was, she could listen to him all day. Stevie was drooling again.

'Come on, I'll take you through to the Ladies' Lounge,' he suggested.

He grasped her upper arm gently and Stevie's skin burned at his touch. This is so clichéd, she thought. I'll be melting into his embrace next. She shrugged to free her arm, not because she didn't want him to hold her (on the contrary, she quite liked it), but because she really didn't want, or need, to be escorted to the Ladies' Lounge.

'Sorry.' He backed off immediately. 'I didn't mean to offend you.'

'Aye, she's a feisty one. You can tell by that red hair of hers.' The wizened little man at the end of the bar had suddenly come to life again.

'It's not red, it's chestnut,' Stevie fired back automatically, flicking said hair away from her face.

'Eh, you don't want to get too friendly with that one, Nick, because she'll eat you for breakfast. Now, *I* likes 'em with a bit of spirit. Pass her over.'

'In your dreams, old man,' came another voice from the gloom at the other end of the bar.

The banter flew around the room and the volume gradually returned to what it had been before Stevie had shown her face.

'See? They're not a bad bunch. Merely set in their ways,' the Adonis said, shepherding her towards the door to the lounge.

'Hang on, a minute.' Stevie stopped defiantly. 'What if I don't want to drink in there?'

'There are two more pubs in the village you could try. You're new here, aren't you?' He squinted at her, and once again she had the feeling they'd met before, or maybe she'd seen him around. No, she'd remember if she had. He was too yummy to forget.

'Yes. So?' she replied, a tad belligerently. What difference did new make after all?

'Only making conversation.' He held up his hands, palms facing her, clearly taken aback by her tone. And so he should be, suggesting she should take herself off to another pub!

'I want a pint in *this* bar,' Stevie said, stubbornly, her chin jutting out and her eyes sparking.

'You won't get one.' There was laughter in his voice, and it wasn't doing anything to stop her quick temper from rising. For the record, she snarled inwardly, my temper has nothing to do with the colour of my hair.

'Why won't I?' Stevie said this through gritted teeth. Her feminist sisters would have been proud of her stance.

'Because Mads won't serve you,' her knight in shining armour replied, reasonably.

'Well, he should!' Stevie stamped her foot.

Mads, catching the drift of the conversation, looked up from his newspaper and frowned at her. She had a feeling he wouldn't be averse to picking her up and physically removing her if she didn't leave.

'OK, OK, I'm going,' she called.

There were several grunts of satisfaction from the men.

'Happy now?' Stevie demanded to the Adonis, as she stropped into the Ladies' Lounge, the gorgeous man at her side.

'Ecstatic,' came the sarcastic reply. 'Enjoy your drink.'

And before she knew it, he had turned around and was walking away from her. Nice bum, she thought, admiring the way his backside filled out his cargo pants. She liked a nice backside—

'Oh!' Her face turned scarlet. I've seen that one before, I'm certain of it, bouncing up and down on top of a skittish horse. She never forgot a bum, a face maybe, but not a bum. Talking of faces, his looked much better when it wasn't screwed up in temper.

She pulled herself out of her thoughts and realised he'd returned to the depths of the men-only sanctuary.

It's like a bloody sheikh's harem there, only in reverse, Stevie thought crossly. Surely refusing to serve someone because of their gender was illegal? She could sue, that's what she could do, but first she wanted a drink, and she was determined to have it.

Stevie propped up the bar and looked around, the difference between the two bars obvious. This was no spit and sawdust joint, like the room she had just left. This one had "ladies" in it, drinking what looked like sherry, or Babycham, or similar other "womanly" drinks. She shuddered. Then there was actual carpet on the floor, not floorboards, and nice pictures on the walls, and gentle lighting and comfy chairs. And there wasn't one person under fifty, man or woman. Unfair, she thought; women weren't allowed in the other bar, but men were allowed in the Ladies' Lounge. Perhaps she ought to start a petition?

However, there were two things both bars had in common. The first was that all eyes were still on her, although not as obviously this time, and the second was that Mads was behind the bar.

'Are you his evil twin?' she asked the large man, sweetly.

'What can I get you, love?'

Stevie opened her mouth to give him a piece of her mind and to insist he stopped calling her "love", then hesitated. Mads was no longer gruff and unfriendly. In this bar, he was all charm and service.

'A pint, wasn't it?' he asked, before she could force the words out.

She nodded.

He pulled the pint, and Stevie paid, not taking her eyes off the man in front of her. Mads indicated for her to take a sip. Stevie dutifully obeyed.

'Nice brew,' she said, licking her lips, appreciatively.

'House speciality. It's called Hairy Dog.'

'Do you serve food?'

'It depends.'

'On what?'

'What time is it?'

She checked her watch again. 'It's coming up for nine-thirty.'

'No, then. We stop serving at nine. The chef has gone home.'

Wonderful. Stevie sighed.

A yelled "Service!" from the other bar caught Mads's attention. As he disappeared through the hatch, he turned towards her and said, straight-faced, 'His name is Nick Saunders.' Then he winked.

Stevie smiled, finished her pint slowly, then went home and opened a tin of soup, eating it absently and thinking it might be a good idea to make some homemade soups for the lunchtime trade, especially nearer the winter.

Although, when she finally fell into bed, her thoughts weren't on the shop – she found herself thinking about Nick Saunders, and wondering if he was single…

Chapter 15

'You like her,' Jenkins, the man in the flat cap observed, sucking on his unlit pipe. Although The Hen and Duck appeared to be firmly entrenched in the past, even that old-fashioned pub was subject to the laws of the land and Mads vigorously enforced the "no smoking" rule, much to Jenkins's disgust. Which was why, Nick knew, Jenkins was usually found with his teeth clamped around the stem of the unlit pipe like a toddler with a dummy, as a form of silent protest.

'I like who?' Nick asked absent-mindedly. His thoughts were on the girl. He knew her from somewhere, but he simply couldn't think where. Something about her red hair rang a bell…

'The girl.' Jenkins huffed out a sigh and Mads chuckled.

'What girl?' Nick took a swig of his pint. He'd only popped out for an hour. He needed to get back; Tia would be wondering where he was.

'The one you just threw out of the bar.'

'I didn't throw anyone out of anywhere,' Nick protested.

'Escorted, then,' Jenkins amended.

'Her? Nah, not my type,' he replied. She was very pretty and he admired her spirit, but there was no way he would admit it to this bunch. 'Who is she, anyway?'

he asked. He rubbed a hand tiredly across his face. God, but he was exhausted. He should be getting ready for bed, not standing in a bar, gossiping.

'I don't know her name,' Jenkins continued, 'but she took over that café down the street.'

'I can't remember seeing a café there,' Nick said, frowning. He didn't venture into town too often though, and when he did it was usually only as far as The Hen and Duck.

'It wasn't open long. There was some kind of fuss or summat, I can't quite recall. The last I heard, the owners put it up for sale, and your lass bought it.'

'She's not my lass,' Nick pointed out.

'She could be,' Mads joined in. 'I saw the way she was looking at you.'

Nick didn't say anything. There was nothing *to* say. It had been nearly two years since he'd had any interest in the opposite sex, not since Tia's accident. And although his sister didn't need him as much now as she had done in those first months after she'd been released from hospital, he still didn't have any spare time to start dating again. He was rushed off his feet as it was…

There was silence for a while, then Mads asked, 'How is Tia?'

Nick shrugged. 'Not good.' Unbidden, the guilt swept over him again and he closed his eyes for a second. Everyone said it wasn't his fault, but how could it not be when he'd been the one to raise the top rail on the oxer, knowing Tia wasn't too keen on jumping the fence. But damn it, she had been ready, the horse had been ready, and he had wanted to push her, to make her the best she could be, because that's what he did, that's what he was good at – training riders and horses alike, bringing out the best in them.

Instead, he'd destroyed her life when the horse, not liking the extra height, had baulked well before the jump and lost its footing, throwing Tia from the saddle. He could still hear her awful scream as the animal rolled on her.

'Sorry to hear that, mate. If there's anything we can do…?' Mads trailed off, glancing around the bar for support. Muttered agreement and the nodding of heads was the response.

'Thanks, lads, but I'm not sure anyone can do anything.'

'I was under the impression she was doing OK. Although it can't be easy, a youngster like her in a wheelchair.'

'No, it's not,' Nick replied shortly, then sighed. Mads was only being friendly – there was no need to take his frustration out on him.

A few of the bar's occupants cleared their throats or coughed. Someone called for another round of drinks and the sombre mood was thankfully broken. Nick could have kicked himself. He didn't like airing his troubles, and the men didn't come here to listen to them. He was normally so reserved – he didn't know what had come over him tonight. He didn't usually suffer from bouts of self-pity, but for some reason life had been getting on top of him lately. It was all work and very little play, as Tia had pointed out, especially now his sister wasn't doing much of the paperwork. He hadn't realised how much he'd come to depend on her until she'd stopped.

Perhaps he should tell her how much he appreciated her. Maybe that was the reason for her mood – she felt unrecognised and unacknowledged. I could take her out for dinner, or something. She'd like that, he thought and hoped.

Chapter 16

Stevie sagged against the stainless-steel counter and wiped a trembling, floury hand across her face. She was so exhausted, she didn't know what to do with herself. In an ideal world, she should be in bed, but she had a ton of baking still to do and she hadn't cleaned the shop yet, or checked the sugar bowls to see if they needed refilling, or cut up the fruit for the smoothies she now offered or—

The list was endless, and she was just one woman... How on earth she ever thought she could run a business all by herself, she didn't know. She must have been mad.

'OK, think – baking first,' because then she could do some of the other stuff while the oven was doing its job. So she set about stirring and mixing, working more or less on autopilot simply to get the job done. What she had once revelled in doing was now becoming a chore, one more item to be ticked off an impossible list.

When she'd put the last of the butterscotch buns in the oven, she shoved all the dirty bowls, pans, and utensils in the dishwasher, and wiped the countertops down. Cleaning the floor would have to wait until morning, she was too tired to deal with it now.

Instead, she tackled another mound of washing up by hand, savagely regretting her decision to buy bone-china cups and saucers, and pretty but not-dishwasher-safe plates with gold leaf around the edges. If she could have stuck them all in the dishwasher, it would have made her life so much easier. And she'd give anything for easy right at this moment.

She left the washed dishes to air-dry (it was beyond her to dry them herself when she had so many other things to do) and she plodded into the café area and pulled fifteen pristine tablecloths from the cupboard of a lovely Welsh dresser she'd found online. It was painted turquoise and cream and complemented the pale rose walls perfectly. Only right now, she was too tired to enjoy it. It was simply another thing she had to clean and dust.

It took her a good half hour to remove everything from the tables, whip off today's tablecloths, put fresh ones on and replace the sugar dish, the salt and pepper pots, and the little vases of flowers, after checking none of those items needed filling up, of course, and that the flowers would last another day without being replaced. She made a mental note to give them clean water in the morning. She really couldn't be bothered to do it right now.

A buzzer sounded and for one moment Stevie wondered what it could be.

Oh, it was the timer on the oven! Her brain was so addled she was having trouble with even the simplest of tasks. She'd heard buzzers like this one practically every day of her working life, and here she was, so tired she wasn't sure of her own name. Was it only thirteen days since she'd opened the tea shop door to her first customers? She vaguely recalled being full of enthusiasm and hope…

Luckily nothing was overdone or (God forbid) burned, but it was only luck she realised when she noticed the timer on the second oven was set to two hours instead of the twenty-two minutes it should have been set for. She whisked out the apricot and almond gallets and felt like crying – not because they were ruined, but because she'd caught them just in time.

This was ridiculous. Something was going to have to give, because she couldn't keep this up.

She put the pastries to cool, gathered up all the soiled tablecloths and napkins and shoved them in the washing machine, then decided to sweep and mop the tiled floor after all. It was only when she was brandishing her mop near the customer toilet, she realised she'd forgotten to clean it. There was nothing worse than dirty customer toilets in a restaurant, pub, or café (unless it was a dirty kitchen) and Stevie took great pains to ensure that hers was spotless. She could think of nothing more off-putting for a customer than eating in a premises, only to pop to the loo and find it disgusting, leading to thoughts of how clean the kitchen might be.

Stevie slid down the mop and collapsed onto her just-cleaned floor.

She wasn't going to cry. She wasn't!

But what she *was* going to do was go to bed and start again in the morning. Apart from being so tired she didn't know what to do with herself, her feet and legs were aching from being on them all day, she had a headache, and she hadn't eaten since... when? She couldn't remember. Certainly nothing but a couple of cups of tea and coffee had passed her lips since breakfast, and she couldn't actually remember if she'd had breakfast or not. She vaguely recalled holding a piece of toast, but that might be yesterday when she'd eaten it and not today.

She went to bed with so much on her mind that her sleep was broken and fitful, her brain too full of the things she needed to do, which explained why she was up and dressed well before her alarm went off despite her exhaustion.

Three and a half hours sleep, that was all she'd managed, and she wondered how long a person could live on so little. If she could get through today and tomorrow, she could spend all day Sunday in bed, she promised herself, and to hell with ordering supplies, or doing the accounts, or the washing, or anything else which didn't involve snuggling under her duvet.

'But what kind of a life was that?' she asked herself after downing a quick cup of very strong coffee, cleaning that pesky customer loo, taking everything she needed for today out of the enormous fridge and arranging it in the display cabinet, then setting off to the bakers for some fresh bread (she really had no time to make her own) and the grocers. Both shops were open early, and she dived into the first one she came to, a list in her hand. She was rapidly becoming the list queen of Britain and she had no idea how she had managed to live her life before without one.

Oh, yes, because she hadn't been run off her feet every second, that was how.

'What can I get you today?'

'Hello, Mrs Evans. How are you?'

'Better than you, by the looks of it.'

'Excuse me?' She must have heard the other woman wrong.

'You look worn out. Good night was it?'

'Eh?'

'I said, last night was a good one, was it? Where did you go, somewhere nice?'

'Er, no. I stayed home.'

'Oh, sorry, I just thought… Don't mind me, my mouth can run away with me sometimes. Here, let me see that.' Mrs Evans took the list out of Stevie's hands and scanned it.

'That's OK. I didn't realise I looked so bad.' Stevie gave a weak laugh. She must remember to put some make-up on before she opened up, otherwise she might scare her customers. Another job to add to the list…

'I don't mean to pry, love, but are you all right?'

'Just tired. Really, really tired,' Stevie said. 'It's not easy running your own business, is it?'

Mrs Evans owned the greengrocers with her husband. In fact, nearly all the shops and businesses in Tangle-wood were privately owned; Stevie hadn't seen a big-chain anything since she'd been here. It was what gave the place its charm, and she guessed Mrs Evans would know exactly what she meant.

'You're doing it all by yourself, aren't you, dear?' the shopkeeper asked, weighing up some grapes and popping them into a brown paper bag.

'Yes.' The word came out as a sigh and Stevie shrugged an apology. She didn't mean to be so down, but she was seriously beginning to wonder how long she could carry on like this. Peggy's Tea Shoppe hadn't even been open two whole weeks yet and already Stevie was almost at the end of her tether.

'You need someone to give you a hand. It's too much for one person.' Mrs Evans lowered her voice, even though there was only the two of them in the shop. 'I mean, how do you manage if you need to pop to the loo?'

Stevie laughed. She wasn't really sure how she managed some days, either.

Hang on… That was it! She had an idea. She didn't have to be one person – she could be two! If she hired someone to take orders, serve, clean tables, and so on, then Stevie would be able to spend some of the day in her kitchen, instead of doing what she usually did after the tea shop closed.

She needed an assistant!

Chapter 17

The very next morning, saw Stevie sitting in her kitchen surrounded by the aroma of warm croissants, and working on an advert. She intended to put it in the window and see what response she got. Ideally, she'd prefer someone who was a little older than her, someone with a sensible head on their shoulders, who she could leave in charge now and again. Someone she could gel with.

With a wry smile, Stevie realised what she was searching for was a friend. What she also realised was, having an employee for a friend wasn't recommended. How bizarre – she was rushed off her feet, didn't have a minute to herself, yet she realised she was lonely.

Yes, she talked to customers all day, every day, but it wasn't the same as having someone to go out for a drink with, or who'd pop in for a cup of tea and a chat, was it?

Thinking about a chat, she checked the time. It was rather early but she'd give Karen a call anyway. It seemed ages since she'd spoken to her, although they'd texted like it was going out of fashion.

'Long time, no hear,' Karen said, as soon as she answered. 'Is everything OK?'

'You don't fancy a job, do you?' Stevie asked her.

'You're not thinking of quitting already?'

'No! But I need an assistant. I can't do this all on my own.'

'Of course, you can't,' Karen said. 'You need to advertise.'

'That's what I'm going to do. I just feel as though it should be easier than it is. I've worked in a top London restaurant, for goodness' sake! This running a café business should be a piece of cake – excuse the pun. But it isn't.'

'It's just a different type of hard work. If you can survive working for Corky Middleton you can survive anything. I only hope I can survive Freddie French,' Karen added, naming her own devil-chef of a boss. 'Sorry, I should have said "Frederique" – he thinks it sounds more continental.' She snorted with derision. 'He's only got me moulding caramelized sugar around thimbles, then filling the little blighters with a crushed biscuit base, creamed cheese, and rose-hip coulis on the top. And he wonders why the punters complain it's not even a mouthful. I could understand if he served several them on the same plate, and maybe in different flavours, but he gives the customer one. *One*, I ask you! The man's so far up his own backside, he should wear a headtorch.'

'Work is going well, then?' Stevie said, smiling. See, this is what she missed – being able to have a good moan when things weren't going right. Being able to share the highs and lows and the silly bits in-between. 'You should suggest it to him,' she added.

'The headtorch?'

'Several different flavours on the same plate.'

'I did. He got me emptying the bins.'

'But you're a sous chef and a darned good saucier to boot!'

'Yeah, I know.' Karen's sigh floated down the airwaves.

'Come work for me,' Stevie pleaded. 'I promise I don't own any thimbles.'

'As tempting as it sounds, I like my life here. I'd miss London, being able to get a crepe at three in the morning; going to all the shows the minute they come out and not having to wait for them to appear in whichever remote part of the country you happen to live in; the designer shops; the weird and wonderful coffees; being able to hop on the Tube. Don't you miss it?'

Stevie did, but she wasn't going to admit it. 'No, I'm too busy,' she replied. 'And since when have you been to a show? You hate them. And you can't afford designer shops. All your stuff comes from Primark. It's Oxfam not Oxford Street for the likes of us.'

'Yeah, but the potential is there,' Karen argued. 'Besides, I don't want to work for my best friend – it would be a recipe for disaster.'

Karen was probably right Stevie admitted, after they'd chatted for a bit until Karen had to dash off to get ready for work. She imagined her friend in her tiny flat, which she shared with three other people, and she was glad she had a two-bedroom flat all to herself. It might be above the shop, so switching off from work wasn't always easy, but at least she didn't have an hour commute each way. And at least she owned the place. It might not be in the centre of a throbbing metropolis, but it was all hers.

Suddenly homesick, Stevie picked up the phone and dialled her mum's number. Her mother answered on the first ring, and Stevie felt a surge of love when she heard the familiar voice.

'Mum. It's Stevie.'

'Who?'

'Stevie. Your daughter.'

'Oh, so you are. It's been so long since I heard from you, I'd forgotten I had another daughter.'

'Very funny. How are you?'

'Fine, but my varicose veins are playing up again, and your father has got a nasty cold. He decided to take up fishing and fell in. Oh, and your nana's gone to live with a man she met in Tesco. Since she's had her hip done, she's acting like a teenager.'

'Well, well, good for her.'

'You won't say that when you know he's twenty years younger than her, comes from Bolivia, has got no pension, and lives in a caravan. Fern says he only wants her for a visa, but I can't see any bank giving *him* a credit card, can you?'

Stevie stifled her giggles.

'And he's probably only after her money,' her mother continued.

'I didn't think she had any.'

'Exactly,' came the indecipherable reply.

'Mum, let her be. She's having fun.'

'Fun? Fun! She's eighty-three! It might kill her.'

'So? She'll at least die happy,' Stevie pointed out.

'I don't know why she couldn't have found someone her own age.'

'There aren't many men her own age still alive, Mum. Perhaps she's in love.'

'Love? Huh! You would have thought she'd have grown out of all that. Your father and I certainly have.'

'Too much information,' Stevie thought, cringing. She spent another few minutes listening to how well Fern and Derrick were doing, and then she said her goodbyes.

An intense feeling of discontent engulfed her as she put down the phone. Here she was, doing what she had always wanted to do (well, almost, she conceded – Peggy's Tea Shoppe wasn't exactly a Michelin star restaurant, but at least it was hers), and she still wasn't happy. She spent every minute of every day working, was miles away from home, and had no social life. Even her nana was getting more action than her, Stevie thought, as she re-read her advert.

Satisfied with the wording, she stuck it on the window, changed the sign from "Closed" to "Open" and prepared to face another day.

A little bit later on that morning, she was bending over, peering into the display cabinet to check everything looked as good as it possibly could, when someone said, 'I could do that.'

The quivery voice made Stevie jump, and she glared accusingly at the bell above the door. Now and again it failed to ring, and she was convinced it had a mind of its own.

'Do what, Mrs George?' Stevie asked, as she placed a teapot on a tray, and selected an English Breakfast tea bag. Mrs George had the same thing every morning, as regular as clockwork.

'That there job. I could do with a bit of extra cash.' The old lady hobbled to her favourite table in one of the bay windows and eased herself into a chair. She usually sat facing out, but this time she took a seat which gave her a good view of the shop and Stevie.

Stevie watched as she carefully propped her stick up and stuck her bad leg out in front of her and wondered how to break the news to the old dear.

'Pah! With your memory? You'd have forgotten the order before you'd got to the counter,' a voice from the corner said. It belonged to a woman of around eighty-years-old, dressed bizarrely in a flowing multi-coloured skirt, a T-shirt, and a floor length purple cape. She had been in several times and Stevie was beginning to think of her as a regular. 'Now, *I* could do it with my eyes shut,' the woman continued.

Not wanting to offend Mrs George, Stevie said, 'We could give it a trial run, if you like. How about giving me a hand for an hour after you've had your tea?'

'Oh, no dear, I can't do Thursdays. I go to the doctors on a Thursday.'

'Every Thursday?'

'Mondays are too busy, what with all those people who were ill on the weekend, Tuesday is my Salvation Army day and Wednesday I like to go to my bridge club. I go to the doctors on a Thursday.'

'I'm surprised you can get an appointment,' the purple-caped woman piped up. 'They're always full when I ring for one.'

'Oh, I don't have an appointment,' Mrs George said, airily. 'I just like to sit in the waiting room and have a natter. Thank you, dear.' This last was said to Stevie who had just placed the pot of tea in front of her. 'And I think I'll have one of those scones with jam and cream, or maybe a slice of cake. What are those?' She pointed to a selection of individual tarts in a variety of flavours.

'Would you like to come up to the counter and choose one?' Stevie offered.

'Not with my leg,' she refused, firmly. 'I can't walk far, and I like to rest it as much as possible.'

'Do you think you'd be up to being on your feet for a few hours every day?' Stevie asked, gently.

'I was thinking, I could sit here and shout the orders over to you,' Mrs George suggested.

'That's great,' Stevie said with a pained smile, 'but what about serving, or clearing the tables.'

'You can do that.' Mrs George nodded to herself, as if the whole thing was a done deal.

'Actually, Mrs George, I need someone who can run the shop while I'm in the kitchen.'

'That's no way to run a business,' the old woman stated. 'Lounging around while you get a poor old woman to run about for you.'

'That's not what—'

'Don't be an idiot, Mary,' the woman in the corner said. 'You can't work here, and that's final.'

'Er…' Stevie said.

'Keep your nose out of my business, Betty Roberts. Go get your own job,' Mrs George said.

'This *is* my job,' Betty replied loftily. 'You're just too stupid to see it.'

'Er… ladies…' Stevie tried to intervene.

Betty got to her feet, and Stevie realised that she was actually quite tall and lanky. She had orange wellies with big yellow flowers on her feet, and a pink beret completed her outfit.

'Let me know when you want me to start,' she said to Stevie and swished out of the door, her cape billowing out behind her, reminding Stevie of a geriatric, multi-coloured Batman.

Mrs George had also risen to her feet and was wrestling with her walking stick. 'I don't think I'll be taking the job, after all,' she called to Stevie from the doorway. 'I don't like cats.'

Eh? What was the old dear talking about? What did she mean, *cats*?

Stevie watched them both as they hurried down the street, not giving Mrs George a hope in hell of catching the sprightlier Betty Roberts, but at least their joint departure had removed the sticky issue of the job.

After thinking for a moment, Stevie removed the advert, added, "Please apply with a CV" and put it back up.

Then she screamed as something soft rubbed against her leg.

It was a little black cat.

At least that explained Mrs George's parting comment.

'Where did you come from?' Stevie asked the feline, bending down to stroke it. 'You can't stay here, oh, no you can't, no matter how cute you are.'

She opened the door, to usher the cat out but instead of leaving, the animal wove a figure of eight around her ankles.

'Go on, shoo,' Stevie said, trying to extricate her feet from the determined feline, and hopping on one foot as she tried to avoid stepping on it, and when that didn't work, she picked it up and popped it on the pavement outside. 'Be a good kitty and go home. I've got nothing for you here.'

The cat ignored her and shot back inside the tea shop. Stevie dashed after the animal, but there was no sign of it. Where did it go?

'Here kitty, kitty.' Stevie bent down to peer under the tables.

'Here's my CV.'

'Arrgh!' Stevie straightened up and banged her head on the underside of a table.

'Sorry, but the door was open, so I assumed the café was too,' a female voice said.

'It is,' Stevie rubbed her head and took the sheet of paper the woman was holding out. 'That was quick.'

'I always carry a few around with me. You never know when a job opportunity will arise. Like today.' The woman laughed, a little nervously, Stevie thought.

Stevie scanned the CV. Cassandra Curtis, aged thirty-four, was more of an executive type than a waitress, if her employment history was to be believed.

'All your previous jobs have been in London,' Stevie noticed. 'You've worked for a couple of big companies.'

'And you're wondering why I'm answering a "Help Wanted" ad in a little village in the middle of nowhere, right?'

'Er... right.'

'Because my husband and I live here. We both got fed up of the rat race and wanted a simpler way of life. Yeah, we got that all right.' She sounded sad.

'I'm sorry?' It came out more of a question than an expression of sympathy.

'We simply can't afford all the repairs to the house and let's not even begin talking about the outbuildings and the land. You see, we bought a smallholding, with grand ideas of being almost self-sufficient. If we could grow roof slates, I'd be a happy woman.' Cassandra paused. 'I know none of my previous jobs qualifies me for this one, but I'm a dab hand at mixing cement, and I'm a quick learner. Please, I need this job.'

Stevie didn't like seeing anyone beg and the woman seemed nice enough. 'One month trial?' she offered.

Cassandra bit her lip and Stevie wondered whether she was going to laugh or cry. 'You won't regret it,' she promised. 'I scrub up well, honest.' She gave an apologetic wave at her attire of muddy hiking boots, scruffy old Barbour jacket, and worn jeans. 'I was off to the Post Office when I saw the advert. Then I was going home to wedge some buckets in the attic.' She saw Stevie's puzzled expression. 'Rain is forecast for later. When do you want me to start?'

'Oh, um, tomorrow?'

'Great!' Cassandra was beaming broadly, and Stevie noticed how pretty she was without the worried expression on her face. 'Would a white shirt and black trousers be OK?' the woman asked. 'I've still got most of my old work clothes somewhere.'

'Perfect. Welcome to Peggy's.' Stevie stuck out a hand and the two women shook on the deal.

'I can't wait to tell Aiden the good news,' Cassandra cried as she headed for the door. 'See you tomorrow, Peggy.'

'I'm not Peggy,' Stevie said. 'My name is Stevie.'

'Sorry, I just assumed… is it the cat's name?'

'What cat?'

Stevie had forgotten all about the little black cat, until she saw where Cassandra was pointing. The cat was perched quite serenely on top of the display cabinet, washing its face.

'It's not my cat,' Stevie objected.

'It seems to think it is,' was Cassandra's parting words as she skipped out of the door.

Stevie took the advert down and marched over to the cat. 'You can't be in here,' she said, scooping the animal off the display cabinet, and making a mental note to disinfect both it and the counters. 'What will the Health Inspector say?'

The cat meowed and rubbed its face against hers. It was certainly very friendly.

This time, when she put it outside the door, it stayed outside, jumping onto the windowsill and peering into the tea shop. All through the day, Stevie was conscious of those pleading green eyes following her, so it was inevitable the last thing she did before locking up was to pick the little bundle of fur up and take it upstairs to the flat.

'OK, Peggy, you win,' Stevie said, thinking the name was as good as any for now. 'You can stay here for the night, but tomorrow I'm taking you to the vet, and seeing if you belong to anyone.' Stevie didn't know much about animals, but she did know that by law all dogs had to be microchipped – maybe cats did too.

Chapter 18

'No microchip,' the vet said. 'But you'll be pleased to know she's healthy. About six months old, I'd say. Do you want her spayed?'

'Do I want her what?'

'Spayed, neutered. She's about to come into season any minute, and if you don't act now you'll have lots of kittens running around the place.'

'I don't want to do anything with her, except to find her owner.'

'I don't recognise her and I never forget a face,' the vet said, tucking a stray strand of hair back into her messy bun. 'You can put up posters and hope someone gets in touch.'

'Or?' Stevie sensed an "or".

'Take her to an animal shelter and see if they can rehome her.'

'What if they can't?' Stevie asked, her arms tightening protectively around the cat. Peggy purred loudly.

'It depends on the shelter. Some will keep her indefinitely, others will…' The vet thumped her hand on the table, making Stevie jump. Peggy gave a piteous mew.

'I'll try the poster route,' Stevie decided, and took the cat home with her, stopping off at the supermarket on the way to buy food, a couple of bowls, a litter tray, some treats, and the odd toy or two. Not that the cat was staying or anything, but while the animal was under her roof, the least she could do was to look after it properly. She even bought it a little red collar with a bell.

As she put it on the cat, she said, 'Now I'll know where you are. No sneaking downstairs. You're not allowed in the shop or the kitchen,' she warned. 'If I catch you in either of those places, I'm taking you to the animal shelter.'

Peggy mewed softly and rolled over onto her back, batting her paws in the air.

The cat was really cute, Stevie acknowledged, and it would be nice to come home to a friendly welcome after a day slaving over a hot oven.

She thought back over the day. Cassandra had arrived promptly at nine, and after being shown how to use the coffee machine (a degree in engineering was needed to make the darned thing work), she set about taking orders and serving them as if she'd been doing it all her life.

Stevie had been so impressed with her that she'd left Cassandra on her own in the front of house after the lunchtime rush and had taken herself off to the kitchen to rustle up tomorrow's batch of goodies. Which was why she'd had the time to take the cat to the vets this evening.

On the flip side, she now had several hours before bedtime when she had nothing to do. After heating up a tin of soup and eating it, Stevie decided to work on the idea she'd had of offering homemade soup when the weather began to turn. So she popped downstairs, grabbed some ingredients and returned to the flat, where she set about peeling and chopping.

As she worked, she hummed to herself, and every now and again had a one-sided conversation with Peggy.

The cat, for her part, sat and watched her with an inscrutable expression.

Chapter 19

'I'm all done.' Cassandra took off her rubber gloves and placed them on the gleaming steel worktop.

'How about a coffee before you go?' Stevie asked. 'I'll let you have a piece of that marble cake,' she added, enticingly.

'Oh, don't. That damned cake bypasses my stomach and plasters itself all over my behind. Do you realise how much weight I've put on since I started working here?' Cassandra slapped her ample rump. 'And most of it is because of that marble cake.'

Stevie patted the seat of the chair. 'Come on, you know you want to.'

'All right,' Cassandra sighed, resigned to her fate, 'but just a normal Nescafe for me, none of that fancy latte stuff with a shot of caramel, or whatever rubbish people stick in their coffees these days. I don't need the extra calories.'

Stevie laughed. 'That's like ordering a burger with extra fries, and a diet Coke.'

Cassandra narrowed her large, dark eyes at her boss. 'Careful, or I might swap this job for one at McDonald's.'

'Yeah, yeah.' Stevie handed Cassandra her cup and cut her a slice of cake. 'Enjoy.'

'Oh, I intend to,' Cassandra mumbled, her mouth already full of her first bite of the cake.

Stevie sat down at the small table she'd installed in the kitchen. As much as she could, she tried to separate work life from home life, although that wasn't so easy, she conceded, when she lived in the same place as she worked. But since she'd taken Cassandra on, she'd developed a routine of preparing everything the afternoon before if the ingredients allowed, so she was able to stack it all in the ovens or the fridge to cook fresh first thing in the morning. While her ovens were busy, she would concentrate on other things, like chopping copious amounts of salad, washing berries and whipping cream, and the smells of cooking would gradually permeate the tea shop, mingling with the aroma of freshly ground coffee. Stevie wished she could bottle that particular mixture of scents – it was mouth-watering.

Seeing Cassandra shovelling marble cake into her mouth, wearing one of the tea shop's pinnies and with a cloth draped over her shoulder, Stevie found it hard to envisage Cassandra in her old life as a personal assistant to the managing director of an engineering company. She wondered what had happened to the power suits Cassandra once wore: Stevie thought she probably used them to mop the floor, knowing her. There was no doubt Cassandra had gone native when it came to embracing her new lifestyle, although the couple were a long way from becoming self-sufficient. Stevie, selfishly, was glad they weren't, because otherwise Cassandra wouldn't be working here and Stevie didn't know how she'd ever managed without her.

'How's the house coming on?' Stevie asked, when she no longer had to compete for Cassandra's attention with a slice of cake.

The waitress wiped her mouth on a napkin. 'I don't think the roof leaks any more,' she replied, brightly. Whenever there was even the slightest hint of Welsh drizzle, Cassandra and Aiden had to rush around with assorted buckets and bowls to catch the drips. 'Do you remember I said I wanted a wet room? Well, I didn't mean I wanted one in every room in the house,' she added.

Stevie laughed, imagining her friend's dilapidated three-bedroomed cottage with a state-of-the-art shower. Hell, the couple barely had hot and cold running water.

'Actually, it's becoming quite habitable,' Cassandra continued. 'If Aiden manages to finish that commissioned piece he's been working on for the past one hundred years, then we will be able to afford to buy the new boiler.'

Aiden had found a newly-discovered ability to carve wood, and was busy making interesting woody things to sell to supplement their income. Stevie had bought a couple of large ladles from him, and they hung from hooks behind the counter, ready for when she offered soup for sale.

Cassandra scrunched up her nose. 'I can't face another winter here with a fair-weather boiler. And we'll need proper heating, especially if…'

She trailed off. Stevie knew how much Cassandra wanted a baby, and she and Aiden had been trying since they moved to Tanglewood.

Stevie smiled sympathetically. 'Your body is probably waiting until you have got that damned house fit for a baby. Unless, of course, you actually *want* the baby to be born in a barn.'

'Ha, ha, very funny. The thing is,' Cassandra said, becoming serious, 'if we wait for the right moment, we'll never get pregnant. There's always something that needs to be done – the house is a wreck, Aiden's business is not established enough, we can't afford it. Anyway, I want a baby now! I'm thirty-four. I can't wait much longer: all my eggs will have gone off.'

'Ugh. That's not a very nice thought.' Stevie paused, then she said softly, 'I can't imagine what it must be like to want a baby so much.'

'You're young yet, twenty-six isn't it?'

Stevie shook her head. 'Nope. I turned twenty-seven not long after I bought this place.'

'You're still a baby, yourself. Anyway, this is the way it generally goes; first you get your man, then you want the wedding thing, then there's this house you've simply got to have, and then you want a baby. Some women do the dog or cat bit in between the house and the baby, and some skip the house, or even the man part, entirely. But the odds are Mother Nature will get her way and your hormones will start playing up. The only thing that can quieten them down is to get pregnant.'

'That is *so* not going to happen to me!' Stevie declared, with total certainty. 'For one thing, I'm nowhere near finding a man, and more to the point, have you *seen* the men around here?'

'There are quite a few nice ones, if you could be bothered to look.' Cassandra began ticking them off on her fingers. 'There's William Ferris, Lord Whatshisname's son, out at the Manor. He's not married and he's rich, or he will be when his daddy pops his clogs. Then there's the guy who owns The Furlongs but unless you're a horse, he probably won't notice you. And there's—'

'Enough, already!' Stevie laughed. 'OK, so there are some eligible ones floating around, but I haven't met any of them yet and it doesn't look like I'm going to. Hang a sec, did you say "horse"?'

'Yeah, Nick Saunders is quite a famous show jumper. Have you heard of him?'

Unbidden, his face flashed into her mind. She hadn't seen him since she had tried to get served in the men's bar at The Hen and Duck. So that's what he did for a living. But still, he never should have been riding one of those animals on a main road. Being a show jumper was no excuse.

Maybe she should pay the pub another visit…

Chapter 20

Nick looked up when he heard a car trundling over the cobbles and sighed in exasperation. Gently placing the horse's hoof back on the ground, he straightened up, prepared to do battle. Firstly, he'd told Miranda several hundred times not to drive around the back, but to use the driveway by the house (he wasn't being pedantic – he had sound reasons for the request, namely that it could startle the horses), and because he hated it when she turned up unexpectedly.

This time she had her good-for-nothing brother in tow.

'Hello, darling,' Miranda trilled as she slid gracefully out of the car. 'I've brought William. I hope you don't mind, but he insisted on coming.'

Nick did mind – the bloke was a waster and a nuisance – but manners got the better of him and he tried for a smile instead. There was no point in annoying the future Lord Tonbridge, and especially since the present Lord and Lady Tonbridge thought the sun shone out of the lad's arse.

"Lad" was rather incorrect. William was only a couple of years younger than Nick, but his attitude and lifestyle was that of a student, staying up until the wee small hours partying, and then lying in bed until midday, if local gossip was to be believed. Nick wondered, not for the first time, what the bloke actually did, and came to the same conclusion he always arrived at – nothing.

William had his sister's innate grace and Nick watched him with narrowed eyes as he too, slipped from the vehicle. The old Land Rover wasn't an easy thing to get in and out of and most people tended to clamber.

Nick's eyes narrowed even further when he noticed what the siblings were wearing. The brother had a three-piece suit on and a cravat around his neck (a cravat for God's sake! Where did the idiot think he was – on a catwalk?). His sister had a flouncy dress and high-heeled strappy sandals.

Nick watched her pick her way over the cobbles, wobbling on those long legs of hers, and he couldn't help but appreciate her looks. Miranda was one attractive lady. But the problem was, she knew it.

'Can't stop long, we're on our way to Cheltenham,' she trilled.

Ah yes, the races. That explained why the pair of them were dressed up to the nines.

'Don't let me hold you up,' he replied.

'You aren't, dahling. We can spare a bit of time.' Miranda sounded as though she was doing Nick a favour by turning up at all. 'How's Domino?'

'See for yourself.' Nick jerked his head at the horse's stable.

'Can you be a love, and get him out for me? I don't want to risk breaking a heel.'

Nick sarcastically tugged at his forelock. 'Yes, madam.'

'Oh, you!' Miranda let out a tinkling laugh. 'Don't be so beastly.'

Nick tied a lead rope to the horse's halter and led him out of the stable.

'He looks good, doesn't he?' William said.

'What did you expect him to look like? Whipped and beaten? Starving?' Nick said.

'Take no notice, Wills. Nick is nothing but a grump.' Miranda laughed.

'Where's Tia?' William asked, looking around as if he expected her to be hiding behind a water trough.

'Indoors,' Nick replied, shortly.

'Do you mind awfully if I pop in and say hello?'

Nick did mind, but before he could think of a reason to refuse, William had darted towards the office door and disappeared into the depths of the house. At least Nick had one consolation – Tia hated being surprised. She'd soon give him short shrift and send him packing.

Miranda tottered closer, being careful where she placed her feet, and patted Domino on the neck. She was close enough for Nick to smell her very expensive perfume.

'How is he doing?' she asked, sounding more serious. She had good reason to be concerned, Nick thought, because the horse had been almost uncontrollable when she'd brought it to him. She'd told him she'd got Domino from some fellow who was going to send him to the knacker's yard, and the poor animal had been in a terrible state. Once Nick had sorted out the horse's physical problems, he'd started on the mental ones – which hadn't been quite so easy to deal with. It had been a case of two steps forward and one step back. He thought he'd cracked it at one point, but roadwork had proved to be a bit too much for the nervous gelding, especially when bright yellow

Beetles appeared out of nowhere and scared the animal half to death.

'Good,' he said, pushing the image of the Beetle's feisty owner out of his mind. 'You can have him back next week. I just want to take him through Tanglewood one last time to check his reaction to traffic, to make sure the throbbing hub of the village doesn't put him off his stride.'

Miranda patted his arm, much the same way she'd patted her horse a few seconds ago. 'I really appreciate what you're doing for me, Nick,' she said, and now her voice was lower, throatier.

'You're paying me to do it,' Nick pointed out.

'Stop it! You sound like a real bad boy, and you make me sound even worse!'

Nick rolled his eyes. The woman was incorrigible and such a tease.

'Aw, I've embarrassed you. Sorry, Nickykins, but you're so easy to wind up.'

Nickykins! Arrgh! Nick ground his teeth. And where was that sodding brother of hers? Tia should have sent him away with a flea in his ear by now.

'Haven't you got a race to go to?' he growled. 'Go and lose some money.'

'You're such a grump.' Miranda laughed again. 'That's what I love about you.'

Short of telling her to piss off, Nick didn't know how else to tell her to leave him alone. He didn't really want to hurt her feelings, but she was too in-your-face for his liking, too sure of herself, with the sort of confidence which comes from breeding and money. He knew for a fact that both she and her brother had gone to the best private schools, had mingled with all the right people, and had been seen in all the right places. Their whole lives seemed to give them a sense of entitlement and it grated on Nick a little.

He was realistic enough to understand some of his antagonism was envy – the siblings had had it so easy, never having to work for anything, never having to rough it, never knowing hardship. Unlike Nick, who'd had to fight every inch of the way for what he wanted.

Not that he regretted the fight, or where he was now – one of the top show jumpers in Britain – but show jumping was a rich man's (or woman's) pastime. Horses cost money. Good horses, the kind that take you to the Horse of the Year Show, or to the Olympics, cost a great deal of money indeed, and he wasn't just talking about the initial outlay, either. Stabling, training, transport, entry fees, vets' bills… they all added up.

Nick had been lucky. From the first time he'd set eyes on a horse, he knew what he wanted to do. At sixteen, with little or no experience, he'd persuaded a yard to take him on as a stable hand. He'd really wanted to be a jockey, but was simply too tall, and too well built, but he'd got lucky when he'd despondently traipsed into a show jumping yard expecting to be turned away and had been hired instead. Bed and board, and a couple of pounds a week to live on, he was worked to the bone and had loved every minute.

Once the yard's owner had spotted a smidge of talent in the young Nick, he'd teased it out, and Nick hadn't looked back since. Two medals in the Olympics and numerous other wins to his name later, sponsorship from some big names had enabled him to set up on his own.

If it wasn't for Tia, he'd have absolutely no regrets.

Thoughts of Tia led to thoughts of William. Where *was* the blighter?

As if thinking about the man had made him magically appear, William sauntered out of the office and towards the car, with an inscrutable look on his face.

'Did you find Tia?' Nick called.

'Yes, thanks.' William got in and made a "wind-it-up" motion to Miranda.

'We'd better be off,' Miranda said, leaning in to peck Nick on the cheek. 'Ciao, dahling. Lovely to see you.'

Nick watched her pick her way back to the Land Rover then returned the horse to the stable and went inside to find Tia.

'What did posh-lad want?' he asked, his tone scathing.

Tia shrugged. She was in the living room, her wheelchair parked in its usual spot. From there she could look out of the window, watch TV, and see into the kitchen – all at the same time if she wanted to.

Right now, she appeared to be staring into space. Her hands were twisting in her lap, and Nick noticed how pale she had become, despite a spot of high colour on both cheeks.

'Did he upset you?' Nick wanted to know.

'No, of course not. He just wanted to ask how I was.'

'Strange,' Nick mused. Why would the bloke want to ask how Tia was? He barely knew her.

'What do you mean, "strange"?' The spots of colour had spread and Tia's face was now quite pink. 'Strange that a man should want to call to see *me*? Is that it?' She was beginning to shout and she thumped her fist on the wheelchair's armrest. 'Is that what you meant?'

'Wait… I… *what*?'

Tia almost drove over Nick's toes as she spun the wheelchair around and made a dash for her room.

'Tia—?' he called after her.

'Piss off!'

'Great. Where the hell had all that come from,' Nick wondered. All he'd said was "strange" and she'd blown up like a landmine.

He'd give her some time to calm down, then go and apologise. He had no idea what he would be apologising for, but he'd do it anyway. It was the least he could do, because if it wasn't for him, Tia would still have the use of her legs.

Chapter 21

Stevie breathed in the heady scents of the florist shop with her usual delight, as she gazed around her at the variety of blooms on display. It was like being inside a jewellery box, surrounded by velvet gems on stalks.

Leanne, its owner, had a flair for colour and instead of arranging the flowers by type, she displayed them by colour; starting to the left of the door with pristine white carnations, roses, lilies and other assorted blooms, the flowers merged into pinks, reds and purples, then into blues, yellow and orange. And everywhere amongst them were swathes of green.

Stevie watched Leanne as she served a middle-aged woman who was rather overdressed for a Wednesday morning, in a pale lemon suit and matching handbag and shoes. She must be going to a wedding, Stevie guessed.

'No, no, no, not those, dear, they remind me of death,' the woman warbled, in a cut-glass voice. She jabbed a manicured finger at some inoffensive tulips. Stevie caught Leanne's eye and made a face. Death? They were tulips, for goodness' sake! What was so funereal about them?

'I'll have some of those lovely irises, a large bunch, mind, nothing measly. And do me an arrangement of yellow roses for the drawing room.' She leaned in close and whispered loudly, 'We've got guests – relations of the Queen, arriving on Friday for the weekend.' She straightened up, glancing around to make sure all the other customers had heard. Her disappointment when she saw only a solitary Stevie was written clearly on her carefully made-up face.

Leanne jotted down the order. 'Certainly, Mrs Ferris. I mean, Lady Tonbridge.'

Her ladyship sniffed her disapproval but rallied gamely. 'You may deliver them on Friday morning,' she instructed graciously. 'Ten o'clock. Sharp.' She glided to the door. 'Please put them on Lord Tonbridge's account.'

With a tilt of the head and a regal smile, she swept out.

Stevie stared after her with her mouth open. She had never seen anyone actually *sweep* before. 'Please tell me she's going to a wedding,' she pleaded.

'No, she always dresses like that when she meets her public.'

Stevie gazed at Leanne in amazement and demanded, 'Who is she?'

Leanne affected the woman's stance and put on a fake posh accent. 'Lady Tonbridge, aka Julia Ferris, of "The Manor".'

Stevie shook her head, none the wiser.

Leanne started plucking flowers out of their pots and placing them into a vase. Stevie stared at her, waiting for an explanation.

The florist stopped what she was doing for a minute and scrutinised her customer. 'How long have you lived here?' she asked.

Stevie quickly counted in her head. 'Coming up for two months now.'

'You obviously don't get out much then,' Leanne observed astutely.

'You've got that right. I hardly get out at all. OK, never, actually,' she admitted.

'I can tell. *Everyone* knows Lord and Lady Tonbridge. The Manor has been in the Ferris family for generations. Lord Tonbridge, Edgar Ferris, spends most of his time in London. Lady Tonbridge stays here and plays at being a member of the aristocracy.' Leanne picked up some gypsophila and slid the stems expertly into the vase. She stood back to check her work, nodding in satisfaction.

'I take it you don't like her much,' Stevie guessed.

Leanne shrugged. 'It's not that I don't like her, it's that I know her background. She's no more "lady" material than you or me. No offence.'

'None taken.' Stevie grinned. 'I freely admit I'm as common as a cowpat.'

Leanne smiled back. 'Do you want your usual?'

'Yes, please, and add some of those tulips.' Stevie pointed to the very flowers that Lady Tonbridge had rejected. 'I quite like them.'

Leanne gathered an armful of flowers and wrapped them in paper.

'So why the snooty attitude?' Stevie asked curiously. 'She can't be serious?'

'Oh, she's deadly serious. She tries really hard to be what she thinks someone in her position ought to be. But the sad thing is, everyone knows she comes from a council estate in Talgarth, and that she worked in a department store before she met Lord Tonbridge. The people in the village despise her because she puts on airs and graces, and from what I can gather, she doesn't fit in with the lah-di-dahs either, who really *have* got the breeding.'

'So why did Lord Tonbridge marry her, knowing what she was like?' Stevie asked.

'The story has it, he married her for love. He even defied his father and nearly got himself written out of the will. I bet he never thought she would turn out to be like that!'

Leanne placed the flowers on the counter and Stevie paid for them, then she continued, 'She doesn't half throw some great parties though, and there's an open invitation to a couple of them for all the villagers. You should try to go.' Leanne gave Stevie her change. 'In fact,' she added, 'Why don't you come out with me on Friday? Get to know the locals a bit better? Have a drink?'

'Not The Hen and Duck,' Stevie said, warily.

'Good lord, no! It's full of old women, and that's just in the men's bar!'

'Yeah, so I found out.' Stevie grimaced at the memory. 'Mads refused to serve me, and made me go into the Ladies' Lounge. I'm not sure which was worse.'

They agreed to meet at The Duke's Arms at eight-thirty the following Friday. Stevie was absurdly pleased with the prospect, and she realised to her chagrin just how much her world had shrunk since she had bought Peggy's Tea Shoppe.

Chapter 22

'I'm shinging in the rain, just shinging in the rain!' Stevie yelled at the top of her voice as she ran through the puddles as delicately as a hippo charging into a river. Her jeans were soaked to the knee and she squelched every time she put a foot to the pavement.

Her chestnut hair (*not carrot – definitely not carrot!*) normally a wild mass swirling around her head and down her back, hung dark and heavy with rain, almost to her waist. Mascara clowned her eyes and drops of water trickled off the end of her upturned nose. It was dark, raining heavily and Stevie was plainly very drunk and having a ball.

Leanne leaned weakly against the side of a parked car, her legs and her eyes crossed. 'Stop it. I'm going to wet myself,' she laughed, crossing her legs even tighter.

'Don't matter,' Stevie called back, dancing into a particularly large puddle in the middle of the road. 'You're wet enough anyway. Who'd know?'

'I would.' Leanne hiccupped, and tried to focus, but Stevie noticed her pupils were pointing in different directions. 'By the way, there's a car coming.'

Headlights lit up the street, catching Stevie in the spotlight. She twirled around, kicking up water, which sparkled into droplets as it splashed back down.

'My public loves me,' she shouted, and with arms outstretched, she bowed low. 'Thank you, thank you.'

The four-by-four drew to a halt in front of her and beeped its horn. Stevie blew expansive kisses in response, as Leanne bent almost double with hysterical laughter.

The vehicle idled in the centre of the road, black and shining, growling ominously and tooted again. Stevie took another bow and Leanne clapped enthusiastically. Neither of them heard the whine of the window.

'Will you please get out of the middle of the road?' an exasperated male voice called out.

Stevie ignored the car for a moment, raising her face skywards and opening her mouth to catch the raindrops. Then she smiled sweetly at it, but the drunken squint spoiled her attempt at an angelic expression.

'No. Why don't you go around me?' she asked reasonably.

'Because there's not enough room,' came the equally reasonable reply. 'Now, will you please move?'

'Why?'

'Because you're in the middle of the road.' The voice was rising slightly in irritation. It was still a very nice voice, Stevie thought, disjointedly.

'Why?' she repeated.

'*I* don't know why you're in the middle of the road, do *I*? You're probably mad, or stupid.' There was a pause. 'Look, I'm on the way to see a man about a horse. It's urgent, so will you please get out of the way?'

The car revved, backing up its owner's request with a snarly growl of the engine.

Stevie stood rooted to the spot, doing a rabbit in the headlights impression, reluctant to relinquish her puddle, however sexy the voice was.

Suddenly the engine noise changed, and the vehicle began to reverse up the street, the driver finally losing patience.

'No! Come back, I've moved. See?' Stevie shouted, finally leaving the puddle and moving to the side of the road. She waved her arms frantically to attract the car's attention, when, all at once, her legs shot out from underneath her body and she landed on her back with a sodden splash. Winded, she felt more than a little dizzy from the effects of too much alcohol and her head hitting the tarmac, and she lay immobile, spread-eagled on the road.

Leanne slid down the side of the car she had been leaning against and sat on the pavement, her legs stuck out in front of her. 'Now, I really am going to wet myself!' she cried. 'And my stomach aches. It's all your fault because you're making me laugh so much.' Leanne pulled at her sodden jeans, her squeals of laughter interspersed with hiccups.

Stevie hadn't moved. She was happy where she was, thank you very much. She could stay here all night, watching the rain fall. Why was there so much water up there in the first place, anyway?

The car stopped its backward motion and, with a loud, 'Aw, shit!' the driver got out and raced up the middle of the road towards her.

Stevie remained on her back, watching what she thought must be shooting stars. 'They are so beautiful,' she mused, dreamily, watching the light catch the raindrops as they plummeted towards her face. I didn't think shooting stars would be wet, though, she thought, and she stuck out her tongue to catch one.

'Are you all right?' the man asked, crouching beside her.

'Uhgugh.' Stevie couldn't talk properly with her tongue protruding from her mouth. She felt strong hands patting her from her head all the way down to her feet.

'Geogh!' She grunted, as she tried to push the man away. His head was deflecting those tiny wet stars.

'Oh, God! She's having a fit!' the man cried, and tried to roll her on to her side.

Stevie objected to this most strongly, and she drew her tongue back inside her mouth where it belonged and let out an almighty bellow.

'Aaagggh!' the driver of the car shouted in surprise. He shot backwards, lost his balance and sat in her puddle.

'This one is mine,' Stevie said, matter-of-factly, staring up at him with wide unfocused eyes. 'Go find one of your own.'

'What?'

'Go away. It's mine,' she repeated.

'Incoherent and rambling,' the man muttered. He got to his feet. 'Can you stand? I want to get you out of the rain,' he said to her.

'Can I stand what?'

'*What?*'

'Yes, what?'

'What are you talking about?'

'Exactly,' Stevie stated, satisfied she had managed to get her point across.

The man gave an exasperated sigh. 'Are you hurt?' he asked.

'Nope. Can't feel a thing.'

There was another sigh. He really ought to get that sighing seen to by a doctor, Stevie thought, as Leanne pushed past him and dragged Stevie's arm, pulling her into a sitting position.

'No! Don't move her!' he shouted.

'I have to. I need a pee,' Leanne said.

'But she could be seriously hurt.'

'Nah.' Leanne hauled on Stevie's arm, and Stevie clambered unsteadily to her feet.

'Are you all right?' the man asked again, peering at her.

Stevie burped loudly, then giggled. She leaned into Leanne, clutching at her for support. The world was definitely not as normal as it had been earlier on in the evening.

'You're drunk,' her would-be-rescuer said accusingly.

'Give him a gold star,' Stevie said. 'I'll catch one for you,' she offered, sticking her tongue back out. 'Ish ee-hy, ook.'

The driver of the car snorted. 'You two should be ashamed of yourselves.' He turned back towards his car, the light from the street lamps illuminating his face.

'Oh, it's you,' Leanne giggled at him. 'Superman to the rescue.' She thrust an arm into the air. 'Hello, Nick.' She squinted at him, her eyes still slightly crossed. 'You're wet.'

Nick glared at her. 'It's raining,' he said.

'Ooh, he's clever, isn't he?' Stevie sang.

'Oh, for Pete's sake! Wait there!' Nick strode back to his car, and both Stevie and Leanne watched as he got in, found a space and parked the vehicle. Then he got out again, strode up to the two women, grabbed each one by an elbow and frog-marched them both to the pavement.

'Where are we going?' Stevie enquired, pleasantly.

'*You* are going home,' Nick replied.

'Don't want to.' Stevie stopped and dug her metaphorical heels in.

'Tough!'

The nasty man pinched the tender flesh just above her elbow. 'Ow! That hurts,' she cried.

'Good.'

Stevie studied his profile carefully as he dragged the two of them swiftly along the street, towards his car 'It's you, isn't it?' she panted.

'Yes. It's me.'

'Thought so. And I'm me,' Stevie announced.

'Yes. I know.'

'Good. So, we are all who we are spossed... suspossed to be. Good. I think. Maybe.'

They reached his car, and Nick opened the door. 'Get in,' he instructed.

'Why?' Stevie wanted to know.

'Because I'm taking you home.'

'There's no point.'

'Yes, there is,' he retorted. 'I can't let you wander off in your condition.'

'I won't wander. Promise.' Stevie made the sign of the cross.

'Where do you live? I'll drive you.'

'No point,' Stevie repeated.

Nick opened a rear door and pushed Leanne in. She went willingly enough.

'Traitor,' Stevie mouthed at her.

'Leanne, where does she live?' Nick asked.

Leanne pointed. 'There.'

'Where?' Nick asked, squinting at the row of shops. Stevie squinted along with him.

'The shea top. Shea shop,' Leanne attempted.

'Tea shop?' Nick asked.

'Yes!'

'You stay here,' he said to Leanne. 'Don't touch anything. You,' he grabbed Stevie by the elbow, 'come with me.'

He marched her along the street and stopped outside the tea shop. 'Keys,' he demanded, holding out his hand.

Stevie puffed a bit and stared forlornly at him.

'Never mind.' Nick patted at Stevie's pockets.

'Gedoff! I don't do that on a first date,' Stevie cried, slapping his hands away, but not before he had pulled a set of keys out of her jacket pocket.

He propped her up by the door and Stevie waited for him to search for the right key. The door opened on the second try, and he pushed Stevie inside, handing her the keys.

'Go to bed,' he instructed.

'I told you, I don't do that on a first date.'

'Yeah, yeah.' He shut the door, leaving her dripping on the mat. 'I'll take Leanne home!' she heard him shout through the glass and she watched as he stomped off up the road.

She waved goodbye, her nose squashed against the window, watching him disappear into the rain-drenched night.

Then she staggered lopsidedly into the kitchen, climbed onto the pristine steel countertop of the island and went to sleep.

Chapter 23

Nick rubbed a hand across his face, grimacing at the rasp of stubble. He was so tired he could sleep for a week. A horse with colic wasn't his idea of fun, especially when it involved a very expensive hunter and a notoriously irascible owner. Apparently, the horse had rolled in the stall and got itself stuck. It was imperative a horse with colic doesn't lie down, but if did and didn't quickly get back onto its feet, then it might die. With the vet on another call and with time being of the utmost importance, Edgar Ferris had called Nick, who was driving back from an event in his car with the horsebox following behind. Luckily, he was only just outside Tanglewood, so he had left the lumbering horsebox to make its way back to The Furlongs and had hightailed it to The Manor.

Unfortunately, he had been delayed a little when, as he drove up the main street, he had encountered two rather inebriated girls and his conscience simply couldn't leave them there. He had made sure Stevie got home safely, then had driven Leanne to the farm where she lived with her dad, mum and two older brothers. Her parents hadn't been best pleased to see the state she was in, but after explaining he'd had nothing whatsoever to do with her present state, he'd dashed off to The Manor for three hours of hard labour.

Nick glanced at the illuminated time on the dashboard – three forty-nine in the morning. He groaned, wanting nothing more than a hot shower and bed. But before that his conscience once again got the better of him, insisting he had one more task to perform – to check on Stevie.

When he had seen her earlier, he had recognised her immediately, even sopping wet and cavorting like a mad witch in the middle of the road. He'd not forgotten either of their previous meetings but he had determinedly put her to the back of his mind; romantic entanglements were not on his agenda right now. If ever.

Anyway, Miranda was enough of a problem. Even after he'd made it clear he had no interest in her, she still pursued him ruthlessly. Tonight had been no exception. He had to admire her, though – even in the middle of the night, with a valuable horse with colic and an apoplectic father shouting at everything and everyone (except the horse), she had managed to look as though she had just stepped out of a page three version of *Horse and Hound*.

Boy, had he been glad to get out of there with only a vague promise of dinner next week. Battle of the sexes, be buggered! It was all out nuclear war! She'd flirted with him outrageously, despite her father being there, and at one point he'd been seriously worried Lord Tonbridge was going to retrieve one of the rifles from his gun cabinet and shoot him with it. Nick guessed the only thing stopping the older man, was that Nick was there and the vet hadn't arrived yet. Nick was cheaper than the vet too, and Edgar Ferris wasn't a man to spend a pound when he could get away with spending a penny. Not that Nick would see any payment for his efforts tonight – this was on the house, so to speak.

He pulled into the kerb outside the tea shop and peered through the car windows. All was in darkness, but that didn't necessarily make him feel any better. He should never have left a drunken woman alone, and he wouldn't have done, if it hadn't been for the horsey emergency.

He sighed loudly, got out of the car and rattled the café's door. To his surprise and alarm, it opened to his touch and his heart fell; she hadn't managed to lock up after he had left her. What else had she not managed to do?

He soon found out.

'Hello? Stevie? Are you there?' he called.

There was no answer, so he ventured further inside and made his way past the counter, into the kitchen, and called again.

'Stevie? It's Nick. Are you OK?'

He was reluctant to venture upstairs without her knowledge. For one thing, a strange man suddenly appearing in her home would terrify her. And for another, from what he had seen of her so far, she was likely to brain him with a frying pan first and ask what the hell he was playing at later.

'Why am I doing this?' he muttered darkly, his hand groping across the wall for a light switch. She was probably in bed, sleeping it off.

Bloody hell, where was the damned switch? He groped some more. Nothing, but at least his eyes were starting to adjust, and he could make out a pile of clothes on the island in the middle of the kitchen, and hear a steady drip of water coming from them, landing with a plop into a puddle underneath.

Thank God! At least she'd had the sense to take off her wet things, he thought.

Then the clothes moved.

'Aaagggh!' he screamed, as a disjointed body jerked upright in front of him. It had no face!

The marionette raised a hand to its head and parted the strands of limp hair and Nick stumbled backwards, staggering towards the door.

'Wha? Whoos'ere?' it said.

Nick didn't believe in ghosts, or anything else supernatural for that matter, but some of the houses in and around Tanglewood were old, as were the stories that went with them. He had a sudden, awful thought there may be some truth to them.

'Uggg,' the figure groaned, and Nick made an answering moaning noise in his own throat without realising.

The thing was trying to get off the counter. It was coming for *him*.

He turned and fled.

He had got as far as three steps into the shop when something tangled in his legs and sent him crashing to the floor, and he narrowly avoided hitting his head on one of the tables. It had caught him, dear lord, the thing had caught him. He could feel bony hands grasping his ankle and working its way up his shin.

He squirmed onto his back, fists clenched, prepared to go down fighting, and let out a shriek when the "hand" jumped onto his stomach.

A loud meow followed.

The fight went out of him and he sank back onto the wooden floor, like a deflating balloon.

It was a cat, a bloody cat.

And now the damn animal was kneading his chest and purring contentedly. He lifted it off and put it on the floor, then scrambled to his feet a little unsteadily and peered into the darkness of the kitchen, his heart thumping.

The hand-on-his-ankle issue might have been resolved logically, but there was still the problem of the hideous, ragged puppet-like thing in the room beyond.

He listened hard, hearing nothing. Even the cat stopped its kneading and sat there, its head cocked to one side.

Silence.

Nick debated whether he should venture into the darkness, decided it must have been his imagination, over-wrought because he was so tired, and he took the coward's way out. He scuttled back to his car, looking over his shoulder as he went and didn't breathe properly until he was in the driver's seat with the doors securely locked.

Then he slapped a hand to his forehead.

Stevie was still in there.

–

Stevie peered groggily out from behind a curtain of tangled wet strands. Something had woken her and she wasn't happy about it. She'd been having a lovely sleep, then crashing, banging, and screaming.

A movement in the shadows caught her eye and she gasped, shrinking back on her table. She realised what it was when it began to meow plaintively.

'G'way, Peggy,' she slurred. 'I'm shleeping.'

Peggy sprang onto the table and snuggled against Stevie, before realising her mistress was decidedly damp and jumping back down again, with a yowl of disgust.

Stevie noticed how wet she was at the same time as the cat did. She lowered her feet to the floor and sat on the edge of the counter, her head hanging, and shivered violently.

The least drunken part of her brain urged her to get out of her wet clothes and go to bed, and so, clambering awkwardly off the table, she lurched and staggered across the kitchen, discarding various pieces of clothing as she went.

By the time she reached her bedroom, she was almost naked and her teeth were chattering so hard she thought they might shatter. Grabbing her dressing gown off the hook on the bedroom door, she wrapped herself in it, fell on the bed, and was asleep again in seconds.

–

Nick was totally ashamed of himself. He'd never run away from a fight in his life (not that he'd had many, but a lad couldn't live on a council estate and go to one of the roughest schools in the area without having an altercation or two along the way).

Yet, here he was, a man who, on a daily basis handled horses weighing more than half a tonne, sitting in his car, trying to build up the courage to go back into the building.

'It's a fecking tea shop, for God's sake, not a haunted mansion. Get a grip, Saunders,' he muttered. He couldn't really have seen what he thought he'd seen. It simply wasn't possible. And if it was, then Stevie was in danger and he had to go back in there and do something about it.

'Shit!'

He got out of the car, slammed the door and rolled his shoulders. Here goes nothing, he thought, and taking a deep breath he marched towards the tea shop's door.

Look at how he'd thought someone (some*thing*) had grabbed his ankle, when it had only been a stupid cat and his even more stupid imagination. He must have imagined the figure on the table, too. After all, it was dark in the kitchen, and all that reflecting steel made for some odd shadows thrown by the street lights filtering in.

He deliberately didn't want to think about the noises the imagined figure had made when it had clapped its hellish eyes on him.

Reaching the door, he eased it open, his gaze darting around the room. It was clear of cats, ghosts and anything else that shouldn't be there. Reassured, he ventured further inside, creeping as silently as possible. If there actually *was* something in the kitchen (and as time went on, he was less inclined to believe what he saw), he didn't want to alert it to his presence.

He hesitated when he reached the kitchen door. It was open, allowing enough light in to see that the steel counter in the middle of the room was empty. Another slow breath, and he stepped into the room.

When his foot landed on something squishy, he almost let out a yell, before he realised what it was.

A boot.

Its twin lay a few feet away.

At least he hadn't stepped on the cat. Or something worse.

Nick was starting to lose patience, as well as feeling rather daft. Telling himself not to be so ridiculous, he retreated to the door, patting the wall as he went, until he located the row of light switches. He flicked them all on.

Dear God! The light, the light! Nick screwed his eyes shut as the sudden glare blinded him, before opening them very slowly to give his poor eyeballs time to become accustomed.

The kitchen gleamed (literally – all that steel!). It was spotlessly clean too, except for a trail of clothes leading to another door at the side, with a flight of stairs beyond.

Two boots, one pair of jeans, a lightweight jacket – too lightweight for today's, or rather yesterday's, weather, for it had rained solidly for the past forty-eight hours, lay scattered at his feet. He followed the garment trail up the stairs, feeling even more silly than he already felt with each step and each item he found. He had a sneaking suspicion he knew what the hideous, life-sized puppet thing had been…

He found Stevie on the bed, face down, with the cat curled around her head, and he might have been worried if she wasn't snoring quite so loudly.

Not meaning to, but unable to stop himself, he studied her – not that he could see much considering her face was planted in her pillow and the rest of her was wrapped in some disgusting tartan robe. Every now and again, a shudder ran through her.

She's still chilled, he realised, and she could do with being under the duvet and not on top of it, too.

Thinking it unlikely, but you never know, Nick went into the little kitchen (a far cry from the industrial one downstairs – this one was cosy and homely) and rooted around for a hot water bottle.

Five minutes later he was back at her bedside with a hot microwaved neck- warmer (the closest thing he could find), a glass of orange juice, and another glass containing water.

The mound on the bed was still shaking.

Nick slid the neck-warmer into the bottom of the bed, took a fortifying deep breath, and prepared to tackle Stevie.

First, he tried tugging the duvet from underneath her, but she was having none of it, gripping onto it with unconscious determination, while the cat looked on placidly. Then he wondered if she had a spare duvet he could simply throw over her.

He quickly checked around. She didn't have one in the room and he didn't want to explore the rest of the flat.

Finally, he decided there was nothing for it, but to pick her up, pull the duvet back, and put her into bed.

He didn't bargain for a very sleepy Stevie wrapping her arms around his neck when he turned her over and lifted her off the bed. Neither did he bargain for the grubby old dressing-gown to fall open, revealing a lacy pink bra, matching knickers, and Stevie's body underneath.

He swallowed and averted his eyes, but not before he'd seen more than he wanted to. Actually, he *did* want to, which was why he hastily looked away, and had to force himself not to look back down at her curves.

Quickly pulling the now-free duvet aside, he lowered her gently onto the bed. Stevie murmured a protest when he disentangled her arms from around his neck, but when he pulled the covers up to her chin, and her feet found the heat-source at the bottom of the bed, she soon snuggled down.

He stayed long enough to satisfy himself she was properly asleep and not in a drunken stupor (he didn't want to risk her being sick in the night), and that the shivering had stopped, then he went off to his own cold bed, knowing he'd have to get out of it in a couple of hours.

But as he drove back to The Furlongs, all he could think of was how right Stevie had felt in his arms, how beautiful she'd looked and how much of a pervert she'd think he was when she woke up.

Chapter 24

Stevie thought she was dying and that was before she risked moving her head. As a matter of fact, she didn't think she *could* move it, without it dropping off and rolling away. Her stomach gurgled unpleasantly, her mouth was drier than a dust storm on Mars, and to top it all off, some sadistic little elf must have superglued her eyelids shut during the night, because her lids were impossible to open. And something was compressing her chest.

She knew what it was when a paw patted her on the nose. 'Peggy,' she murmured. 'Geddoff.'

Peggy gave a little mew and suddenly the weight lifted off Stevie's chest as the cat jumped to the floor. Blindly, Stevie struggled out of bed, trying to force her eyes open while wrestling with her dressing gown, which had got itself tangled up in her legs during the night.

She paused in her efforts. Dressing gown? Why was she wearing her dressing gown in bed? She hunted feebly around in her throbbing head for an answer but couldn't find one. She must have been drunker than she had thought – not a great deal of the end part of last night made any sense.

She prised one eye open with her thumb and index finger and groaned. 'Ow.'

The early summer sun shot through her eyeball and skewered her brain. She quickly shut the eye again, carefully peeled her tongue off the roof of her mouth and tried to wet her lips. It was like rubbing an armadillo's backside.

'Cooeee.' Cassandra's voice floated up the stairs.

What time was it? Stevie rubbed her eyes and tried to focus on the alarm clock on her bedside table. Late, that was what it was. Very late.

With another groan, she levered herself upright, took off her dressing gown and hunted for some clothes. She really should have a shower, but the thought of hot water hitting her head made her wince. She settled for splashing some cold on her face instead, cleaning her teeth, and tying her hair into a bun.

She looked a mess, she thought, as she stared at her reflection. Bloodshot eyes, sallow skin, wounded expression, and no wonder, because she dimly recalled downing several glasses of beer before Leanne had suggested gin. Stevie didn't even like gin!

'Stevie, are you OK?' Cassandra sounded worried.

'Yeah, I'm fine. I'll be down in a sec.' Stevie took one last look, vowed never to touch another drop of alcohol again, and teetered gingerly down the stairs.

'You look awful,' Cassandra stated, taking one look at her.

'Thanks.'

'Are you ill? Can I get you something?'

'Paracetamol and a coffee would be lovely. Don't bother firing up Bert, use the instant stuff.' The coffee machine would need to be switched on soon, but Stevie couldn't face it just yet. It usually made one hell of a racket and tended to blow out the odd cloud of steam.

'Do you want me to put these in the oven for you?' Cassandra pointed to the trays of ready-prepared pastries. She looked worried.

'Thanks, that would be great.' No wonder she was concerned – Stevie had normally baked the breakfast batch and was usually working on the more elaborate cakes and fancies for the elevenses crowd by now.

'Summer flu, do you think?' Cassandra asked as she switched the ovens on.

'Leanne.'

'Ah.' Cassandra filled the kettle. 'Then I've got no sympathy for you; the woman can drink like a whale.'

'I found out,' Stevie replied mournfully, her head in her hands. 'She had me on gin.'

'Homebrew?'

'Regular stuff.'

'Phew, you've had a lucky escape. She usually brews her own and it's lethal. Whatever you do, never go to her place for a meal. She'll have you so drunk on it you won't remember your name.'

'She's done it to you, hasn't she?'

'Yup.'

Stevie accepted the coffee gratefully, scalding her mouth on the hot liquid. As the caffeine worked its magic and began to revive her, Stevie saw one of her boots lying on the floor. What was it doing there?

The other one lay a little further away, and now she came to think about it, she remembered seeing the odd garment or two lying on the stairs as she came down them.

Vague images of last night floated on the edge of her mind – rain, and a sexy voice, and being very, very cold. Oh, and arms, strong ones, picking her up. But that couldn't be right, because she clearly remembered walking out of the pub with Leanne. Then the fresh air hit and the memories became somewhat hazy.

The bell above the door tinkled and Stevie grimaced. She wasn't in the mood for customers this early. It was only just gone eight o'clock – they didn't open until eight-thirty, and the croissants weren't cooked yet, and the coffee machine had to be switched on, and—

'Good, you're still alive.' A figure filled the doorway.

'Huh?' Stevie squinted at it.

'Hello, Nick,' Cassandra said calmly. 'We're not open yet.' She made to shoo him out of the kitchen. 'Sorry, I forgot to lock the door behind me.' She turned to Stevie. 'You do realise you left it unlocked all night?'

Stevie had realised no such thing. 'Damn. I could have been murdered in my bed.'

'My fault, I should have locked it behind me when I left,' Nick said, 'but I was so tired, I couldn't have been thinking straight… what?'

Both women were staring at him, mouths open.

'Well, well, well, you dark horse,' Cassandra said to Stevie, breaking the silence.

'You were here? Last night? In the tea shop?' Stevie was flabbergasted, scrambling through the disjointed images of the night before, and not finding him in any of them. But there was that voice…

'Sort of, yes,' Nick replied.

'Why?' Even as Stevie asked the question, she dreaded the answer. Surely, she'd have remembered if she'd slept with him? Shame reddened her cheeks and she stared at him, horrified.

'I couldn't leave you on the counter.' He gestured to the stainless-steel island in the middle of the kitchen and shrugged. 'You would have caught a chill, or worse,' he added darkly.

'What was I doing on there?' she asked.

'Sleeping, apparently.'

'Yes, of course,' she replied, as if it was the most normal thing in the world to use one's kitchen island as a bed. 'How did you know I was sleeping on it?' She'd have to disinfect it before she used it again. 'Cassandra, could you switch Bert on, please?'

'Sure,' Cassandra replied, staying exactly where she was. She had an avid look on her face and her eyes were wide with astonishment.

'I saw you,' Nick said. 'You gave me the fright of my life – I thought you were some kind of…' he paused. 'Never mind. Anyway, I had to take you to bed.'

'I bet you did!' Cassandra declared. 'Nick Saunders, I'm ashamed of you, taking advantage of a drunken woman.'

'I didn't!' Nick protested.

Stevie wished they would both shut up and leave her alone.

'I merely made sure she was OK and was warm enough,' Nick retorted loftily.

'Was she?' Cassandra waggled her eyebrows at him.

'Yes.'

'Go away,' Stevie said. 'I don't feel well.'

'She was out with Leanne from the florist shop,' Nick said, by way of an explanation.

'I know,' Cassandra replied. 'I'm surprised she can remember her own name this morning.'

Stevie put her head in her hands as the conversation sunk in. 'You put me to bed,' she said in a disbelieving tone. 'Did you undress me too?'

'No, you did that all by yourself.'

That would explain the trail of clothes up the stairs. She must have taken them off, one soggy item at a time, as she went. 'You should have stopped me.'

'I wasn't here at the time.'

She lifted her head to look at him. 'I thought you said you were.'

'I'd… um… popped back to my car for a second. By the time I came back, you were wrapped in a dressing gown and lying on the bed, shivering.'

Stevie let out a sigh of relief. He'd not seen her in her half-naked glory after all.

'I tucked you in,' he continued, 'gave you a hot water bottle (neck warmer, actually) and went home.'

The look of anticipation on Cassandra's face faded into disappointment. 'You didn't sleep with her, then?'

'Cassandra! No, he didn't!' Stevie was shocked her friend could think such a thing.

Cassandra turned her attention to Nick. 'How come you were in a position to put our lovely pastry chef here, to bed?'

'I was on my way to The Manor and there she was, dancing about in the middle of the road in the rain, then she fell over, so I saw her safely into the shop and took Leanne home.'

'On the way to The Manor, eh?' Cassandra sent him a significant look.

Nick sighed. 'Edgar's hunter had colic.'

'Was Miranda there?' she asked.

'Yeah, so?'

'Just asking.'

Stevie's ears pricked up. Who was this Miranda person? And why did Nick look so sheepish? She was about to ask, when the bell above the door tinkled; their first customers had arrived and nothing was ready.

'Excuse me,' she said to Nick, 'we've got work to do. Cassandra, please see to Bert, I've got to check on the oven.' She stood, scooping a passing Peggy up as she did so and deposited the cat on the stairs, shutting the door to the flat with the moggy firmly on the other side. 'Thank you for what you did last night,' she said stiffly, as Nick turned to leave. 'I can assure you it won't happen again.'

With that, she opened the oven door, letting out a blast of mouth-watering steam, and completely missed the look of disappointment on Nick Saunders's face.

Chapter 25

Late spring bled imperceptibly into early summer and Stevie basked in the knowledge she was actually making a go of things. Business was brisk, with her regulars in the morning and hikers and ramblers throughout the day. She'd started offering snacks as an addition to the cakes and pastries, and she was in the middle of making a batch of lentil and vegetable pasties when she heard a strident voice in the tea shop.

'Too much sugar, that's the problem. I don't know why we come in here.'

Stevie put the rolling pin down and edged closer to the door. Through the crack between the door and the frame, she could see a familiar gaggle of women at a table in one of the bay windows. They visited the tea shop every Tuesday and Thursday after doing the school run and usually had a slice of cake and a coffee each. Except for the one who'd just spoken – green tea for her, and she always turned her nose up at the delicious array of yumminess in the display counter.

'Because there's nowhere else to go?' one of the other women suggested, in a timid voice.

'Nonsense! I'm sure there are other, *more suitable* places.'

'Saffron loves it here,' another said. 'I bring her for a treat on Saturdays when I collect my meat from the butchers.'

'All children love sugar if they're allowed.' The strident voice was scathing. 'No wonder they're getting fat and lethargic.'

Stevie shuffled, trying to see Saffron's mum. The woman looked chagrined, as if she'd just been told off by a bossy headmistress.

'I don't mean *your* children,' the obnoxious mum added, with enough saccharin in her voice to sweeten a ten-tier wedding cake. 'I mean children in general. I never give my two anything artificial and certainly nothing with the white death in it.'

Stevie's eyes nearly bugged out of her head. White death? She sincerely hoped Obnoxious Mum didn't give her children drugs— Oh, the woman meant *refined sugar*, Stevie realised, with a shake of her head. White death, indeed! How ridiculous. A sweet treat now and again never hurt anyone. Stevie had to admit though, that *now and again* was hard to stick to when it came to *her* products. They were simply too good not to be moreish.

Cassandra was deliberately not getting involved in the conversation, Stevie noticed, calmly taking orders and serving the drinks, but Stevie saw the effort it was costing her by the hardening of her friend's jaw and the set of her shoulders.

'I wouldn't bring my two anywhere near this place. It's as bad as making them eat fast food.' Obnoxious Mum shot a scornful glance at one of the other mothers, who bent her head and appeared to find the contents of her coffee cup extremely fascinating.

'It was just the once though, wasn't it, Bev?' Timid Mum said to the one who had just been so roundly chastised. 'I'm sure you'd never do it again.'

Bev shook her head vehemently. 'It was a one-off, a cousin's birthday party. There was a play area. I couldn't say no. Besides, Claude hated it. He had one chip, sorry *fry*, and left the rest.'

Even Stevie, from her odd angle behind the kitchen door, could tell Bev was lying through her dentist-perfect, alarmingly-white teeth. She bet the kid had wolfed down every mouthful and demanded more. Not that Stevie condoned too much fast food (although she was partial to a particular brand of pizza herself, especially when it was delivered right to her door so she didn't have to change out of her pyjamas and go fetch it), but once in a while was OK.

'You're not seriously going to eat *that*, are you?' Obnoxious Mum belted out.

Stevie squinted, trying to see what the woman was referring to. "That" was a Religieuse – two tiers of fluffy choux pastries, each filled with chocolate crème pâtissière, and covered in a generous ganache, also chocolate. A swirl of buttercream icing topped it off. It was a food group all on its own and absolutely delicious, even if Stevie did say so herself. What could possibly be wrong with it?

'Er…' The fourth woman in the quartet, who had so far managed to escape Obnoxious Mum's notice, stared down at her plate. She looked like a rabbit caught in headlights.

'You'd be better off with a few less calories, wouldn't you say?' Obnoxious Mum was the slimmest of the little group of mothers and obviously proud of the fact. She was done up to the nines, too, as if she was off to a board meeting. Maybe she was, Stevie thought. Perhaps dropping the kids off at school and having a quick pit-stop with her friends (although Stevie wasn't sure the others thought of her as a "friend", if their body language was anything to go by), was a prelude to a high-flying day filled with important business decisions and meetings.

Obnoxious Mum turned to Cassandra. 'Do you have anything gluten-free? Oh, and I don't want refined sugar in it, either.'

'Try one of our savoury scones,' Cassandra suggested in a deceptively pleasant voice. Stevie wished she could see her assistant's face – she'd bet any money it had a fake smile plastered on it.

'What's in it?' The degree of suspicion in Obnoxious Mum's voice couldn't be any greater than if Cassandra had suggested she eat rat poison.

Oh no, talking of unwanted pests, Stevie spotted Peggy slinking through the tea shop, aiming for her favourite place on the windowsill. At least five times a day either Stevie or Cassandra had to retrieve the cat from the windowsill and put her back upstairs. Stevie had yet to figure out how the feline escaped from the flat, but what she did know was that animals in places where food was prepared and served, was a no-no.

Taking a deep breath, Stevie marched into the shop, brushing the flour from her hands. 'Hi, I'm Stevie, the owner. Can I just say, I use the freshest ingredients possible in my cooking. The savoury scones are an excellent choice – gluten-free and the cheese is local, extra-strong and rich.'

Obnoxious Mum shuddered. 'Did you say "cheese"? I'll have you know I'm lactose intolerant. Are you trying to kill me?'

I'm trying to put some flesh on your skinny bones, Stevie wanted to say, realising the slimness she'd noticed from afar was more akin to Skeletor than a Vogue model when viewed up close. The woman could do with a damned good meal inside her.

'I must admit, it narrows the field a bit,' Stevie said. 'How about a chocolate nut ball?'

'Excuse me, but I hardly think chocolate is sugar-free.' Obnoxious Mum delivered her observation tartly then glanced at her companions with a triumphant smirk.

Stevie narrowed her eyes. Game on! She was well aware some people had dietary restrictions and she had been experimenting with various recipes purely aimed at that market. The chocolate nut balls had only gone on sale that very morning and were clearly labelled – *if* Obnoxious Mum had bothered to get down off her high horse and bothered to read it.

'They're made with raw organic cocoa powder,' Stevie said. 'The sweetness comes from the shredded coconut and I use almond butter instead of the dairy version. They are gluten-free, sugar-free, and dairy free. Have one on the house. In fact, why don't all you ladies try one? I'll bring some over.' And with that Stevie strode over to the counter and plated up a handful of the little dark brown balls. They looked a little poo-like, as if a rather large rabbit had done something unmentionable, so in order to make them appear a little more appetising, Stevie added a generous dollop of creamy Greek yoghurt.

'Here you go, ladies.' She put the plate in the centre of the table.

'They look lovely,' the woman with the Religieuse in front of her said. The other two eyed the plate timidly, waiting for Obnoxious Mum to make the first move.

'You eat it, if you want to,' she said to her companions. 'I'll stick with my green tea. *That*,' she paused dramatically, 'looks positively laden with calories.'

Stevie turned away from the table and rolled her eyes. There was simply no pleasing some people.

'I'll have it, if they don't want it,' a voice in the corner said.

Stevie glanced over her shoulder and saw Betty eying up the chocolate balls with a hungry look. 'I'll make you a plate of your own,' she offered and dived behind the counter.

Cassandra had her back to the room and was pretending to fiddle with Bert. 'You should make that awful woman a plate of fresh air,' she muttered, her voice cracking. 'Tell her it's a new recipe.'

'Shhh! Stop it. Can you grab Peggy while I take Betty a plate of chocolate nut balls? And stop laughing,' Stevie added. 'It's not funny.' Stevie didn't know whether to feel sorry for Obnoxious Mum, to be annoyed with her, or to laugh at her.

Cassandra took a steadying breath and squared her shoulders, before she faced the room. 'I can't see Peggy,' she said, after a pause.

'She was heading towards her favourite spot on the window sill. Hurry, I don't want to give Obnoxious Mum any ammunition.'

Cassandra shot Stevie an amused glance. 'Obnoxious Mum, as you call her,' Cassandra let out a snort, 'is Allegra Johnson, and she's a nasty piece of work. You handled her well, though.' She glanced at the window sills. 'I still can't see Peggy.'

Neither could Stevie, and as she took the nut balls over to Betty, she scanned the tea shop as she went. Nope, no sign of the cat, and she breathed a sigh of relief. It must have gone back to the flat.

'A piece of advice,' Betty said, after taking a mouthful of chocolate nut balls and closing her eyes in delight as the flavours exploded on her tongue. 'Don't let the whiners get to you. You can't please all the people all of the time, and you can't please *that one*,' she jerked her head at the quartet, 'any of the time. My lovely, this is really *good*.'

'Thank you,' Stevie said. 'I'm glad you like it.'

'You lot don't know what you're missing,' Betty called, waving her spoon at the group of mothers. 'Bloody gorgeous, this is.'

Allegra Jonson stuck her nose in the air and turned away from Betty, but the one called Bev picked up her spoon to give the chocolate nut balls a go, only to put it swiftly down again when she caught Allegra's eye.

'Another piece of advice,' Betty said to Stevie, diving in for a second mouthful. 'Change the name – chocolate nut balls puts all kind of images in my head.'

Stevie blanched, then blushed. Oh, Lordy, Betty was right, and the teenagers who sometimes came in after school would have a field day with a name like that. What had she been thinking?

'Thanks,' she said to Betty, patting her on the shoulder.

She stepped back and something let out an indignant yowl. Stevie muffled a shriek, knowing exactly what had made the noise and glanced behind her just in time to see a sleek, black shape dart through the kitchen door. Stevie caught a final glimpse of tail before Peggy scooted up the stairs.

When she checked to see if any of her customers had noticed, Stevie was disconcerted to see Allegra staring furiously at her.

Chapter 26

'We'll have fun,' Nick insisted, through gritted teeth. He was trying to keep a hold on his frustration, but he had a feeling he was failing miserably.

'Will we?' Tia said this in a deadpan voice, challenging him. Her arms were crossed and her lips had narrowed into a thin line.

'We haven't been anywhere for ages.'

'I don't want to.'

'Please, for me?' Nick was aware he didn't sound either pleading or begging – he sounded pissed off and at the end of his tether.

'If you can explain what is so "fun" about traipsing up and down the high street on a Saturday afternoon, then I'll happily come with you.'

'Um…' Nick was at a loss. It certainly wasn't his idea of fun (he hated shopping) but he thought Tia might enjoy it. She hadn't left The Furlongs for weeks now. A change of scenery would do her good.

'We could go for a walk along the river, then have a coffee.' He ignored her exaggerated glance down at her legs when he mentioned the word "walk". 'There's a new tea shop opened up in the village. I thought we could pop in there afterwards.'

Tia regarded him steadily, then huffed out a big sigh and shrugged her shoulders. 'If this thing gets stuck in the mud, don't blame me. And if I say I want to go home, we go home. No arguing. Agreed?'

Nick let out the breath he wasn't aware he had been holding. 'Agreed.'

He was about to ask her if she needed any help to get ready but thought better of it. His sister had become incredibly independent since the accident. That wasn't to say she didn't insist on doing most things herself and generally succeeding, but Nick was aware of how much Tia relied on him. Unfortunately, Tia was aware too, and it tended to make her cranky.

He had tried to make it as easy for her as he could – he'd had a bedroom and a bathroom built downstairs, converted from what had once been a storeroom on the back of the house, and fitted out for a wheelchair user; all the kitchen units and countertops had been lowered (although it played havoc with his back whenever he tried to cook in it), he had arranged for ramps on all the doorways which needed them, and had bought a converted car for Tia's sole use.

He knew how much it pained her to watch him ride, to be around horses and not be able to mount one, or to see the grooms doing what she'd once done. Horses had been her passion, her life, and her downfall, and Nick wished with all his heart he could mend her.

Getting changed took Tia an age, and Nick did some work on the computer while he waited. Good, he thought, as he read an email confirming he'd successfully entered a competition with one of his best horses. He'd registered one of his most talented grooms, Sally, to ride

Rougemont Reggie, an up-and-coming stallion of some four years old. He was green but had the ability. Nick was training both horse and rider at the same time. He didn't expect them to be placed, but the experience would be good for his protégé and her mount.

He worked for the next half hour until he heard Tia trundling across the kitchen's flagstone floor. Checking her over, he was relieved to see she'd dressed sensibly in jeans and sweater. Summer might be on its way according to the calendar, but no one had thought to tell the weather. It wasn't raining (which made a change) but it was cloudy, and not particularly warm – a typical summer day in Wales, in fact.

He let her hoist herself out of the chair and into the car, biting his lip to stop himself from offering to help. He knew she could do this on her own and he had to let her. Besides, if he annoyed her now, she was perfectly capable of changing her mind and storming off back to the house. He wished he knew what was really bothering her, apart from the obvious.

Nick whistled to Billy, their border terrier, and Tia opened her arms to let him jump into her lap. As he drove he watched her out of the corner of his eye, as she nuzzled the dog's neck, burying her nose in the wiry coat. She looked so sad and pensive, his heart went out to her.

Plucking up courage and knowing he was probably making a big mistake but going ahead anyway, he asked, 'Do you want to talk about it?'

'Not really.'

'So there *is* something bothering you?' Nick pounced like the ginger cat they'd adopted last year. Marmalade was a good mouser, as the gruesome "presents" left on the doorstep attested. He had a brilliant line in pouncing, too.

'You mean aside from the fact I'll never walk again?' she stated.

Nick grimaced. He knew he was opening a bag of worms when he'd opened his mouth. 'Aside from that,' he persisted.

'Nothing.'

'Come on, Tia, I know you. There's something else on your mind. Tell me.'

Tia shook her head, staring stubbornly out of the window for the rest of the short journey and Nick was forced to drop the subject.

When they pulled into the little car park down by the river and Nick drove into a disabled space, Tia rolled her eyes. She hated the necessity of using one of those parking spaces, but she needed the room to be able to get into her chair. She also hated it when passers-by stared at her whenever she hoisted herself into, or out of, the vehicle, so Nick surreptitiously stood behind her, using his body as a shield against curious or pitying eyes.

The walk along the riverbank did them both good, Nick thought. The path was wheelchair friendly, so Tia didn't need him to push her, and they strolled together in companionable silence for a while. Every so often Billy would drop a stick in Tia's lap and she would throw it for him and the pair of them laughed as he bounded through the long grass after it. The only part of him visible was his head as he leapt up to grab a quick look around; the rest of the time they only knew where he was by the madly waving fronds of grass.

Eventually, they turned around and went back the way they'd come. Nick was relieved to see Tia had some colour in her usually pale cheeks and there was a shine to her eyes. He really should try and make sure she got out more.

'Coffee and a cake?' he suggested. Seeing her hesitate, he added, 'There's plenty of room inside.' He knew how difficult it was to manoeuvre a wheelchair in some shops and restaurants, and this was often the reason Tia would refuse to go in. She frequently said it was bad enough being in the damned thing, without having everyone stop what they were doing to look at the disruption she caused when chairs, and sometimes even tables, had to be moved to let her pass.

'OK.' Her reply was somewhat reluctant, but at least she'd agreed.

Peggy's Tea Shoppe was busy, but there was a table free just inside the door, and Nick made a bee-line for it after holding the door open for Tia to wheel herself through. He eased a chair out of the way to give her more room, then turned to look around the café. He'd not really had much of a chance on the two other occasions he'd been inside.

'It's nice,' Tia said. 'Chintzy and cute.' She peered at a nearby table. 'I love the fact nothing matches,' she announced. 'It's quaint and quirky.'

Nick hadn't really noticed. He was too busy trying not to stare at Stevie, who was this side of the large display counter, bending over it to peer inside. She had a really nice backside, he couldn't help thinking.

As if his thoughts had magically travelled straight from his head into hers, Stevie straightened up and looked over her shoulder, right into his eyes. He swiftly looked away, mortified she'd caught him ogling her. Little did she know, but it wasn't the first time he'd done such a thing, and she'd been wearing considerably less then than she was wearing now.

He picked up the menu and pretended to study it, only to find Tia giving him a strange look. 'What?' he asked.

'I asked you if this place is new but you weren't listening.'

'Oh, I think it's been open a couple of months or so.'

'I recognise Cassandra Curtis, but I don't know the other one. Is she new, too?' his sister asked.

'Stevie? Er, yes, she bought the place.'

'Do you know her?'

'Not really.'

'But you've been in here before?' Tia persisted. 'You clearly know her name.'

'What's with all the questions?'

Tia shrugged. 'Just making conversation.'

'What can I get you?' Stevie said, and Nick jumped. Tia smirked at him.

'Is it OK to bring the dog in?' he asked, gesturing to Billy who was lying quietly under the table and panting like a steam engine.

'It's fine,' Stevie said. 'I don't have a problem with well-behaved dogs. It's climbing cats that I disapprove of.'

Nick wondered what she was talking about but before he could think about it too deeply, she said, 'I'll bring him a bowl of water, if you like?'

'Yes please. This is my sister, Tia,' Nick said, trying not to look at Stevie. He had no idea why he was so *twitchy* around her. She was attractive, certainly, but he'd met other attractive women before, so why was he acting like a fifteen-year-old, all gauche and self-conscious?

'Hi, Tia, nice to meet you.' Stevie stuck a hand out to shake Tia's. 'What can I get you?' she asked her.

'I'll have an Earl Grey.' Tia said. 'Do you have any cake? Nick promised me cake.'

Stevie smiled. 'Do we have cake!' she exclaimed. 'We have lots of it! There are the staples like Victoria sponge and carrot cake, or the special today is a pineapple upside-down cake. Or we have eclairs, and custard slices, or if you're feeling a little more decadent we have clafoutis, or macarons, or dacquoise, or—'

'Slow down,' Tia laughed. 'You lost me at éclair. What's a dacq-thingy?'

'It's a cake made with layers of hazelnut and almond meringue, with buttercream and a bitter-sweet chocolate ganache, and to give it a little tartness, I've added a drizzle of raspberry coulis.'

'It sounds divine, I'll have a slice of that please.'

'Nick, what would you like?'

'Er, just coffee for me please.'

Stevie batted her eyelashes at him. 'Can't I interest you in anything?'

'Just coffee. A strong one.'

'Yeah, you strike me as the strong and silent type,' Stevie said back at him. 'Coffee, it is, but when you see what your sister is eating, you'll wish you had a slice, too.'

'I won't,' Nick muttered under his breath, as Stevie went back to the counter. He watched her go, wishing she didn't wiggle quite so much. It was rather distracting.

'You like her, don't you?' Tia said.

'Eh? What?' Nick forced his gaze away from Stevie's swaying hips and back to his sister.

'Stevie. You like her. She seems nice.'

'She's OK I suppose. I hardly know her.'

'This is on the house,' Stevie said. 'For rescuing me the other night,' she added, immediately repudiating Nick's statement in one sentence, as she balanced a tray in one hand and relieved it of its teapot, small jug of milk, and cup and saucer, with the other. 'I was rude to you the other day when you came to check on me, and I'm sorry. I blame the hangover. And I was rather ashamed I needed a knight in shining armour to look after me.'

Nick didn't know where to look or what to do with himself. On the one hand, he was delighted Stevie had thawed towards him (though he had no idea why he'd been so bothered about it), but on the other, he didn't want Tia to get the wrong idea. For years, before her accident, she'd been trying to pair him up with this friend or that, and sometimes he'd gone out with one of them – he told himself it was only to get his sister off his back for a while, but the real reason was that he was a hot-blooded male and sometimes female company was exactly what he needed. But since the accident she'd not tried to set him up once (although he was aware she thought he and Miranda had a bit of a thing going on) and he'd not dated anyone of his own volition, either. He'd been too busy with Tia's needs, the stables, his career – and his guilt, he couldn't forget the guilt, because it reared its ugly head every time Nick saw Tia, or the wheelchair, or the ramp leading up to the front door, or any of the numerous other adaptations which had been made to the house.

Tia was giving him a very odd look indeed, and when Stevie went to fetch the cake and his coffee, she said, 'I thought you didn't know her?'

'I don't! Not really.'

'You know her well enough to "rescue her" the other night.' Tia did quotation marks in the air. 'What sort of looking after did you do?'

'She was lying in the road and I made sure she got home safely, that's all.'

'What was she doing lying in the road?'

This was the most animated he'd seen Tia in a long time, so instead of clamming up, which was what he would have preferred to do, he told her the story of how Stevie had gone out for a drink with Leanne and had come off rather the worse for wear.

'Leanne!' Tia laughed. 'Poor Stevie. Even *I* know better than to try to keep up with Leanne. She drinks like it's going out of fashion.'

'I've learned my lesson,' Stevie said, appearing at their table with two slices of the dacquoise, despite Nick's insistence on only having coffee, and catching the tail end of the conversation. 'Try it,' she added to Nick. 'If you don't want it, don't eat it.'

'Then what?' Tia persisted, once Stevie had left.

'I drove Leanne home and went on to The Manor to deal with Edgar's hunter.'

Tia gave him a narrow look, and Nick squirmed. 'You told me about the hunter, but not about being a hero,' Tia teased.

'Oh, that's not all,' Stevie said, appearing at their table again and catching the last snippet of the story. 'He came back after he'd sorted the horse out to make sure I was OK

170

and he tucked me in and got me a hot-water bottle,' she said over her shoulder, as she went back to the counter.

Tia shot Nick an accusatory stare and Nick felt his cheeks grow hot. Wonderful. Now he really did look like a total berk.

'I had a responsibility,' he muttered. 'I'd have done the same for anyone.'

'Would you, though?' Tia asked. 'She's really pretty. Have you noticed the colour of her hair? It's gorgeous.'

Nick had noticed, all right. It reminded him of the flames when he lit a fire in the hearth on a cold winter evening. He'd noticed her eyes too, a sort of smoky grey, and he'd noticed the smattering of freckles across her nose. And her lips—

'What about Miranda?' Tia interrupted his musing.

'What about Miranda?' he countered.

'She likes you, really likes you.'

'Does she?' Nick rolled his eyes. Not again…

'Don't tell me you haven't noticed, because I don't believe you.'

Nick sighed. 'I don't feel the same way about her,' he said.

'Why not? She's beautiful, and great fun, and intelligent and rich.' Tia waggled her eyebrows at the rich part. 'What's not to like?'

'She's not my type,' Nick protested.

'What is your type, then? Stevie?'

Nick let out another sigh. 'Stop trying to matchmake, Tia. I'm not interested.'

Tia was silent for a moment. She picked up her fork and took a small mouthful of cake, before returning the fork to her plate. Her face was pale, apart from two spots of colour, one on each cheek. Her eyes were downcast and her lips had narrowed. He'd clearly upset her, and he was annoyed with himself for doing so, but he wished she'd butt out of his love life. He didn't have one, didn't want one, and didn't have time for one. Not now, not with the way things were. Romance was the last thing on his mind.

'It's because of me isn't it?' she said eventually. 'I'm the reason you don't want to get involved with anyone.'

'Nonsense. I'm simply too busy. The stables take up all of my time.'

'That's just an excuse.' His sister looked him straight in the eye and Nick's heart plummeted to his feet when he saw the expression on her face.

She took a deep breath. 'I'm going to move in with Mum,' she announced.

Nick's heart almost stopped at the unexpected news. 'With *Mum*? But why?'

'Because I'm holding you back, stopping you from living your life. It's not fair on you, Nick. Besides, I'm fed up with living at The Furlongs,' she added.

'You love it there,' he began, but Tia didn't let him finish.

'Do you realise how hard it is for me, watching you ride every day? I can't do it anymore!' she cried.

'But you *can*, we talked about this. There are some great horses out there who work with disabled riders. We can get you a hoist, and a special saddle and—' He paused. 'What I'm saying is, you can still ride.'

'It won't be the same.'

'No, it won't,' Nick agreed, 'but at least you'll be riding again.'

Tia put a hand on his arm. 'I want to go back home, Nick, to Mum's. Can't you see that? I don't want to stay here any longer.'

He closed his eyes for a second and thought about what she'd just said. She'd hate it, but if living at The Furlongs was such torture to her, then who was he to try to make her stay? She might be his little sister, who he'd cared for and looked out for ever since she was born, but she was a grown woman and he had to stand back and let her make her own decisions.

'Is it what you really want?' he asked.

Tia nodded emphatically. 'Yes.'

'OK, then, I'll arrange it.' He looked at the ceiling, a sudden sting of tears in his eyes.

He'd tried everything to help her, but it wasn't enough. Maybe he'd tried too hard, suffocating her with attention, not letting her get on with things in her own way, trying to always be there for her.

Bloody hell! Anyone would think they were a married couple talking about getting divorced. Nick gave a sad smile, at the thought. It would take a couple of months to sort the move out, what with speaking to the council to arrange the alterations, and goodness knows how long that would take. But maybe it would give her time to reconsider, to change her mind…

Chapter 27

Stevie stood in one of the tea shop's bay windows, frowning at the rain and listlessly eating some ice cream. Eating was perhaps the wrong word – trying unsuccessfully to dig a spoonful out of the bowl was probably a more accurate description.

In anticipation of bright sunny days and hot summer weather (huh!), she'd been experimenting with home-made ice cream, only this one was made using frozen bananas as a base, with strawberries, vanilla, a little milk and some sugar. The mixture was then frozen again for an hour or so, and therein lay the problem. If the ice-cream-smoothie-sorbet combo was frozen for any longer than sixty or so minutes, it turned into a brick. Stevie had been forced to hack the first attempt out with a hammer and chisel. For the second attempt, she'd scooped the mixture into balls after the required hour and returned it to the freezer, but the balls had simply stuck together, and when she managed to free a couple from their neighbours, she still had trouble eating them. It was like trying to chew on a marble.

Definitely not one of her better experiments.

Not that she was likely to sell any ice cream in this awful weather anyway, she thought, trying to console herself. It had been raining almost solidly for the past week, and tourists and hikers were thin on the ground. She had what she had come to think of as her regulars, but she needed more customers than that in order to keep the business going.

She'd overheard people saying that this summer was possibly the wettest on record, and she could well believe it. She'd never seen rain like it – it was coming down in sheets and the main road, which led down to the river, looked more like a river itself.

Cassandra had rang to say she would be in late, as their roof had sprung a previously well-hidden leak. 'No sooner we repair one bit, than we find another bit which seems to think it was a shower-head in a past life,' she had declared over the phone. Stevie could hear a faint yell in the background. 'Oops. Gotta go. I think Aiden's fallen off his ladder and into the swimming pool.'

'Swimming pool?'

'There is a massive puddle outside our back door. It's deep enough for sharks.'

Stevie had hung up and sighed, wondering how she was going to manage. Then she'd glanced out of the window again and shrugged. There wouldn't be many people out and about today. She'd cope.

That had been at eight-thirty. It was now closer to lunchtime and Stevie could count the number of customers she'd had on one hand.

Two women, shoulders hunched, heads down, one battling to keep an umbrella over her (Good luck with that, Stevie thought), were dragging a pair of kids down the street. Stevie, with nothing better to do, watched their progress with bored fascination. Every time a car or a van drove by, the four were faced with a wave of water sloshing over their feet and splashing their legs.

They were positively soaked, and although Stevie would welcome their custom if they were to come in, a part of her hoped they wouldn't. She'd already mopped the floor three times this morning, and one of those times had been when she'd briefly opened the door to let a bedraggled and very cross-looking Peggy in.

Stevie was thinking about calling it a day, turning the "Open" sign to "Closed" and joining her cat on the sofa in the flat upstairs where the feline was undoubtedly already curled up fast asleep, when she spied a rather large cobweb up near the ceiling.

If there was one thing she disliked it was spiders, so with grim determination, she grabbed a duster, kicked off her flat shoes, dragged a chair into position, and climbed onto it.

She was stretching as far as she could, flicking her yellow duster at the web, when the door abruptly slammed open, the bell tickled frantically, and a gust of wind swirled around the tea shop, making her jump.

Stevie let out a yelp of surprise and toppled off her chair. As she came crashing down, she grabbed for anything she could get her hands on. The tablecloth did nothing to arrest her fall, and the items on the table itself rained down on her, bouncing off her head like very hard hailstones.

'Ow!' Stevie rubbed her crown where the sugar bowl had struck and sat up.

'Trust you, Stevie Taylor. We've come all this way and this is how you greet us.'

'Mum?' Stevie peeped over the top of the table. 'Fern?'

'It's not as big as I thought it would be,' Hazel sniffed, looking around her, shaking the umbrella and sending droplets of water flying across the room.

Stevie winced as Fern's children raced up to the counter, trailing muddy puddles as they went.

The four of them were drenched and so was Stevie's previously pristine floor. To add to the mess, a trickle of water had snaked its way across the tiles and was happily dissolving the fallen sugar cubes into a sticky mess.

Stevie scrambled to her feet and smoothed down her apron.

'It's not very busy, is it?' her mother added. 'Here.' She thrust the umbrella at Stevie. 'Well? Don't just stand there – I could murder a cuppa and a slice of cake.'

Fern had yet to say anything and Stevie was acutely aware of the faint distaste on her sister's face. 'It's a bit of a come down, don't you think?' Fern sneered.

Stevie glared at her. 'No, I don't. This is my place. *Mine*. I work for myself and answer to no one. How can that be considered a "come down"?'

'It's hardly Michelin and considering how much you used to bang on about those silly little stars, I thought they were vitally important.'

'They are, but not in a tea shop,' Stevie growled, and although she would secretly love to be awarded one, she was realistic enough to realise that was never going to happen.

'Well? Where's my tea?' Hazel demanded, taking her coat off and hanging it on the back of a chair, before plonking herself down at a table. 'And why have you called it *Peggy's* Tea Shoppe?' Her mother gave an exaggerated frown and tapped her fingers on her chin. Stevie knew exactly what was coming next. 'I suppose it's because you bought it with her money,' Hazel added.

Yep, Stevie was right. Her mother was never going to let that one go, was she? And neither was her sister.

'*Our* money,' Fern chimed in.

'Give it a rest,' Stevie muttered, opening Bert's hot water valve and filling a teapot.

'Oooh, get her,' Hazel chorused, as Stevie placed the pot, a jug of milk, and a cup and saucer in front of her mother. 'What's wrong with a tea bag and a mug, that's what I want to know.'

'If you want it in a mug, I'll give it you in a mug,' Stevie offered, while imagining pouring the contents of the teapot over her mother's head. 'What would you like, Fern?'

'Coffee, no milk, no sugar, no foam, no nothing.'

'Black, then?'

Fern scowled at her. 'Jade and Macey will have a glass of cola.'

'Sorry, I don't sell it.'

Her sister shot her an incredulous look. 'Orangeade? Lemonade?'

'I've got milk, orange juice, apple juice, pineapple juice, raspberry cordial, or I could rustle up a smoothie…' Stevie trailed off at Fern's shudder.

'They won't drink any of that rubbish.'

'Well, they'll have to go without then, won't they?' Stevie retorted, beginning to lose what little patience she had left. If her family had come here for the sole purpose of putting her down, then they could jolly well sod off back to London.

'What are you doing here, anyway?' she asked. 'You should have phoned and let me know you were coming. You've not picked the best day for it.'

'Day? We're staying for three,' her mother said, blowing noisily on her tea.

Three!? Stevie thought and took a deep breath. At least she had to work and so only had a limited amount of time to spend with them. They'd have to amuse themselves most of the time, so hopefully she didn't have to see much of them. It was awful to feel that way about her own flesh and blood, but she simply couldn't help it.

'Where are you staying?' she asked, hoping it wasn't too near.

Even as Hazel opened her mouth to say, 'Here, of course,' Stevie guessed from the expression on her mother's face and she steeled herself for what she knew was coming. Her heart headed south to her feet at a rate of knots and her sanity quickly followed.

'I haven't got the room,' she began, thinking furiously for any excuse.

'Nonsense!' Her mother smirked. 'You said you had two bedrooms. Fern and I can share one, the kids can have the other.'

Great, Stevie thought, where do they suggest I sleep? They clearly didn't know and didn't care, and she found herself looking forward to three nights on the sofa with as much enthusiasm as a duck looked forward to its pond being frozen over. And talking about ducks, it was still raining hard and the thought of being cooped up with her family for the rest of the day was daunting.

'What the hell is that?' Fern screeched, suddenly.

Stevie jumped, dropping the plate of cakes she'd been preparing. 'What?'

'A rat! A rat!' her sister yelled. 'Kill it!'

Stevie shot out from behind the counter, clutching a spatula and preparing to do battle, but came to an abrupt halt when she saw what was making her sister so hysterical. 'It's a cat,' she said, flatly.

'Yes, I can see that now, but what's it doing in here? Hardly hygienic, is it?' Fern made shooing motions with her hand. 'Don't touch it, my darlings,' she said to the children. 'It's probably riddled with fleas.'

'Peggy hasn't got fleas,' Stevie protested. 'Anyway, she's not supposed to be in here.'

Fern let out a gasp. 'Rub our noses in it, why don't you?'

'Eh?' What was her daft sister on about now?

Seeing Stevie's confused expression, Fern rolled her eyes before saying, 'Calling the damned thing *Peggy*. You'll end up like her, if you're not careful.'

'Like a cat?'

'No, stupid,' like Aunt Peggy – lonely, batty and with a house full of cats. You've made a start already.'

'I'm not lonely, or batty, and I've only got the one cat,' Stevie objected.

'Is there a boyfriend on the scene, one you've not told us about?' Fern demanded.

'No, but—'

'I rest my case. You're lonely,' Fern reiterated, firmly. 'Sad and lonely, and we all think you're mad to move halfway across the country to run a roadside greasy spoon.'

'Hang on a minute, Peggy's isn't a greasy spoon. For one thing, I don't cook fry ups, and for another, I don't get many lorry drivers popping in for a cup of Oolong.'

'It is on the side of the road though,' Fern continued, 'and you can't deny the cat.'

Of course, it was on the side of a road! Every business in the street was on the side of the road, if you applied Fern's distorted logic.

'Never mind,' her mother said. 'You'll be back home with your tail between your legs soon enough.'

'What do you mean?' Stevie demanded.

'You're not making much of a go of it, even I can see that,' Hazel said, glancing pointedly at the empty tables.

'It's raining, that's all.'

'That's the problem with this part of the country,' Hazel stated. 'It rains all the bloody time, according to the forecast. Oi! Hurry up with that cake, I'm famished.'

Stevie finished slicing new portions, shoved them onto a plate for the terrible twosome, and dabbed it down on the table, noticing absently how her mother took the largest piece. Hazel might not be the most supportive of mothers (not when it came to Stevie, anyway – Fern always fared better), but Stevie was a firm believer in actions speaking louder than words, and her mother normally ate everything Stevie made for her.

She checked that the two dripping children were behaving themselves, and made sure they had an apple juice each, then poured herself a coffee and pulled up a chair.

Her mother, Stevie noticed, was busily inspecting the tea shop and Hazel shot Stevie a penetrating look. 'Are you sure she didn't leave you this café, as well as the money?'

'Perfectly sure,' Stevie said adamantly. 'I bought this myself, fair and square.'

'That's not strictly true,' Fern piped up. Her cake sat untouched in front of her.

The difference between Fern and her daughters was incongruous. Fern was stick-thin, bordering on scrawny, and appeared to resent every calorie she put in her mouth, whereas her children were fed anything and everything they wanted, no matter how bad it was for them, and they were starting to become quite robust. Yes, robust was the word Stevie was searching for, and she noticed the children had already finished their sweet treats and were eying the display cabinet with greedy expressions.

'I said, "that's not strictly true",' Fern repeated.

'I heard you.' Stevie had been trying to ignore the barbed comment.

'Peggy's money paid for this cafe,' Fern persisted. 'It's not fair. We need an extension, and I would have liked to have had a new kitchen, while we were at it.' Fern's sigh was artfully despondent.

'I thought you said you couldn't get planning permission,' Hazel said, and Fern's mouth narrowed into a thin line.

'That's beside the point,' Stevie's sister said. 'It's still not fair.'

She sounded like a spoilt child, Stevie thought, and as if thinking about children had spurred her nieces into life, the oldest one called, 'Mummy, do we have to stay with Aunty Stevie? You said she's a witch and I'm scared of witches.'

Stevie stiffened, her shoulders becoming rigid. It was bad enough having the family talk about her behind her back, but they'd clearly done so within earshot of the girls.

'Don't be silly! I said no such thing,' Fern objected but she was blushing, her cheeks turning an impressive shade of pink.

'Well, I think it's true,' Jade insisted. '*And* she's got a black cat. Do we *have* to stay, Mummy?'

Stevie sighed. This was going to be the longest three days in history, she thought, especially when she heard Macey scream, 'She's poisoned us!'

Swivelling in her chair, Stevie was just in time to see Macey vomiting all over a pile of half-eaten cupcakes which the pair of them had stolen from the cabinet.

Lovely!

Chapter 28

'What can I get you?' Leanne asked.

Nick stared around the shop in confusion. He'd never bought flowers before. Actually, that was a lie – he'd bought the odd bouquet, but the purchase had always been over the phone, and he'd never actually seen what he'd bought until after the event. Sometimes not even then, if it was an "It's not you, it's me" bouquet. Not that he'd sent many of those, but there was one memorable occasion when he'd been dating a fellow rider, and after their third date she'd started dropping hints about wedding venues. He'd tried to let her down gently, hence the flowers after he broken it off with her, but...

'Who are they for, and what's the occasion?' Leanne tried again.

'Oh, I, er, sorry Leanne, it's just I've never been inside a florist shop before, and it's just so... *flowery.*'

'It would be, wouldn't it,' Leanne said dryly. 'I mean, that's what florists do, sell flowers. And the odd plant.'

'Yes, well.' He glanced about helplessly. There were just so many to choose from. Was he expected to grab a handful himself, or pick some from each and somehow put them together so they didn't look like he'd raided the nearest hedgerow?

'Who are they for?' Leanne persisted. 'Mother? Girl-friend? Roses always go down well. Red ones for love, pink ones if you're not sure. White are classy, but they tend to say "marriage", so unless you want her to get the wrong idea…?'

'Er, Tia. They're for Tia.'

'Flowers for Tia, eh? So, tell me, Mr Saunders, what have you done that you feel you need to say sorry for?' Leanne crossed her arms and glowered at him.

'Nothing!' Nick objected, then clarified it with, 'Not that I know of.' He hesitated then let out a sigh. 'If you must know, she's decided to go back to Mum's.' Leanne would find out sooner or later anyway, so he didn't see the point in keeping it a secret. Besides, he mused, she might be able to help.

Leanne uncrossed her arms, her expression sympathetic. 'Really? Why?'

'I don't know,' he replied miserably. 'She's not been happy for a while, but she won't tell me what's wrong.' Even as the words left his lips, he wondered why he was airing his dirty laundry to Leanne. She and Tia were friends of sorts, but Tia hadn't really encouraged their friendship to continue since her accident. It was as if Tia was pushing away everyone from her previous life, despite Leanne's best efforts.

'Hiya, Lea.'

Nick jerked around at the sound of a new voice. Stevie from the tea shop down the road was closing the door behind her, giving him time to arrange his face into a neutral expression. He was trying not to show he found her attractive, in a scatty, ditzy way, and was also desper-ately trying not to remember the feel of her soft body in his arms and the sight of her scantily-clad curves. She looked quite delectable right now, actually, with her hair dripping down her face.

'Awful weather,' she announced to the shop, then stopped as she saw him.

It was probably the awful weather she'd just mentioned, combined with coming in out of the rain and into the warmth of the florist, which caused her cheeks to pink up and her eyes to widen.

Nick was glad he'd had time to compose himself first and had tamed his reaction to her before she'd noticed him. Then he caught Leanne's knowing glance and it was his turn to blush.

'It's the worst rain in living memory. I blame global warming,' Leanne said, raising her eyebrows at him and sending him a meaningful look, which Nick chose to ignore.

'I don't know why I bother putting fresh flowers on the table, because there aren't any customers to appreciate them,' Stevie grumbled, directing her comments to a bucketful of creamy, frilly flowers. 'The weather is scaring them off. Still, it's an excuse to get out of the flat. My mother is driving me mad, and don't get me started on my sister and those horrid brats of hers.'

'Don't you like kids?' Nick blurted out, then wished he'd kept his mouth shut. Or if he absolutely felt the need to talk, the good old British weather was a decent option and that was a line which was already being explored. What was wrong with him?!

Stevie looked at him for the first time since she'd entered the shop. 'I do like children actually,' she said, 'and I love my nieces, but I'd love them more if I hadn't been crammed in a two-bedroom flat with them for the past day and a half.' She shook her head. 'I'd also love them more if they weren't so spoiled and I hadn't had to sleep on the sofa for two long, lumpy nights.'

'Oh, um, I see. I didn't mean anything by it, just making conversation,' Nick stuttered, wishing Leanne would get a bloody move on with his order. She seemed to be deliberately slow. Surely wrapping a few stems shouldn't take this long?

'Getting on your nerves, are they, love?' Leanne said. 'When are they going back?'

'Tomorrow morning, thank goodness. I don't think I can stand another day. There are only so many things you can do indoors to keep a pair of lively kids entertained, and my poor little flat is hardly child-friendly. Once I'm done here, I'll pop to the newsagents and see if they've got any crayons. Although I suspect it will only keep them quiet for ten minutes.'

'Do they ride?' Nick found himself asking, without meaning to. The words just slipped from between his lips without any instruction from his brain.

'Excuse me?' Stevie said.

Even Leanne paused in her slow bouquet-making to look from him to Stevie.

'Ride, as in horses?' he clarified, wishing he would shut up but not seeming able to control his mouth.

'I've no idea,' Stevie replied. 'But I suspect they don't. In fact, I'd be surprised if they know what a horse looks like.'

'Do *you*?'

'Of course, I do. What do you take me for?'

'I mean ride, not do you know what a horse looks like.'

187

'Oh. No, I don't.'

'Why don't you come up to the stables this afternoon and bring your nieces. I've got an indoor arena, so they won't get wet. And two of my horses are quiet, old lads; they'll be gentle with the children.'

'I think you probably need to worry about the kids being gentle with your horses, rather than the other way around,' Stevie quipped, then became serious. 'Thank you, it's a kind offer, but—'

'Go for it!' Leanne cried. 'At least it gets them out of your hair for an hour, and you never know, you might enjoy yourself.'

'Um, OK, then, if you're sure?' Stevie said to him.

Nick was never more unsure than he'd been in his life. 'I'm sure,' he said. Maybe he could rope Tia into helping, even if it was only with digging out the old riding hats they'd acquired over the years and finding a couple to fit small heads. It might do his sister good. He gave Stevie the address and the phone number of The Furlongs and watched as she keyed it into her phone. A little part of him wished she'd give him her mobile number in exchange, but before he could suggest it, Leanne spoke.

'That's today sorted out,' the florist said to Stevie, 'and tomorrow you should come to Sunday lunch with us.'

'Really? That's wonderful, thank you!' Stevie beamed, and Nick watched the way her eyes crinkled slightly at the corners, and her nose crinkled too, like a happy puppy. She had freckles across it, and for some reason he had an urge to kiss them.

He cleared his throat and said to Leanne, 'How much do I owe you?'

'Seventeen pounds thirty-five, please, and give Tia my love. Tell her I'll ring her later and arrange an evening out, just us girls. You'll come too, won't you, Stevie?'

Nick was chuckling to himself as he left the shop. The expression on Stevie's face had been priceless and he bet she was remembering the last time she'd gone out for a drink with Leanne Green.

But he did find himself hoping he'd be the one to tuck her into bed again.

Chapter 29

'They'll be fine,' Stevie said for the fortieth time. 'Nick Saunders is a well-known international rider.' Stevie knew this because she'd Googled him – more than once. 'He's not going to let anything happen to them. Anyway, why don't you come with us?'

Fern screwed up her nose. 'Ugh. I can't think of anything worse than standing around in the mud and the rain, getting cold and soaked in a barn.'

'If it's in a barn, you're hardly likely to get rained on,' Stevie argued. As much as she was looking forward to seeing Nick again, she wasn't looking forward to super-vising her wayward nieces.

Fern waved a languid arm in the air. 'You go. You're more used to the outdoors. I'm going to have a nap.'

'Mum? Do you want to come?'

'No chance. I'm going to watch *Give us a Clue* on TV and have a nice cuppa. If you've *got* normal tea, that is.'

'You know I have. You've been drinking it for the past two days.' Stevie marched into the kitchen, yanked open a cupboard, got out a box of "normal" teabags and slapped it down on the table. 'Help yourself to cake,' she added. Not that her mother needed any invitation – she had practically eaten Stevie out of house and home since she'd arrived, all the while insisting she needed to lose weight. Stevie thought her mother was eating for two – herself and Fern!

On the way through the practically empty tea shop, Stevie whispered to Cassandra, 'Wish me luck. If you need anything, call me.'

'I can manage,' Cassandra said. 'We're hardly over-flowing with customers.'

'Don't remind me. At this rate the business will be sinking along with the village.'

'It'll perk up, you'll see,' Cassandra promised, but Stevie saw her friend cross her fingers.

With a heavy heart, she bundled the children into the car, and set off into the wild.

A couple of miles later she saw a sign for The Furlongs, and she turned off the main road. A series of twisting turns down a narrow lane and one false turn into the drive of someone's secluded bungalow later, and they had arrived. Thankfully, the rain had eased off so she could actually see out of the windscreen, but she was still grateful to leave those nasty lanes behind. You never knew what you might encounter around the next horseshoe bend – give her London traffic any day. Not that she had driven much in London (too hard to find a parking space), which was why she'd been on foot the day a big red bus had taken a bit of a shine to her.

Impressive, Stevie thought, her gaze darting around as she drove the car slowly up the drive and parked it next to a humongous horsebox, all shiny and sleek. It looked more like one of those big American RVs she'd seen in a film, than a vehicle for moving horses from one place to another.

So far, so good.

She was further impressed with the yard itself. An L-shaped, one-storey run of stables (she knew this because some of them had horses' heads poking over the top of the half-doors) was flanked by the side of the house, and the yard in front was cleaner than her kitchen floor. She'd expected mud and grass, and other stuff (horse poo, mainly) but it was pristine.

Even the kids were overwhelmed, because she hadn't heard a peep out of them since they'd got out of the car.

'That's a horse,' Jade said, breaking her silence and pointing to the nearest stable.

'Yes, it is,' Stevie agreed, wondering if they should wait here or go up to the house and knock on the door.

'It's very big,' Jade added in a small voice.

It certainly was. The damned thing towered over them, its enormous black head tossing up and down, its nostrils flaring. It appeared ready to gobble them up. Thank goodness it was in its stable, Stevie thought, although she had an awful feeling it could get out if it really wanted to.

'I see you've met Ebony,' a voice from behind said, and Stevie whirled around, seeing Nick walking towards them. 'She's only a baby, just two years old, but she's a sweetheart.'

Yeah, Stevie had met sweethearts like that before – playground bullies who fooled adults into thinking butter wouldn't melt when they were, in fact, the spawn of the devil.

'You can stroke her if you like,' Nick said. 'She won't bite.'

Stevie stared at him doubtfully, as he lifted Jade up, taking the child to within an inch of the creature's nose.

'Here, let me show you, then you can do it,' he suggested, and the little girl nodded.

Nick patted the long nose, then scratched the animal under the chin, as if it were a huge dog. Then it was Jade's turn.

'It's warm and hairy,' she said in wonderment.

'Stroke the end of her nose,' he suggested.

Jade did so and giggled. 'It's very soft.'

'Horses have quite delicate noses and lips,' Nick explained, 'and just like you and me, they'll jerk back in surprise if you make any sudden movements around their head because they're worried you might hurt them.'

'I'd never hurt it,' Jade vowed solemnly. 'Can I get on it, now?'

'Not this one, she's too lively for a novice like you.'

'What's a novice and can I be one?' Macey asked, tugging at the hem of Nick's jacket.

Stevie met Nick's gaze and they smiled at each other. Maybe this wasn't going to be so bad after all, Stevie hoped.

'Let's get you kitted out, then I'll show you which horse you *can* ride,' Nick said.

As he led them across the yard, Stevie leaned in close. She'd intended to ask him a question, but ended up sniffing him instead, as the glorious scent of man and aftershave reached her nose.

She took another deep breath, then realised he was giving her a quizzical look.

'Er, um, aren't the horses a bit big for the girls?' she asked, coming to her senses. He had smelled really nice, though, and for some reason it seemed familiar. Giving herself a mental shake, she tried to concentrate on his answer.

'I've got a couple of Shetlands,' he said, as if that was supposed to make sense to her. Were they jumpers, like Argyle and Fair Isle, and if so, why was the choice of knitwear important?

'Old Mrs Bont had to give up her smallholding a couple of years back and she was desperate to find them a good home, so I offered to take them in, along with Sydney, the donkey. She still comes to visit them when she's feeling well enough.' It was Nick's turn to lean in close. 'Cancer,' he said in a low voice. 'Such a shame.'

Stevie was still grappling with the image of a donkey wearing a pullover.

'Tia,' he called, as the little group came to a halt outside an open door. Stevie checked out the inside – no horses, thankfully, but lots of shelves and things dangling on hooks.

Tia appeared at the top of the slight ramp leading from the house to the yard and wheeled herself slowly down it. Stevie wondered if she should offer to help, but took her cue from Nick, who remained right where he was.

'Nice to see you again,' Stevie said politely. Tia turned as if to go back inside.

'Are you going to help sort the kids out, or what?' Nick asked his sister.

'Or what?' Tia retorted.

Stevie felt distinctly uncomfortable. There was a subtext going on, and she had no idea what it was. 'Maybe we should come back another time?' she suggested. Like never.

'No!' brother and sister shouted in unison.

Jade jumped and Macey's little hand stole into Stevie's larger one, gripping it tightly.

'Let's find you a hat, shall we?' Tia said to the girls with a smile which didn't quite reach her eyes. She looks sad, Stevie thought and wondered if she'd been crying. There was a slight redness around her eyes, but for all Stevie knew, she might have hay fever, or had been chopping onions, or was allergic to horses. It could be anything, but whatever it was, it was certainly none of her business.

Nick grunted, 'I'm off to saddle up.' Stevie watched him leave, wondering what all that was about.

'Are you going to ride, too?' Tia asked, breaking into her thoughts, and Stevie shook her head.

'No, thanks, I'll keep my feet firmly on the ground. I can't risk breaking an arm if I fall off. I've already broken my leg once this year.'

Stevie saw Tia's mouth tighten, and she had an awful idea she knew how Nick's sister had ended up in a wheelchair. Oh God, she'd just put her foot right in her mouth.

'Who would do the baking?' she trilled, trying to turn the subject away from broken bones, but not doing a very good job of it. She waved her arm and waggled her fingers. 'You need both hands to cook. At least I do.' Shut up, Stevie. Please.

Stevie followed her own advice and clamped her lips shut.

'I meant to congratulate you on the tea shop,' Tia said, wheeling into the store room and glancing up at the shelves. 'It's lovely. Come here, poppet,' she said to Jade. 'Let me have a look at you.'

The girl moved closer and Tia peered at the girl's head. Jade peered back.

'Why are you in a wheelchair?' she asked, with a child's uninhibited frankness. 'Can't you walk?'

'No, sweetie, I can't.' Tia said this with a smile, and this time it did reach her eyes. She was really beautiful when she smiled, Stevie thought; a feminine version of Nick, with her dark, curling hair and her blue eyes. Where his features were planed lines and rugged handsomeness, hers were delicate and pale, but the family resemblance was still there.

'Sorry,' Stevie said, remembering her manners. 'I forgot to introduce you. Tia, this is Jade, and this is Macey.' Stevie put a hand on the youngest child's head.

'What lovely names!' Tia exclaimed, putting a hard hat on Jade's head, and wiggling it about, before taking it off again and reaching for another. 'There, that one should do it.' She gave the second hat a tug and checked the chin strap. 'It's got to be tight, otherwise it won't do its job,' she said to Jade. 'Your turn,' she turned to the younger child.

Macey stepped forward for her own hat fitting.

'My mummy says Aunt Stevie will end up an old maid like Peggy.'

'Who's Peggy?' Tia asked, as Stevie let out a snort of disgust. She really must have a word with her darling sister about her ridiculous stories when she got back. Fern was filling her children's heads with nonsense.

'Peggy was old and had lots of cats,' Jade said. 'And she didn't have a husband, and no children either. Mummy said she was lonely.'

'She most certainly wasn't!' Stevie said. 'She had loads of friends, and I used to visit her all the time in London.' She stopped short of saying, "unlike your mother".

Jade turned an innocent face to Stevie and announced, 'Mummy said you only did that to get your hands on her intetrihance.' She stumbled over the word, but the meaning was clear, and Stevie seethed. How dare Fern say that!

Taking a deep breath, and trying not to let her annoyance show (it wasn't the children's fault their mother was such a bitter cow), Stevie plastered a false smile on her face.

Tia saw Stevie's expression and gave her a gentle smile. 'You're not exactly an old maid; you're probably younger than I am. There's plenty of time to prove them wrong.'

Suddenly all the light went out of Tia and her expression closed up. Stevie noticed her hand gripping the armrest of the wheelchair.

'It doesn't help that Peggy left nearly everything to me,' Stevie said, trying not to disrespect Fern in front of her own children. 'That's bound to cause some friction.'

'Is that how come you own the tea shop?' Tia asked, wheeling out of the storeroom and heading across the yard in the direction Nick went earlier.

'Yes. Peggy left me enough money to buy it, and it's doing well so far, fingers crossed, although this darned rain doesn't help.'

Tia glanced up at the sky. The rain was still holding off for the moment, but ominous black clouds roiled in the distance. 'We usually get a spot of awful weather in summer,' Tia said, 'normally as soon as the kids break up from school, but nothing like this. Look, girls, there's Nick with your ponies.'

Nick was waiting in the arena, holding the reins of two small orangey-coloured horses.

'That horse is really small,' Jade said. 'It's Jade-size.'

Tia laughed. 'It certainly is! This is Pickles, and that one there is Marmite. They're Shetland ponies, not horses. They're too small to be horses.'

'Will they get any bigger?' Macey asked. 'I'll get bigger, and one day I'll be as big as Jade.'

Stevie smiled. Jade was only a few inches taller than her sister, but to someone as little as Macey, Stevie guessed every inch must count.

The next hour or so was spent following Jade on Pickles, who was led by Nick, around and around the arena. Stevie led Marmite with Macey on board and the little girl wore the biggest smile Stevie had ever seen.

Nick let his sister do the talking and Tia proved to be an excellent instructor.

'Hold the reins, like this,' Tia had said, 'and pull gently this way if you want him to turn, but don't worry about that for now because Nick will keep a hold of Pickles until you're confident enough to steer him yourself.'

'Look, Aunty Stevie, I can drive it!' Jade called when Nick finally relinquished his hold on the reins and let Jade ride by herself.

He stood to one side, while Stevie carried on leading Marmite ("Don't let go, Aunty Stevie. I'm not a big girl like Jade"), and she missed watching him striding ahead of her.

Finally, the lesson was over, and the children were tired but happy, and dying to tell their mother all about their adventure. They were actually quite sweet when you got them away from Fern, Stevie decided.

'Thank you both so much,' Stevie gushed to Nick and Tia. 'I'm grateful to you for letting them come here and ride. It's been the highlight of their visit.'

It most certainly was, because with the waterfall pouring down from above, the poor little mites had hardly been out of the flat since they'd arrived. Tanglewood and surrounding areas were lovely if the weather was good, but if the weather was poor, activities were rather limited unless you wanted to go shopping, and even that wouldn't take more than an hour, although you could always drive to the nearest big town if the situation became desperate.

Stevie had noticed how most people had tended to barricade themselves into their houses, only venturing out for necessities like bread and milk, or to go to work, or visit the doctor. A few intrepid locals walked their dogs, but Stevie guessed the walks were briefer and further apart than normal.

Thanking Nick and Tia again, Stevie was deep in thought as she left The Furlongs. She'd really enjoyed herself today, but that wasn't what was playing on her mind. Something was clearly bothering Tia, and she was such a lovely person that Stevie was concerned about her.

Chapter 30

'She's lovely,' Tia said, on their way to the Ferris's place. 'You should ask her out.'

'I don't think so.' Nick seriously didn't want to discuss this right now. He was too busy trying to push the image of bright hair, laughing eyes and a wonderful smile out of his mind.

'Why not? She's lovely!' Tia repeated.

Nick shot a swift look at Tia's hopeful face 'Because I'm not interested in anyone, that's why.'

'You seemed to connect with her.'

Darn it, his sister could be very persistent when she wanted to be! 'Will you please give it a rest, sis. I neither want, nor need, a woman in my life right now.'

There was a long pause, then Tia whispered, 'It's because of me, isn't it?'

Nick thumped the steering wheel. 'No, it's not because of you. I'm talking about the business, my career. I keep telling you, I haven't got time for love and romance.'

'That's so sad.' She sounded wistful, and he was well aware that she, on the other hand, had all the time in the world because she had little else to occupy her, despite his efforts to get her involved.

There was a tiny light at the end of the tunnel she'd retreated into, though. He'd been pleased when she'd

200

agreed to help Stevie's nieces with their helmets. He'd made the excuse that it was probably best if a woman did it, and because Stevie wouldn't be able to tell if the helmets were a good fit or not, it had to be Tia. He'd had difficulty hiding his delight when Tia had accompanied them to the arena, and then went on to play the part of a riding instructor. It was a long time since she'd done that.

'Why do you think Edgar and Julia have invited us for dinner?' he asked, deliberately changing the subject. 'I was only over there a couple of weeks ago.'

'Perhaps they like you?' Tia suggested. 'Maybe they see you as son-in-law material.'

Nick growled. 'I damn well hope not.'

'Miranda has made it clear how much she fancies you. It's no secret,' she added, but both brother and sister got the surprise of their lives when they pulled up into The Manor's sweeping drive to be met by Miranda folding her long legs into a tiny sports car.

'Nice,' Tia drawled out of the window.

'Oh, it's not mine. It belongs to Roger.'

'Roger?' Tia called, as Nick lifted the chair out of the back and positioned it next to Tia's open car door.

'Yes, you must remember Roger. He's one of the Smythe-Cuthberts. You met him at last year's summer ball. Mummy introduced you. *You* remember, don't you, Nick? He was quizzing you about martingales.'

Nick vaguely recalled some posh bloke wittering on about assorted bridles, but he hadn't been taking an awful lot of notice to be fair. He'd been too busy worrying about Tia, who had looked lost and forlorn, like a child who was only able to talk to the waistbands and elbows of adults. She'd spent most of her evening trying to slip off into a corner, and he'd spent most of his trying to get her to mingle. Oh, and avoiding the over-clingy attentions of Miranda, who constantly patted and pawed him like he was some kind of lap-dog.

'Here he is,' Miranda said. 'Dahling, I was just telling Nick and his sister that this lovely little car is yours.'

Nick checked out the man trotting out of the wide front door. Now he remembered him. He'd met him a couple of times since, too, but the details were fuzzy.

'Saunders,' Roger grunted.

No way was Nick going to call this man by his surname. 'Roger, nice to see you again.'

From the expression on Roger's face, he clearly didn't think so. 'Can't stop. I'm taking Mirry to London.' He squeezed into his car and started the engine.

Mirry? Nick winced. There was no way Miranda was a *Mirry*.

'Yes, we're off to see his parents,' Miranda yelled over the roar. She had a big smile on her face. 'He's already asked Daddy, so before we announce our engagement to the world, Roger thought he'd better let his lot know. Do me a favour, Nick, dahling, and don't say anything to anyone for a few days. Ciao, got to run.'

She blew them a kiss and waggled her left hand at them, as Roger spun the car around and headed down the long drive, gravel spewing from the tyres.

Tia had her mouth wide open. Nick mirrored her expression.

'Well, that's a turn up for the books,' Tia said eventually. 'You've missed your chance. Dodgy Roger nabbed her.'

'Dodgy Roger?'

'Let me put it this way, he's worse than an octopus.'

'The nasty little sod! Did he try anything on with you?' If anyone laid so much as a finger on his little sister, Nick would—

'No, not the touchy-feely sort of octopus, the steal-anything-he-can-get-his-hands-on sort of octopus. I'm surprised the Ferrises allow him in the house. They'd better check the silver.'

'He's not a thief, is he?'

'He doesn't call himself that. Apparently, he says he "borrows" things.'

'But I got the impression he's quite well off,' Nick said.

'He is. His family are rolling in it. The rumour has it that his father kept him on a bit of a short leash when it came to spending the family fortune, so he used to help himself to trinkets from other people's houses to supplement his allowance. I've heard that one lord actually had his butler pat Roger down before he left, just in case.'

'How do you know all this?'

'I listen. It's surprising how many people think that because your legs don't work, your ears don't either,' Tia said, dryly.

'Last year's ball?'

'Yep.'

'I'm sorry. Look, we won't go to this one.'

'Yes, we bloody well will. Edgar and Julia would be offended. Although,' she paused, 'I might well be gone back to Mum's by then.'

To stop himself from sparking up an argument, Nick grabbed hold of the back of her chair and began to push, ignoring her huff of annoyance.

'Nick, darling, and Tia! So glad you could join us.' As usual, Julia Ferris was dressed as though she was off to Ascot, although at least she wasn't wearing a hat. She breezed into the hall, a billow of expensive perfume wafting around her, and leaned in to give them both a double kiss. 'You've just missed Miranda and Roger. They have *news*.' This last was said in an exaggerated whisper.

'We know, Miranda told us,' Tia said.

'Don't worry, we'll keep it quiet until it's official,' Nick added, seeing Julia's startled expression. At least, he thought the slight widening of her eyes and the parting of her bright pink lips indicated startlement. With the amount of Botox Julia had had done, it was difficult to tell.

She waved an elegant hand in the air and gave a little pout, simpering at him. 'I did hope… oh well, as long as my little girl is happy, that's all I care about.'

Yeah, and marrying into the Smythe-Caruthers family was nothing but a bonus, Nick thought. Julia Ferris was renowned for her social climbing, but to be fair to her, she did seem to genuinely love Edgar. Nick hoped so, because if local gossip was to be believed, Edgar had been practically disowned by his father when he'd fallen in love with Julia. Which was sad and ironic, since rumour had it, Edgar's father had been forced to give up the love of *his* life by *his* own father. Talk about history repeating itself. Nick would have thought Edgar's father knew how it felt to have love denied and wouldn't have wanted to inflict that on any son of his.

Not so. From the fragments Nick had overheard, mostly in The Hen and Duck, Edgar's father had been of the opinion that if he'd survived being separated from the woman he loved, then Edgar would too. But he'd not made allowances for Edgar's stubbornness nor his determination to marry Julia. Good for you, Edgar, Nick thought, as he shook the older man's hand.

He didn't see William until he heard a sharp intake of breath from Tia and he turned to see him straightening up from kissing her. His sister didn't look pleased about the contact. Her shoulders were hunched and a little tick played at the corner of her eye – a sure sign she was nervous.

Why did William make Tia nervous, Nick wondered?

'Hi, Nick, have you heard the good news? Miranda is engaged.' William smiled, but Nick thought he looked a bit strained.

'Yes, we bumped into her outside,' Tia said. Nick thought she sounded slightly odd, too.

Julia said, 'Tia, tell me, how *are* you, dear? Well, I hope? I must say, you're looking a bit peaky, isn't she, Edgar?'

'What?' Edgar asked.

'Tia, she's looking a bit peaky. You're not coming down with anything, are you? Let me get you a jar of honey to take home with you. Edgar swears by it, don't you, Edgar?'

'Hmm?' Edgar was too busy shaking hands with Nick.

'He doesn't listen to a word I say,' Julia continued, guiding Nick and Tia into the "small" dining room, which was actually large enough to seat twenty – more at a push. 'His mind is elsewhere, so you'll have to excuse him.'

'That's what I wanted to talk to you about, Nick,' Edgar began, but Julia shushed her husband, claiming there would be enough time to discuss business after dinner, so Nick had to sit through three rather long courses before he could discover the reason why Edgar Ferris had actually invited him to dinner. It certainly wasn't to make up the numbers, or to keep Miranda company, this time.

'Do you mind if I borrow your brother for a half an hour?' Edgar asked Tia, and although Nick could see she was also dying to know what was going on (and rather annoyed that "the women" had to remain behind while the men talked business – Nick knew he would pay for the slight later, even though it wasn't of his making), his sister nodded and poured herself another glass of wine. A large one.

She'd had two already and it wasn't like her to drink. Something was obviously bothering her, and Nick vowed to get it out of her by the end of the evening.

'The Manor isn't doing too well, you know,' Edgar began, closing his study door behind them. Nick almost expected the other man to pour them both a brandy and offer him a cigar, but Edgar simply sank into one of the winged chairs and rested his head against the back.

'No, I didn't know,' Nick replied. He was sorry to hear that, because he genuinely liked Edgar and Julia.

'We can't keep going the way we are. Something's got to give. We're not financially viable, you see.'

Nick nodded, although he wasn't sure he did see, because he had no idea what any of this had to do with him.

'We're opening the place up for weddings and stuff,' Edgar confided. 'It's not my idea of course – I can't stand the things – but I've been outvoted.'

Nick tried to see Edgar organising a wedding and failed. But Julia? She could certainly do it; after all, she'd been running the hunt and annual summer balls for years.

She'd be a perfect wedding organiser, and The Manor was a perfect venue.

But Nick still couldn't see what all this had to do with him.

'I've got a bit of a proposition,' Edgar continued. 'It's William's idea actually, but we need your help. Weddings aren't going to be enough to keep the wolves from the door, I'm afraid. We're opening the house and the grounds up to the public, of course, but at six quid a pop entrance fee, we'll have to get people in by the shipload to make any decent money. Then William came up with a plan. You know he's heavily into conservation?'

Nick raised his eyebrows. He didn't know. The man had a reputation for being out all night and in bed all day, and not necessarily his own bed, either, Nick guessed. Only last week, Mads had mentioned he'd seen William slinking back home at seven in the morning. It looked as though he'd spent the night in a hedge, Mads had said. No wonder Nick didn't want the man anywhere near Tia.

'Yes.' Edgar nodded. 'He's been working with The National Trust to reintroduce beavers into the area and it was his idea to dedicate some land for the purpose. I've never seen a beaver dam before,' Edgar added. 'Bloody marvellous thing. You ought to have a gander at it yourself.'

Nick's eyebrows rose even further. He wasn't even aware there *were* any beavers in Wales, let alone on his doorstep.

'Poor chap's been hard at it most nights,' Edgar was saying. 'Apparently, the damned things are most active at dusk and dawn. The project is doing well and they've had an effect on other wildlife already. It's all terribly exciting.'

Nick was astounded. So that was why William had been out and about at night, and why Mads had said he had looked like he'd slept in a hedge – he most probably had! It seemed like Nick had totally misjudged William.

'It certainly is, but how can I help?' he asked.

'You youngsters are so impatient – I was just getting to that. We've got a few spare bedrooms in the house for the wedding side of the business, but William wants to convert some of the old outbuildings to cottages too, and run residential courses, rural, countryside stuff, like basket-weaving and coppicing, plus some more exciting things like archery and clay pigeon shooting. This is where you come in.'

The logic was lost on Nick. 'I can't shoot,' he protested, 'either with a bow and arrow, or a gun, and I certainly can't weave baskets.'

'*I'm* going to run the shooting,' Edgar said. '*You'll* do the riding.'

'I will? What riding?' By now Nick was thoroughly confused. It all sounded wonderful, and he was pleased to see Edgar so enthusiastic, but Nick had no idea what he was on about with regards to riding.

'Horse-care classes, riding lessons, trekking,' Edgar said, sitting forward with excitement. 'Are you in?'

'In?'

'Yes, on board, with the programme, *in*.'

'Um, I'm not sure. I don't think so, I mean, I'm a show jumper, not a riding instructor.'

'Nonsense! You train other riders, don't you?'

'Yes, in *show jumping*.'

'I haven't made myself clear – it won't be for any old common or garden riders, it'll be for—'

x

208

The door slammed open with a bang and Tia shot into the room. 'Take me home, now!' Her eyes were red and suspiciously damp. She'd clearly been crying.

Nick leapt to his feet. 'Why, what's wrong? Has something happened? Are you hurt?'

'I'm fine. Nothing's happened. I just want to go home.'

Nick glanced helplessly at Edgar, who shrugged. 'Tia—' Nick began.

'Please, Nick, don't ask any questions, I just want to leave.'

He shook his head, confused and concerned. 'OK, I'll just say goodbye to Julia. Thanks for dinner, Edgar. You've certainly given me a lot to think about.'

Even as he uttered the words, Edgar's proposal slipped from his mind. The only thing Nick was interested in, was finding out what had upset Tia.

'Wait by the car,' he said to her. 'I'll go and find Julia.'

'She was in the sitting room the last time I saw her,' Tia called after him.

What did she mean "the last time I saw her"? If Tia hadn't been with Julia, then where had she been? And, more to the point, who had she been with?

Julia was reading the newspaper, her glasses perched on the end of her nose, but she swiftly removed them when Nick poked his head around the door, and Nick smiled a little at her vanity. Julia Ferris was a handsome woman, with or without her spectacles, but he pretended he didn't notice as she stuffed them down the side of her chair.

'Thank you for a lovely dinner, Julia, but I'm afraid we must be off.'

'Did you have a nice talk with Edgar?'

'I'm not sure…?'

'Give it some thought, won't you? There are very few places in the country offering what we'd like to offer – with your help, and Tia's, of course.'

'I will,' he said, but he wasn't making any promises. Riding schools were ten a penny, and he simply wasn't interested. And Tia certainly wasn't!

Julia tilted her head for a kiss and Nick dutifully air-kissed both cheeks. Then he strode into the hall and out to the car, only to pull up short at the scene in front of him.

Tia was in her chair, waiting by the car. William, hands on hips, towered over her. Nick couldn't see his face, but he could see Tia's, and tears were streaming down it. Her cheeks were blotchy, her eyes red, and she looked so distraught, Nick's heart went out to her. He hated seeing his sister upset, he always had done ever since they were small children. He was the eldest, it was his duty to protect her, and if William Ferris had done anything to hurt her…

'Tia? What's wrong?' In a few quick strides, he was at her side and kneeling in front of her chair.

'Nothing. Just take me home,' Tia insisted, burying her face in her hands.

He stood up. If she wouldn't talk to him, then he'd make sure William damned well did.

'What have you done to her?' His voice was low and menacing as he took a step towards him. 'If you've touched her…'

'Leave him alone, Nick.' Tia stared up at him. 'Just take me home,' she repeated.

'Not until I find out what's going on.' Nick was adamant.

'Please, Nick.'

'What did he *do*?' Nick persisted.

'Nothing!' Tia tugged at his sleeve, but Nick didn't move.

He glared at William. William was staring at Tia with a stricken look on his face.

'Then why are you crying?' Nick demanded. 'Please, Tia, you've got to tell me.'

'Because… because… I love him, if you must know!' Tia cried and promptly burst into fresh tears.

Nick was dumbfounded. 'You *love* William Ferris?'

Chapter 31

'I'm singing in the rain,' Stevie chortled once more, but this time she was as sober as a nun. 'Just singing in the rain. What a wonderful feeling to have my flat back again.'

Her visitors had left that morning, her mother fussing she'd forgotten something and her sister complaining constantly from the minute she'd woken up to the second she'd darted out of the door, but nothing could dampen Stevie's spirits. Not even the incessant, persistent, never-ending, ceaseless rain. And her nieces had both given her a hug, *without* being told to.

She had her flat all to herself again. She could sleep in her own bed, watch whatever she liked on TV without being criticised for her taste in programmes, eat stuff out of a tin if she wanted (she was sick and tired of cooking), and she could slob around in her PJs all afternoon if she felt like it. Bliss.

But first, she fully intended to enjoy a Sunday roast which someone else had prepared. She wasn't turning up empty-handed though – she'd rustled up a tiramisu, (which didn't count as cooking) and had bought a bottle of wine. She really, really hoped Leanne wouldn't drink it all by herself, she thought as she drove cautiously down the winding lanes to the farm, trying to avoid the bigger puddles and wishing her wipers had an additional, faster speed.

'Come in, come in,' Leanne gushed, shepherding Stevie into the farmhouse. 'Meet my brothers and their wives, and my brothers who don't have wives yet, and my niece and nephews, and my mum and dad.'

Gosh, but there were a lot of people crammed into a not very big space.

Stevie smiled nervously as she was introduced to Martin and his wife, Janine, Stuart and his wife, Lisa, three children (two boys and a girl, but Stevie couldn't remember their names, or which child belonged to which set of parents), two more brothers, Murray and Saul (both wifeless) and Mr and Mrs Green ("call him Geoff and me Iris," Leanne's mum had said). By the time everyone had smiled and nodded, and made the odd quip or three, and Iris had dragged Geoff into the kitchen to help her dish up, Stevie's head was spinning.

Room was made for her on the sofa and Stevie found herself squashed between Murray (about her age, nice eyes, a bit on the tubby side) and Saul (a little older maybe, even nicer eyes, and fit, very fit – and not just in the fitness sense of being fit either. He was actually rather scrummy).

'Leanne has told us all about you,' Saul said, with a twinkle in his eye.

'Oh dear, nothing bad, I hope.'

'No, more's the pity.' There was that twinkle again and a flash of a bright smile. Was he flirting with her? 'She tells us you've opened up the old café down by the river.'

'Yes, I bought it a couple of months ago.' She couldn't believe it – the time had gone by so quickly. It was weird though, because on the one hand she felt as though she'd been here forever and on the other, it seemed like only yesterday she was arguing with the sign writer.

'Settled in OK?' one of the wives, Lisa, asked.

'I have.' Stevie nodded. 'It's a lovely spot and I've got some regular customers.'

'So I heard,' Lisa said. 'Allegra Johnson and her little gang, for one. I also heard you had a bit of a run in with her.'

'Oh?' News had a way of travelling fast in small communities, Stevie was discovering. The one thing she missed about London (apart from the shopping, the fab restaurants, and the social life, of course) was the anonymity. No one had a clue who you were, and no one wanted to know, either. It was both awful and wonderful at the same time.

She felt the same way about life in Tanglewood – Stevie loved that everyone knew everyone else, (it was actually quite comforting) but it was rather intrusive and a bit scary too.

'She's telling everyone not to go to your café because it's unhealthy,' Lisa was saying, and Stevie gasped.

'She's *what*!'

'Don't worry, no one listens to a word she says, except for those hangers-on she surrounds herself with, and I think they're only friends with her because they're too scared of her not to be.'

'What exactly has she been saying?' Stevie asked, horrified. The prick of tears stung the back of her eyes, and she blinked fiercely.

'Now, Lisa, I told you not to say anything.' Iris bustled in with a jug of steaming gravy in her hand. 'Lunch is served,' she announced, 'unless your gossip has driven poor Stevie's appetite away.'

It had rather, but Stevie didn't say anything. It was lovely to be invited and she didn't want to upset Leanne's mum.

'Mmm. Beef, my favourite,' Saul said. 'Ladies first.'

Stevie shuffled to the edge of the sofa and lurched out of her seat. For a second, she felt a swift push on her bottom, then she was free of the sucky squishiness of the sofa.

Saul was grinning at her. 'Sorry, but you looked as though you were stuck there for the duration. Someone should have warned you about our ancient sofa. I'm sure if you squish too far into it, it'll drag you into an alternative universe. Oh, and don't listen to Lisa, she's nothing but a gossip.'

Stevie smiled gratefully at him, as her hand was engulfed by his far larger one, the heat of his skin warming hers, then she gasped as he added, 'Nice arse, by the way.'

'Cheeky sod!' she cried, but she couldn't help smiling. Leanne's brother was rather too forward for his own good.

'It took your mind off Allegra Johnson for a minute though, didn't it?' he said with a laugh.

'Ignore him,' Leanne said, 'the rest of us do. He loves shocking people, which is probably why he can't keep a girlfriend.' She stuck her tongue out at him and Stevie chuckled. Why was it, that no matter how old you were, when your family all got together everyone reverted to about twelve? And your parents treated you as such, too.

Saul whispered in Stevie's ear as he played the gentleman and pulled out a chair for her, 'She's just jealous because she hasn't had a date for months. No one can afford to take her out; have you seen the amount of wine she can pack away?'

'I heard that,' Leanne said, 'and yes, she has. Our Stevie isn't backward in coming forward when it comes to a glass or two either. She had to be taken home by our resident celebrity showjumper the other night.'

'If I remember rightly, so did you!' Saul replied, helping himself to a huge spoonful of mashed potatoes. 'Poor Nick Saunders spent ages trying to explain to Dad that it wasn't him who had got you into such a state, and he was simply picking up the pieces.'

Stevie was trying to take it all in, but there were at least five different conversations going on around her, plus the noise from the children, and everyone was busy lunging for the serving dishes or passing things around the table, so she just sat there, waiting for things to calm down.

She'd never seen such friendly chaos. Arms, spoons, plates, forks ('You'll have someone's eye out with that, my boy,' Iris said, on at least two separate occasions), all were waved around and passed up and down the table. Then there was a squabble over the gravy boat, until Iris, who had yet to put anything on her own plate, heaved her ample frame out of her seat and toddled off to the kitchen to fetch some more.

Finally, there was some semblance of order and Stevie picked up a serving spoon intending to fill her own plate, only to find Saul had sneakily swapped plates, and he had the empty one and she had one piled so high with food it almost reached her chin. She looked like a proper greedy-guts.

'You've got to be quick in this family,' he warned, 'otherwise the rest of them will have stripped the table bare like a swarm of locusts.'

There was still plenty left in the tureens, but she didn't say anything apart from "thank you". If she was honest, she felt slightly overwhelmed. It was all so very different from her own small family. There were so many Greens, and to have them all squashed around one table, with elbows touching and hardly any room to wield a fork, rendered Stevie speechless.

She made up for her silence by tucking into her lunch. The beef was flavoursome and so tender it melted on her tongue; the roast potatoes were crispy and fluffy with just the right amount of seasoning, and each vegetable was superbly cooked. Iris certainly knew her way around a Sunday roast and before long Stevie found she'd nearly cleared her plate and was wishing she'd worn stretchy leggings instead of jeans.

The noise level had abated somewhat as everyone concentrated on their food, but as bellies gradually filled, the noise returned to its former pitch.

It also looked like Saul had taken it upon himself to be her protector, so with him on one side of her and Leanne on the other, Stevie didn't feel quite as awkward as she might otherwise have done by being surrounded by so many people she didn't know.

'Your mother is a good cook,' Stevie said, chasing the last few peas around her plate. 'I'm glad she's not in competition with me.'

'She can't bake for toffee,' Leanne said. 'But she's a dab hand at traditional meals. She has to be, to feed this lot! Murray and Saul still live at home, and the other two are back and fore for their dinners so often I don't think Lisa and Janine ever feed them.'

'Shut up, Lea, you make it sound like we're a couple of mummy's boys,' Murray interjected. Until now, he'd been fairly quiet, but clearly this was an insult too far.

'If the cap fits, Murray-Man,' one of the married brothers called.

'Go boil your head, Marty,' Murray retorted.

'Boys! Behave yourselves, you're embarrassing Stevie.' Iris banged her hand on the table and the noise dropped to a more acceptable level as everyone stared at Stevie.

If she hadn't been embarrassed before, she certainly was now.

'Sorry,' Murray and Martin muttered in unison. Leanne gave her a smirk, licked the tip of her forefinger and held it up, making a "one" gesture.

Saul said, 'Murray and I converted one of the old barns into a proper house. We live there, not here.'

'You might as well live here, because you're never at your own place,' Iris pointed out. She had an indulgent smile on her face and clearly loved having her family around her.

'We are! It's not our fault you keep feeding us,' Saul replied.

Iris raised her arms in despair and gave Stevie a wink. 'Ah, so that's where I'm going wrong? I'll stop making you dinner then, shall I?'

Murray looked worried, but Saul had an ace up his sleeve. 'That's OK, I'll just pop into Peggy's Tea Shoppe every lunchtime and the pub in the evening.'

'I'll refuse to serve you,' Stevie warned, warming to the theme. 'Be nicer to your mother.'

'I'm always nice to you, aren't I, Mum?'

Iris chuckled. 'Sometimes. Right then, you can show me just how nice you are by offering to do the washing up. All you men can lend a hand, except your father. He helped with the cooking.'

There was a chorus of groans, and some murmuring about Leanne's non-existent role in operation clean-up, but Iris's four boys disappeared into the kitchen happily enough, and soon there were sounds of squealing and giggling from the children who had followed their fathers.

'I expect I'll have to go behind them to clean up the mess they'll no doubt make while cleaning up.' Iris sighed. 'Now, Stevie, tell me all about your café.'

'There's not much to tell,' she began, but Leanne interrupted her.

'She's a proper pastry chef, is Stevie. Worked in a Michelin star restaurant and everything,' Leanne exclaimed.

Iris looked from one to the other. 'Is that good?'

'It's bleedin' marvellous,' Leanne said, before Stevie had a chance to open her mouth. 'Go on, Stevie, tell Mum about Corky Middleton.'

'Who's Corky Middleton?' Iris wanted to know.

'Just a chef,' Stevie said, 'no one, really.' And she realised she meant it. After all the work, all the long hours, and all the striving to be the best of the best in the cut-throat world of London cuisine, Stevie found she didn't actually care about that anymore. She was perfectly content being her own boss and running her own show, and even though it might not be up there with the likes of Corky Middleton, she was happy.

Actually, she realised, she really was happy. Mostly. If it would stop raining. And if Nick Saunders's face didn't keep popping into her head.

'So, you see, Great-Aunt Peggy was behind it all, and that's why I called it Peggy's Tea Shoppe, because I owe everything to her,' Stevie said, finishing up her story of how she came to move to Tanglewood. The wives had joined their husbands in the kitchen, ostensibly to check on the clearing up, but Stevie guessed her coming-to-Tanglewood story was boring them to tears.

How Stevie missed her great-aunt and, just for a second, grief reared its head. Stevie would have given anything to have her funny, oddball aunt back in her life. Her house had been nothing like this one (Peggy had no family, apart from Hazel, Fern and Stevie), but her home always felt really lived in, as though people had just popped out for a second or visitors were just about to arrive.

'So,' Iris said, breaking into Stevie's thoughts. 'You and Nick Saunders, eh? Go on then, spill the beans.'

Stevie did a double-take. Where had that question come from? 'There aren't any beans to spill,' she replied, blushing. 'I actually don't think he likes me very much.'

'But you like him?' the older woman queried, and even as Stevie was shaking her head in denial, a part of her was whispering, "liar!"

'Oh, I forgot to tell you, Tia's going to live with her mother,' Leanne said to Iris.

'Leaving Nick to run the place all on his own?' Iris gave Stevie a pat on the arm. 'Well, I suppose it does mean when Nick finally settles down whoever he marries will have that lovely old farmhouse all to herself. It never works with two women in one kitchen.'

'Which is why I never do any cooking,' Leanne stated. 'She won't let me anywhere near her double oven.'

'You don't cook because you *can't*,' Saul said, appearing in the doorway and wiping his hands on a tea towel. 'You do realise the way to a man's heart is through his stomach? It's no wonder you can't get a fella.'

Leanne snorted. 'Sexist crap. With an attitude like that, no wonder women take one look at you and run a mile.' Turning to Stevie, she said, 'He doesn't have any trouble getting a girl, but he can't keep them. Once they get to know him, they're off.'

'Ow, that hurts.' Saul placed a hand over his heart. 'I just haven't found the right one yet,' he explained to Stevie. 'Or maybe I have?' He gave Stevie a big grin.

'Give over, she's got the hots for Nick Saunders,' Leanne retorted.

'Don't they all?' was Saul's reply.

'I haven't!' Stevie protested again.

'So that means you're free to come to dinner with me,' Saul said.

'Saul's got a date, Saul's got a date,' Leanne sang, until her mother elbowed her in the ribs. 'Oof!'

'Leave your brother alone before you scare Stevie off. I like her,' Iris announced.

'I'd like that, thank you,' Stevie said to Saul and she found herself looking forward to a date with him – he was good-looking, amusing, and his family clearly thought the world of him.

But why was the image of Nick's face still seared on her inner eye?

Chapter 32

With no parking allowed on the main street and with no rear access to speak of, Stevie usually parked in the free car park opposite, the one she'd used the very first time she came to Tanglewood.

This afternoon, the view out across the fields and the river from the car park wasn't as pleasant as it usually was. In fact, it was quite disturbing. Feeling a faint twinge of unease, Stevie got out of the car, pulling her hood over her head. The rain hadn't eased at all on the journey back from Leanne's house and was still coming down in buckets.

She peered towards the river and the row of cottages running adjacent to the bank and was surprised to see movement. Lots of movement. At least twenty people were there, carrying what looked like old-fashioned sacks of grain, then her brain caught up with her eyes and she realised what she was looking at were people hauling sandbags. Sandbags meant flood defences, and as she studied the river she realised just how high the water had become. There was almost no space between the arches underneath the quaint humped bridge and the seething dark water.

Stevie, wishing she had something more waterproof in her wardrobe, made her way to the end of the street to offer her help. She wasn't sure how much use she could be, but she was willing to do anything she could.

As she grew nearer, the force and speed of the water took her breath away. The normally placid river churned and broiled, its usually clear water now a muddy brown, and debris caught in the fast current swept past faster than a human could run. If anyone fell in, they'd not stand a chance.

The banks had already overflowed, and the footpath was completely submerged. Even as she watched, the water crept higher, threatening to overflow onto the narrow, tarmacked road and lap at the front steps of the little row of cute cottages.

'What can I do?' she called over the roar of the river.

'Get in line,' a man instructed, pointing to a snake of figures which started at a pile of sandbags where the dead-end road in front of the first house joined onto the main street and ended at the doorstep of the cottage furthest away.

Stevie recognised Henry, the ironmonger, and gave him a nod. He nodded back, his expression grim, and made room for her, patting her on the shoulder as she slid into the line of people. She darted a quick look around, recognising quite a few of them. More than a few, actually, and most of them had been in her tea shop at one time or another. She was surprised so many of the villagers had turned out to help – she couldn't imagine the same thing happening in London. Take the building her old flat had been in for instance – she'd actually had no idea who was living upstairs or what they looked like, and she simply couldn't imagine calling on them for help if she'd needed it. Hell, her own flatmates would have been reluctant to pitch in.

Seeing so many familiar faces simply getting on with it, despite the torrential rain, gave her a warm, comfortable feeling. And the smiles and nods of acceptance aimed at her, made her finally feel as though she was a part of this little community.

She braced herself for the first sandbag. Crikey, that was heavy, she thought, wincing as it was almost thrown into her waiting arms. Twisting awkwardly and taking care not to slip on the wet, and by now rather muddy road, she heaved the bag at the next person. No sooner had she got rid of her burden than she was given another, and another, until her muscles screamed and her legs trembled, but still the bags kept coming.

In no time, she was soaked through. Even her bra was wet, and cold water trickled nastily down her neck and back. She hadn't felt her feet for the last ten minutes or so, and was dimly aware they were just as wet from the river water lapping at her toes as from the water pouring from the sky.

At some point, she noticed a lorry delivering another load, and she could have wept. She'd give anything to stop, but the water was now over their ankles and perilously close to the front of the cottages. She couldn't believe how fast the river was rising.

'We can't stop it, can we?' she gasped to the woman next to her.

'Maybe, maybe not. Depends on how much higher the river rises. We gotta try though, haven't we?'

'But look at all this rain,' Stevie cried, and Henry said, 'It's not *this* rain we need to worry about. It's the rain further up the river. This stuff,' he jerked his head, 'fell a couple of days ago in the mountains in mid-Wales. And I hear it's still coming down.'

Stevie heaved a sandbag onto his forearms and swivelled to face the other way, stretching her spine as she watched the progress of the next bag. Any minute now...

She grunted at the weight of it and turned back to Henry, preparing to hoist it at him. Every bag was taking more and more out of her, and she didn't know how long she was going to be able to keep it up.

A squint through the veil of rain at the cottages gave her new resolution. Those poor people. Imagine if it was her tea shop under threat from flooding? She'd be devastated.

'Effing hell!' a voice called. 'Look at that!'

Stevie and the others in the line stopped for a precious second and what they saw made them all gasp.

The tree was huge. Torn up by its roots, it bobbed in the centre of the river. A pale circle of bare wood, bigger than the front of a lorry, bore down on the bridge, its roots like skeleton's fingers, some of them submerged, others waving in the air, with smaller debris caught in their grasp.

Stevie dropped her sandbag and, with mouth and eyes wide open, watched as the river's momentum carried the tree past the row of cottages and on towards the little bridge.

'God help us, it'll take the bridge out,' someone cried.

The tree slammed into the old stones with a grinding, roaring thump and Stevie swore she felt the ground shake beneath her feet. There wasn't enough of a gap between the water and the arch for the tree to slide underneath, and even if there had been, Stevie suspected the spread of roots at the one end and branches at the other, was too wide to let it through.

With one of the three arches securely blocked and more water-borne debris piling up behind it, there was only one way for the water to go – outwards. Even during the minute or so the workers watched, the water level rose rapidly. Sandbags would be useless against this flood and everyone knew it.

'Get anyone left in those houses out,' a familiar voice shouted and Stevie pushed her sodden hood back off her face to catch a glimpse of the speaker.

Nick, water dripping down his face, banged on the door of the cottage furthest away from the main road. His expression was grim.

'It's empty,' someone called. 'They use it as a holiday home. The owners live down south.'

Nick, without preamble, moved on to the next one.

People darted everywhere. The front doors of the other three were wide open, and Stevie could see shapes moving inside. Shouts of, "turn it on its end", and "I'll take the weight, you steer it", indicated that the helpers were desperately trying to move anything they could possibly salvage to the upper floors. A man (she could have sworn it was Saul) leaned over the stacked sandbags protecting one house and lifted a woman into his arms. Stevie watched as he sloshed through the encroaching water until he deposited the woman safely on the street. Someone else was close on Saul's heels. His arms were full of a squirming toddler, and he was quickly followed by another person clutching a cat carrier.

Stevie stood there, helplessly, wondering what she could do. Shivering and soaked to her skin, now that she'd finally stopped throwing bags of sand around, the chill was settling into her bones.

'You can't stay here!' Nick was shouting up at a first-floor window, where a pale face peered out from behind a curtain. He turned to the nearest helper. 'Who lives here?'

The face at the window tugged at the curtain, shoving it aside for a better look, and Stevie recognised it.

'It's Betty,' she said, wading closer to Betty's front door. The water was now mid-shin and was starting to lap eagerly at the bottom of the stacked bags.

They were running out of time; those bags couldn't keep the swirling waters out for much longer.

'Come on, Betty, open the door and let's get you out of there,' Nick called.

Betty shook her head.

'She's going to be marooned up there, if she's not careful. If she won't come down, we're going to have to force the door,' he said.

'Let me have a go,' Stevie suggested. 'It can't do any harm.'

Nick stepped to the side. 'She's all yours but make it quick.'

'Betty, you have to leave,' Stevie shouted up. 'You can't stay here.'

Betty, with much shoving and banging, managed to heave the old sash window up. 'I can stay and I will. This is my home.'

Stevie's heart went out to her. The old lady sounded determined and pitiful at the same time.

'But it's dangerous,' Stevie argued, ignoring Nick's hurry-up gesture. 'The water will flood the house soon.'

'It'll have to be bloody deep to reach this floor,' Betty said. 'And if it gets that high, you'll have more than my old carcass to worry about – the whole village will be flooded.'

'I'm going in,' Nick said. 'Someone's got to make her see sense.' And with that, he took a couple of steps back and launched himself at the door. His shoulder slammed into the wood with a resounding thud but the door held and Nick bounced back off it, almost landing on his backside.

Despite the gravity of the situation, Stevie had to bite back a laugh.

Rubbing his arm, Nick squared up to have another go.

'Oi, what's that young man doing to my front door?' Betty yelled, leaning so far out of the window, Stevie feared the old woman would topple through it.

'Come down and open it,' Stevie pleaded, 'before he breaks it down.'

'I'll break his head, in a minute,' Betty yelled, and when the old lady's face disappeared from the window, Stevie prayed she was on her way downstairs.

No such luck. Betty reappeared at the window. The old woman leaned out just in time to see Nick rebound off the surprisingly solid door again and promptly threw a bucket of water over him.

To be fair to Nick, he didn't bat an eyelid, and Stevie wondered if he'd even noticed – he was as wet as she was, despite his waterproof Barbour jacket.

'It's not like this in the movies,' he grumbled, wincing. 'I'm going to have one hell of a bruise tomorrow. 'I'll have to break a window.'

'Betty's going to love that,' Stevie thought, then she had an idea. 'Betty?' she bellowed over the roar of the water. 'I need your help. How do you fancy a job?'

'What sort of a job?' the old woman shrieked back. 'If this is a trick to get me out...' she warned.

'No trick, I promise. Cross my heart and hope to die.' Stevie dutifully crossed her heart.

'What do you want me to do?' the old lady demanded, squinting at Stevie out of narrowed eyes.

'I need someone to help me make hot drinks for this lot, before they all keel over from hypothermia, and I'll make some soup too. But I can't do it all on my own.'

Betty peered down at her, and for a second Stevie thought she was going to refuse. 'What will happen to my house?' the old woman asked, after a brief silence. 'If I can't come back here, where am I to go?'

Ah, bless her! So that's what was really worrying her, Stevie realised. Betty was scared that if she left her home, she'd be on the streets. As if anyone would let that happen!

'You can stay with me,' Stevie said. 'I've got a spare room. Pack a bag, just in case, but don't take too long, eh?'

'Right, that's settled, then,' Nick said. 'Let's get to it!'

And get to it, he did. Leaning over the sandbags he took hold of the old lady's bag and thrust it at Stevie. Then he bent forwards, wrapped his arms around Betty and scooped her into his arms. Betty grabbed hold of the back of his neck and held on with worried determination.

He won't drop her, Stevie knew inside, and for a second she had a feeling of déjà vu – she could almost imagine it was her own body being held in those strong arms and not the elderly lady's. From out of nowhere, she had a scent-memory of spicy, citrusy aftershave, leather and yummy man, all mixed into one delectable smell.

'Am I taking her to your place, or was that really a ruse to get her to unlock the door?' Nick asked.

Betty's head shot up from where it had been snuggling into his neck and she gave Stevie an alarmed look. Stevie had a brief flash of envy, as she wished it was her who Nick was carrying, before saying indignantly, 'Of course it wasn't a ruse. Betty is to stay with me. In fact,' she raised her voice even further and bellowed at anyone still in earshot. 'Everyone back to Peggy's. I'll stick the kettle on. It's on the house.'

A cheer went up and the bedraggled rescuers followed her to the tea shop.

Once inside, Stevie flicked the switch on Bert, called to everyone to give her a minute for the machine to warm up, then dashed upstairs to change into dry clothes. There was no way she could serve cake in this state – unless people liked it soggy –because she was dripping everywhere.

She shot Nick a narrow-eyed look as he followed her upstairs, still carrying the old lady, who seemed rather content to continue to be held by him, even though his soaked clothing must be seeping into her relatively dry coat. Betty wore a smug, self-satisfied expression as Nick bumped open the door to Stevie's spare room with his hip, and gently placed her on her feet. She tottered for a second, then caught her balance.

'I enjoyed that, young man. I'll let you carry me again,' she announced, and Stevie slammed her own bedroom door shut so he didn't see her amusement. Her laughter quickly died as she realised Nick had seemed to know exactly which room was the spare bedroom and she blushed as she stripped off, remembering he was no stranger to *her* bedroom, either.

Dry clothes on, a brief rub of a towel over her drenched locks, and Stevie was good to go. She wished she had more time to dry her hair properly, and to put a smidgen of make-up on (the rain had done a good job of washing her mascara off, leaving black smudges around her eyes where she'd rubbed the water out of them), but she had a shop full of cold, wet people downstairs who needed to be fed and watered.

Most of them had shed their steaming coats and the garments hung in a sodden mound on the old-fashioned hat stand near the door, dripping water in a steady, indoor version of what was falling from the sky outside. Stevie shrugged. There was nothing to be done about it and she had all evening to mop up. Right now, she had beverages to serve and cake to slice.

'Thanks, love,' Mr Evans said, as Stevie handed him a hot cup of tea. 'I can't feel my fingers. It's nice of you to invite everyone in.'

'It's the least I can do,' she said, 'what with all the help they've given. I like to do my bit.'

He patted her on the arm. 'You are, love, you are,' and he gave her such a smile Stevie felt like she truly belonged. There was nothing like a catastrophe to bring people together, and this awful flooding had certainly brought out the best in all of them. Her heart swelled with pride as she saw everyone tucking into her cakes and pastries and she didn't begrudge any of them a single mouthful.

At some point during the pouring of endless cups of tea, Stevie became aware of Nick's eyes on her, but whenever she glanced at him, he quickly looked away. A little while later, another pair of hands appeared alongside her own, hands with soft wrinkles and an age spot or two, and Stevie smiled at Betty, who was getting stuck in like she'd been behind a tea shop counter all her life.

Gradually, the crush of people thinned as coats were put back on and goodbyes were said, until only a handful of die-hards remained. There were still some pastries left, so maybe they were hoping for another bite to eat before they went. Stevie realised she would have to do a considerable amount of baking tonight, if she intended to replace what had been devoured today. The empty plates and dishes looked as though a plague of locusts had paid her a visit, but Stevie didn't mind, even though all her profit for the month had probably gone down the plughole. The way everyone had simply stopped what they were doing to come to help those poor people in the riverside cottages, had really impressed her.

Stevie left Betty to see to any remaining requests, while she began Operation Clean-up, ferrying all the used dishes and cutlery out to the kitchen and stacking what she could into the dishwasher. As she closed the door and turned the dial, she sensed she wasn't alone.

Expecting to see either Betty or (hopefully) Nick, Stevie straightened up and was confronted by a widely smiling Saul.

'Oh, hi,' she said, wondering what he wanted; she wasn't particularly keen on the public coming into the private parts of the café.

'I'll give you a hand,' he offered. 'Everyone's more or less gone, but we've left you with a bit of a mess, I'm afraid.'

They certainly had, Stevie saw, as she returned to front of house to assess the damage. With the café nearly empty the true extent of it became clear. The floor was awash with muddy, grey water, splashes of it had managed to find themselves onto the walls and windows, and there were dirty great footprints everywhere. Not only that, but the cushions on the chairs held the imprint of wet, grubby bottoms, so they would need to be washed, and the formerly pristine tablecloths were smeared in mud, and covered in damp crumbs and tea or coffee stains.

Saul had followed her out of the kitchen and he stood next to her with a mop in his hand, as she surveyed the tea shop.

'We've not left you anything to sell, either,' he said, apologetically, gesturing towards the empty cake stands. He really did look very sorry.

Nick, on the other hand, didn't look sorry at all. He simply glowered and Stevie wondered what he was still doing there.

So, apparently, did Saul. 'Nick, mate, are you still here?'

Nick scowled. He really was in a foul mood, Stevie thought, wondering what had caused it. Even Betty, who had the most reason out of the four of them to be unhappy, didn't appear to be as miserable as Nick.

'Are you staying to help Stevie clean up?' Saul continued, seemingly oblivious to Nick's surly attitude. He turned back to Stevie. 'Bet you didn't think you'd see me again so soon, did you?'

'See you *again*?' Nick finally spoke, and from the way he said it, Stevie wished he hadn't bothered.

'She had lunch with us,' Saul said.

'Us?' Nick's eyes glinted.

'The family, although I'll be pleased to get her on my own later this week. I thought we'd try a little place called The Griffin. Have you been there before?' This last part was aimed at Stevie, but she was too busy wondering what had yanked Nick's chain to answer straight away. Crikey, but this Nick guy was one moody git. If she was asked to describe him, she'd say Heathcliff with a touch of Mr Darcy thrown in. If he was like this at home, no wonder his sister wanted to move out!

'Stevie?'

'Eh?' She glanced at Saul. 'Er, yes, I mean no, I haven't been there.'

'Great!' His smile was warm and wide, but Stevie wasn't basking in the glow of it. She was too busy wondering what she'd done to annoy Nick and why he had pushed his chair back with more force than necessary when he got up to leave.

Chapter 33

'What's the river like? Has it burst its banks yet?' Tia was trying to make conversation (which was most unlike her these days) but Nick wasn't in the mood. He had too much on his mind, what with Tia saying she was going back to live with their mother, then announcing she was in love with that weasel William, and now Stevie and Saul...

No, he wasn't going to think about Stevie. It was of no concern to him what she did with her time, or who she spent it with. At least Saul was a decent enough bloke, although he did have a bit of a reputation with women. Love them and leave them, seemed to be his motto, but Stevie was old enough to take care of herself, and it was nothing to do with Nick if she fell in love with Saul only for his roving eye to settle on someone else. She was a big girl, she didn't need Nick to warn her.

'It's high,' he replied, taking his coat off and hanging it on the edge of the door to dry.

'How about the cottages at the end of the high street?'

'Flooded.'

'Oh, those poor people! Did everyone get out all right?'

'Yes.'

'Any injuries?'

'No.'

'What about the damage?'

'What about it?'

'Is it bad?'

'There's no telling, until the river stops rising.'

'Leanne rang and said a huge tree had crashed into the bridge,' Tia said.

'That's right.'

'It is still passable?'

'No idea. I suppose the council will have to get a structural engineer out to look at it.'

'I heard Stevie was there. I heard she offered to put Betty up.'

'You heard a lot. Did you also hear your boyfriend was there?'

Tia's hands twisted in her lap and she looked away. 'He's not my boyfriend.'

Nick took a deep breath, it was now or never. He had to have it out with Tia before she left for good, and it might as well be now.

'Is it because you're in a wheelchair?' he asked, not caring if his bluntness hurt. It had to be said.

'Yes,' Tia hissed through her teeth.

Nick's temper rose. 'The little shit. How dare he?! The next time I see him, I'll— Bugger "the next time", I'm going to go over there right now and give him a piece of my mind. How dare he turn you down because you're in a wheelchair! How—'

'He didn't.'

Nick stopped ranting as Tia's words sank in. What was she on about? She wasn't making any sense at all. 'He didn't *what*?'

'Turn me down.'

'I don't understand.'

'I know and that's the problem, Nick, which is why I want to go to live with Mum.'

The fight drained out of him and Nick sank onto the nearest chair. He still had his soiled, wet clothes on, but he ignored the puddle he was making on the kitchen tiles and focused on his sister.

'Make me understand. How can I help you if you don't let me know what you need?' he said.

'I don't want any help and that's the part no one understands. Yes, I admit, I did in the beginning, and I'm so thankful you were there for me. Wait, let me finish,' she said, when he opened his mouth. 'You are putting your own life on hold because of me and I can't stand it.'

'I'm not!'

'Please, let me talk. You wanted me to tell you, so let me tell you and stop interrupting me.'

Nick bit his lip. It was an effort not to argue with her, to tell her she was wrong about him, but he had to respect her wishes, so he kept his mouth closed and tried to keep his mind open.

'Thank you,' she said. 'Now listen to me. I've seen how you were with Miranda and how much she liked you, but you wouldn't let her in. It's the same with Stevie.'

'I didn't let Miranda in because I didn't want to have a relationship with her,' Nick protested, instantly forgetting his vow of silence. It had lasted all of ten seconds, but he couldn't let Tia go on thinking he had ever felt anything other than friendship towards Miranda, because he seriously hadn't. He hadn't been lying when he said she wasn't his type.

'I notice you haven't said the same about Stevie,' Tia pointed out.

Darn it, but his sister was sometimes too astute for her own good. Stevie was most definitely his type – there he'd admitted it to himself, just when it was too late. 'Stevie's not interested in me,' he said.

'That's not the impression I got.'

'Your impression is wrong – she's dating Saul Green.'

'I expect that's only because you failed to ask her out. Just like Miranda, you'll let this one slip through your fingers, too. And all because of me.'

Nick wasn't quite sure which bit to address first. It didn't matter how many times he told Tia he wasn't interested in Miranda, that he never had been and never would be, his sister couldn't seem to accept it. Then there was this ridiculous notion Stevie was only seeing Saul because Nick hadn't asked her first. He tried to ignore the niggling little fact that even if she had been interested in him, it was too late – she clearly wasn't interested now.

Maybe his sister had a point, though – *had* he been putting his love life on hold because of her? Using the excuse that he was too busy, when in fact it was because he was concerned that if Tia saw him in love and getting on with his life it might make her feel worse about her own lack of a love life?

He had a horrible feeling she was right and far from protecting his sister, his reluctance to become involved with anyone was, in fact, exacerbating the problem.

Now wasn't the right time for him to be questioning this though, because he realised Tia was doing her utmost to deflect him from the subject Nick really wanted to talk about – her and William Ferris.

'What has this got to do with William?' he asked and had the satisfaction of watching Tia blush. 'You tell me you love the man and he didn't turn you down, so what's going on? Why were you crying?'

Tia rolled her eyes. 'Because,' she said, slowly and carefully, 'I'm in a wheelchair.'

Nick's heart turned over and a lump rose in his throat. 'Tia, I—'

'You still don't get it, do you?' she yelled at him. 'I'm holding *you* back from finding a girlfriend and settling down. If I say "yes" to William, I'll be holding *him* back, too. Look, without me here, you can concentrate on you. You can live your life without having me in the background. Without me here, William can do exactly the same.'

Nick stared at his sister in dismay.

'I love William and he says he loves me,' she continued. 'He wants us to be a couple, but I said "no". So, I'm the one turning *him* down, not the other way around.'

'Your being in a wheelchair doesn't make any difference,' Nick pointed out. 'Love is love.'

Tia gave a bitter laugh. 'Of course, it does! His job is all outdoors, extremely physical. I can't share any of that with him.'

'If he worked in a tax office and sat at a desk all day, you wouldn't share that with him, either,' Nick pointed out.

'But it's not *just* a job, is it?' Tia insisted. 'It's a way of life, a lifestyle, and I can't participate in it. How long before he realises that? One year, two, ten? Before we have kids, or after? And that's another thing – I may not be able to have children at all. Do I wait for him to fall out of love with me, to realise what a huge mistake he's made, or do I set him free now, before it's had a chance to take root? I opt for the latter.'

'I bet William doesn't.'

'You've changed your tune. Not ten minutes ago you were wanting to go over there and give him a good talking to.'

'That's because I thought he'd upset you.'

'He had.'

Nick was confused again. It seemed like it didn't take much where his sister was concerned. 'Why? How?'

'Because he asked me to marry him.'

'Oh.'

'I told him my intention of moving back to live with Mum and he came right out with it. I refused, of course. I'm not staying here and ruining two more lives. As soon as the adaptations to Mum's flat are finished, I'm going to live with her and that's final.'

Nick watched his stubborn, opinionated sister wheel herself swiftly away. We'll see about that, he thought. But if he intended to change her mind and make her view her situation differently, then he needed to be honest with himself and with her. It was no use him trying to convince her she ought to listen to her heart, when he was just as guilty of holding back and not embracing life fully because of Tia's accident.

It was just a pity he'd realised this *after* Stevie and Saul had become an item, because the only girl Nick wanted was the bubbly one with the bright hair and soft grey eyes – the one he had let slip through his fingers.

Chapter 34

'Thank you so much. I don't know what I'd have done without you.' Stevie stood on tiptoe to give Saul a peck on the cheek, drawing back quickly when he moved his head to try to catch her on the lips. Now, why had she done that, since she was going on a date with him at the end of the week and when a kiss at the end of the evening might be a very real possibility?

Saul cocked his head to the side, his gaze quizzical, but thankfully he didn't say anything about her lack of enthusiasm. 'I'll pick you up at seven, yeah?'

'That's great, lovely, I'm looking forward to it,' Stevie enthused, aware she had gone to the other end of the spectrum and was now over-egging it.

She locked the door behind him and slumped against it. She'd been on the go since seven that morning and now it was nearly eight-thirty in the evening. Practically everything edible had been eaten and if she wanted to open the café tomorrow, she needed to get baking.

Betty, bless her, had popped upstairs for a little lie down and Stevie didn't blame her – the woman was somewhere in her early eighties, and seeing her so scared and vulnerable made Stevie realise Betty wasn't a spring chicken. She would also give anything to be able to change into her pyjamas and snuggle up in bed with a hot chocolate but instead she was going to don her apron and have a fight with some dough.

She was halfway through preparing a second batch of Danish pastries which she intended to bake fresh in the morning, when she heard Betty trundling down the stairs.

'I thought you were resting,' she said to the older woman.

'Nah, I managed a quick nap and recharged my batteries. That'll do me for another couple of hours. Now, what do you need me to do?'

Stevie was a little reluctant to let Betty loose with anything, but she was hardly in a position to refuse. A simple Victoria sponge shouldn't be too taxing and it would keep Betty occupied while allowing Stevie to judge how capable a cook she was. If she made a hash of that, then there would be no letting her anywhere near the kitchen again.

'How about a Victoria sandwich?' she suggested.

'Right, I can do that.'

'Do you need a recipe?' Stevie didn't have a recipe as such, she simply remembered what was needed and how much.

'I'm good.' Betty reached under the island and withdrew a couple of shallow cake tins, then she rooted around until she had assembled the ingredients. So far, so good, Stevie thought, watching her covertly out of the corner of her eye. In a small bowl, Betty beat four eggs, then set it to one side, while she put the rest of what she needed into a mixing bowl.

Stevie chewed her lip. The flour, butter and caster sugar were all going in without being measured. Not good, not good at all. They all had to be exactly the same quantities, otherwise the sponge wouldn't be right. Two hundred grams of each – lord knows how much Betty had slopped into the bowl. A splash of milk followed, along with a dash of baking powder.

Stevie gave a mental shrug. It was no biggie if the cake didn't work out and at least Betty felt as though she was helping, so Stevie concentrated on folding and rotating her dough, using a pastry scraper to help. She didn't usually need one, but today the dough was a tad on the sticky side. That's what happens when you cook tired and without the love she normally put into her baking, she thought. Tonight, it was more of a chore than a labour of love.

'What does that say?' Betty was peering at the digital display on the top of one of the ovens.

'That one is set to one-hundred-and-eighty. Use the one next to it. Do you want me to show you how to use it?'

'No need.' Betty stabbed at the button, and after a couple of beeps, she nodded to herself, and returned to the mixer. The whirr of it filled the room for a few minutes, then Betty switched it off, and poured the mixture out, dividing it equally between the two tins. Then she popped them in the oven and said, 'What next? I hope you're not going to use a boring old buttercream and jam filling?'

'I was thinking of passionfruit and mascarpone,' Stevie said.

'Compote or curd?'

'Er... curd?'

'Leave it to me.'

This was said with such certainty Stevie was taken aback. Betty seemed to know what she was doing and for

Stevie that was a bit of a shock. She'd assumed the older woman wouldn't have much of a clue in the kitchen, or at the very best, have only amateur baking skills – after all, how to make a Victoria sponge was taught in schools, wasn't it? But she was fairly sure how to make compotes and curds weren't, unless things had been different in Betty's day.

'You didn't learn this at school, did you?' she asked. 'Was it your mum who taught you to bake?'

'Good Lord, no! My old mam did a fine roast dinner, but she'd have turned her nose up at all this. Nonsense, she'd have called it.'

'Where did you learn to bake then?' Stevie asked, measuring out the ingredients for croissants. These little pastries benefited from being made the night before and sitting in a fridge for a good few hours. She'd pop them into the oven in small batches just before the café opened – there was nothing nicer in the morning than a freshly-baked, still-warm croissant. Except for maybe a pain au chocolat, accompanied by strong black coffee to compliment the sweetness. She'd make some of those next, then some scones, and that should be enough to see them through the breakfast rush. If there *was* a rush tomorrow...

'It's a long story,' Betty said, wiping a floury forearm across her face.

'You don't have to tell me,' Stevie said, seeing a sudden flash of sorrow flit across the old woman's face.

'Oh, but I want to,' she said. 'I don't talk about that time very often, but you've been so good to me...'

'Betty, you don't have to,' Stevie repeated. 'It's none of my business and if it's going to upset you, then I don't want to know.'

Both of them concentrated on their tasks for a moment and for a while Betty said nothing. Stevie didn't want to push her; she'd speak when she was ready.

'We didn't have much money when I was growing up,' Betty began. 'My dad worked down the mines and my mam was a cleaner. She was a damned good one too. Woe betide any of us kids if we made a mess on her step. She used to scrub it once a day and sweep the pavement outside our house, too.' Betty smiled, her gaze unfocused as she stared into the distance. Then she seemed to shake herself. 'Anyways, she taught me well, and when I was old enough I couldn't wait to leave home, so I got myself a job in one of them grand hotels on the south coast. Started off as a general help, mostly cleaning, gradually spending more time in the kitchen than I did seeing to the guest rooms. It was there I learned to cook. But it was baking I was best at and I loved desserts, I did.' She patted her tummy. 'I still do.'

Stevie bent her head and tried to concentrate on her flaky pastry to hide her smile. Although fairly tall, no one could accuse Betty of being plump, and the stomach the old woman had just patted was more or less flat. 'Did you work there for long?' she asked.

'A good few years.' Suddenly Betty's face closed up and her mouth became pinched, and Stevie could tell the old lady wasn't going to say any more. She also noticed how tired she looked, and she had a slight tremble in her hands. Poor love, Betty had had a rather traumatic day and it was bound to have had an effect on her. Firstly, being flooded out of her home, then having to be put up for the night by a virtual stranger, then helping in the café when a woman of her age should have been resting (Stevie blamed herself for that – she should have insisted the old lady put her feet up).

'Right,' Stevie said. 'Fancy a brew?' She dusted her hands off and flicked the switch on the kettle.

Betty nodded, a little uncertainly Stevie thought, and without thinking about it, she leaned down and gave the old woman a kiss on the forehead.

'You can stay here as long as you like,' she said to Betty. 'I'm more than happy to have you here, and if I can do anything to help, I will.'

'You're a good girl,' Betty said, patting Stevie's hand. 'You'll make that young man a fine wife.'

Stevie was too scared to ask which young man Betty meant.

Chapter 35

The rain had finally stopped and Stevie woke to blissful silence. No pattering against the window pane, no wind, no distant roar of the river.

She slipped out of bed, padded over to the window and lifted the sash. Leaning out, she craned her neck, trying to see the end of the street and the bridge. Yesterday, she could see the brown-grey churning water quite clearly, flooding the fields and the road alike.

Today, the water was still there, but it was no longer churning, and there were some bare patches which, although covered in mud and debris, were clearly above the waterline. The river was gradually receding.

She breathed a sigh of relief. Perhaps business could finally get back to normal.

Remembering her guest, Stevie crept to the bathroom, had the quickest shower in history, and quietly got ready to face the day.

As she waited for the ovens to reach the correct temperature, she had a cup of coffee and pondered the problem of her house guest. Eventually, after finishing her coffee and popping the trays in the ovens, she decided she had to take her cue from Betty. Stevie had meant it when she said the old woman could stay here as long as she wanted, although she was well aware it could be for some considerable time. She just prayed Betty hadn't lost everything and would be able to move back into her little cottage at some point.

Stevie shoved another tray of the pre-prepared pastries in the oven and thought about breakfast. She ought to feed Peggy, too, but Stevie hadn't seen the cat since...? When? She couldn't rightly remember. Yesterday? The day before?

'Here kitty, kitty,' she called, opening a cupboard door and reaching for the box of treats which she kept in the café's kitchen for the sole purpose of enticing the cat out from wherever it was hiding in order to shoo it upstairs. She rattled the box with enthusiasm, several times.

No sign of the cat.

Stevie was pretty certain it wasn't upstairs because the pesky feline liked to sleep on Stevie's bed, and it didn't matter how firmly she shut the door, the cat always seemed to manage to get in. And more often than not, the horrid little beast would sprawl across her face, making Stevie think she was suffocating.

No, she definitely wasn't upstairs.

Stevie wondered if Peggy was waiting by the front door, cross and bedraggled from being left outside all night, but there had been so many people in the café yesterday evening she hadn't given the cat a thought, so it was entirely possible the feline had slipped outside, to do whatever it was cats did at night.

She opened the door.

No cat.

She peered up and down the street, calling, 'Peggy, puss, puss, puss,' but still no cat.

Oh well, no doubt she'd come back home when she was hungry enough, Stevie decided, and went to rescue her pastries before they burned.

A tinkle alerted her to someone in the shop, and she rolled her eyes. She'd forgotten to lock the door after herself and even though the sign said "Closed", someone had decided to try their luck. Quite a lot of someones, as it turned out.

Rolling her metaphorical sleeves up, Stevie coaxed Bert into life and began to serve.

'Am I glad to see you,' she hissed, when Cassandra arrived half an hour later. 'What's with all these people?'

Cassandra shrugged. 'There's a group of them down by the bridge. I think they're waiting for the council to arrive and inspect it.'

'I didn't realise it would draw the crowds,' Stevie said. 'The usual?' she asked one of her regulars. He liked a double espresso to go. Stevie always assumed he'd be wired for at least an hour afterwards.

'Ah, Leanne, what can I get you? We don't normally see you in here,' Cassandra said, as Stevie gave the gentleman his change.

Leanne was a one-man band running the flower shop all by herself and she generally didn't leave it.

'Cappuccino, please, and a promise that you'll come to the ball with me.' This last bit was directed at Stevie.

'What ball? Do you think you're Cinderella?' Stevie smiled.

'The ball up at The Manor, silly. Remember? I told you they hold one every year and all the villagers have an open invitation?' Leanne was practically bursting with excitement. 'I can't wait! New dress, here I come! You can

249

meet Saul there, so if he asks you to go with him, please say no, otherwise I'll have to go on my own.'

'Saul?'

'You can't have forgotten you have a date with him on Friday and if I know my brother he won't stop at the one. He really likes you.'

'He does?'

'He kept giving you puppy-dog eyes.'

'Oh.' Stevie hadn't really noticed. 'He did stay behind yesterday evening to help clear up the café,' she said. Nick had stayed after everyone else had left too, but she had no idea why. And she also had no idea why he'd left as abruptly as he had, either. He was one strange man.

'So, are we on?' Leanne asked. She took her coffee and tapped her foot, her face alight with excitement.

'On?'

'For the ball?'

'I suppose.'

'Don't sound too enthusiastic, will you? Maybe a new dress will fire you up. Wanna go shopping?'

Stevie said, 'Now? I can't. I've got customers and a rack of chocolate and broccoli cupcakes in the oven.'

'Not now, silly, I've got a business to open too. How about Sunday? We can go to Hereford – most of the shops are open on a Sunday. Or how about Bristol? I'll drive. I haven't been to Bristol for ages.'

It was quite a trek, but Bristol was probably their best bet if they wanted to get something decent. It had more department stores for a start and Stevie had a sudden pang for the hustle and bustle of London. If only she was still living there, she could pop to Covent Garden, or really push the boat out and visit Regent Street.

With a wry smile, she said, 'Bristol, it is,' and her smile broadened into a grin when Leanne let out a loud squeal and did a little jig on the spot.

'We can make a day of it, go to lunch, have a couple of cocktails,' the florist cried.

'You said you'd drive,' Stevie pointed out.

'Darn it, so I did. See you on Sunday.' She turned to leave. 'Do you mind if I ask Tia if she'd like to come. I get the feeling she could do with cheering up.'

'Not at all.'

'What are you planning?' a voice behind her said, making Stevie jump. She'd forgotten about Betty.

'The ball at The Manor,' Leanne said, before Stevie could catch her breath enough to respond. 'We're going to Bristol on Sunday, dress hunting.'

'The ball, eh? It's years since I've been to one of those,' Betty said.

'You should come with us,' Stevie suggested.

Betty shuddered. 'No thanks, I don't like cities. They're too full of people.'

Stevie hadn't actually meant Betty joining them on the shopping trip (she had a feeling Betty would have wanted to visit an entirely different sort of shop to the younger women), but she said, 'That's a shame, but come to the ball anyway.'

'I might just do that.'

Leanne added, 'Do come! The whole village will be there.' She gave Stevie a significant look. 'Including Saul.'

'Saul?' Betty asked.

'My brother. Stevie has got a date with him on Friday.'

Betty gave Stevie a sharp look. 'Have you?' She was frowning as she slipped a teabag into a mug and she waited just long enough for Leanne to leave, watching her hold the door open for a clutch of teenagers, before saying, 'Saul Green isn't the man for you.'

Stevie blinked. 'Excuse me?'

'He's a bit of a lad, if you know what I mean. He'll have your knickers off before you can say boo to a goose.'

Stevie's mouth dropped open, but before she could think of a suitable reply, a buzzer sounded from the kitchen and Stevie went to take her cupcakes out of the oven. She left them on a rack to cool, then plated up the beetroot ones she'd made earlier. Deep pink sponge, topped with a swirl of vanilla and beetroot buttercream, with a tiny mint leaf on top, Stevie had to admit they looked delectable. The colour alone should appeal to children, and when their mums discovered the treats they bought for their offspring actually contained a healthy portion of beetroot, Stevie hoped she was on to a winner.

As she worked she let Betty's words run through her head. Have my knickers off, indeed. As if she'd let him anywhere near her knickers!

Stevie paused, cupcake in hand, as the thought hit home.

Why had she agreed to go out with Saul if she couldn't imagine him getting into her knickers? Not that she intended to do that on a first date anyway, but when she thought about it, she was pretty sure she didn't intend to do anything like *that* with Saul, ever.

She put the final cupcake on the three-tier cake stand and carried it into the café.

'Ooh, they look scrummy. Can I have one?' One of the teenage girls, who was all make-up, long swishy hair, and incredibly tight jeans, pulled a couple of coins out of her pocket. 'How much are they?'

'Eat in or take away?' Cassandra asked.

'Better make it to take away, and the coffee too. My mum will kill me if she catches me in here. I'm supposed to be on my way to ballet.'

'Yeah, Izzie, she'll have a fit,' one of the others said, and the rest of them burst into giggles. 'Got any carrot sticks in your bag?' she asked her, then said to Cassandra, 'I'll have a slice of whatever that is please, and a tea.' She pointed at a cake, then turned to the others. 'I'm not eating this on the bus, I want to eat it here.'

Izzie shot a nervous glance out of the window, hesitated, then nodded. 'OK, but can we be quick? My mum only dropped me off a couple of minutes ago.'

'Find a table,' Cassandra said, 'and I'll bring it over.'

'Wait.' Stevie lifted one of the cupcakes off the stand and put it on a plate. 'You can have this on the house if you'll give me your honest opinion.'

Izzie frowned. 'Why? What's wrong with it?'

Stevie laughed. 'Nothing, I hope. I'm trying out some new recipes and I'd like some feedback.'

'If I don't like it, I don't have to pay for it?'

'You don't have to pay even if you love it. Sit down and Cassandra will fetch your drinks.'

The girls wandered off to the nearest table with muttered comments of how lucky Izzie was, and how they wished they could be tasters too. Stevie smiled, retrieved the next batch from the oven, left it to cool, and tested the temperature of the cakes she'd taken out earlier.

Perfect. They were ready for icing, so she picked up the piping bag she'd prepared and gave each cupcake a swirl of dark salted chocolate and a sprinkle of chopped walnuts. There! Chocolate broccoli cupcakes all ready to go.

She took them with her to the café and walked straight over to the table the girls were occupying. 'Try one of these, too,' she offered, 'on the house.' She popped a cake in front of each teenager, then stood back to watch their reaction.

'Mmm, this is gorgeous, but I think the pink one is nicer. It's so pretty,' Izzie said.

'What about the flavour?'

Izzie bit into hers, the rest of the girls following suit, and the air was soon filled with "mmm" and "yummy" and "delish".

'You like them, then?' Stevie asked, smiling. She was hoping they would, but you never can tell. Now let's see if they still like them once they know what's in them, she thought. 'The chocolate one is actually broccoli and chocolate, and the red one with the pink buttercream is made from beetroot.'

'No! It never is?' Izzie picked up her chocolate cupcake, held it up and studied it. 'Where?'

'It's definitely there,' Stevie said. 'Does that make you like it less?'

The girls thought for a moment, and one of them shook her head. 'I like carrot cake, so it's a bit like that, isn't it? And if it's got some vegetables in it, it's got to be better than not having any at all.'

'Does it count towards my five a day?' another asked, and the rest of them laughed.

Stevie joined in. 'No, sorry. You still need to eat your vegetables. I've got an idea though; if you pop in at the same time next week, I'll have some more hidden-vegetable cupcakes for you to try, as a favour to me. What do you say?'

'Not on your life,' a voice said, and Stevie looked up from the table to see Allegra Johnson's red and annoyed face glaring at her from near the door. 'How dare you bribe my daughter with cake!'

'Mum?' Izzie's expression tore at Stevie's heart. The child looked positively terrified.

'She's supposed to be at ballet, and yet I find her in here being seduced by *that*.' She flung her arm at the empty plates on the table, nearly slapping an old gent in the head. He ducked just in time. 'She's only thirteen!' Allegra cried, as if thirteen was too young to eat cake. 'What are you up to? That's what I want to know!'

Stevie opened and closed her mouth, not knowing where to begin.

'Izzie, get your kit and come with me,' her furious mother demanded. 'As for the rest of you, I'm going to tell your mothers what I caught you doing. Jonelle Jones – you should know better. And as for you, Saffron Dean, I expected better from you too. Your mother's a nutritionist, for goodness' sake. I expect they'll be as disappointed in you as I am. Come, Izzie.' And when Izzie hesitated, her mother yelled, 'Now!'

The poor girl jumped to her feet, her cheeks as red as the beetroot cupcake she'd just eaten, and followed Allegra to the door.

'I'm going to get you shut down for this,' Allegra cried. 'Leading young girls astray, it's disgusting.' And with that, she yanked the door open, the little bell tinkling furiously and stormed out, a mortified Izzie trailing behind her.

'We should have had it to take away.' The girl who'd spoken was the same one who'd insisted on eating in.

'Take no notice of Mrs Johnson. She's always like that. Totally batty. It's Izzy and the other two I feel sorry for. My mum says if she keeps on telling them they can't have this and they can't have that, they'll rebel one day and it'll be carnage in McDonald's.'

Stevie hadn't said a word. Her head was still reeling from the unwarranted outburst. What had she done that was so wrong? It wasn't as though she was forcing alcohol on unsuspecting teenagers. Admittedly, she was guilty of deception on the vegetable front, but that was a good thing, wasn't it?

'Yeah, don't worry about her, she's off her head.' The girl turned to the others. 'Did you hear her say she was going to tell my mother? "Saffron Dean, I expected better from you",' she mimicked in a high-pitched voice. 'My mum will tell her where to go. In fact,' Saffron looked up at the stunned Stevie. 'I'll get her to call in, if you like. I'm sure she'll approve of your veggie cakes. She's always trying to get me to eat more fruit and veg. *And* she'll tell everyone else they're good for you, too.'

Stevie eventually spoke. 'Thanks, that's a really kind offer, Saffron but the cakes aren't exactly *good* for you.' She didn't want people thinking she was making such an outrageous claim. 'Besides,' she added, 'everything will be fine. Mrs Johnson will probably have forgotten all about it by the time she gets home and even if she hasn't, what harm can she do?'

It was only when the girls exchanged anxious looks, that Stevie recalled something Leanne had said yesterday about Allegra Johnson telling people not to visit the tea shop. Stevie began to think she might have a problem.

And she was right.

Chapter 36

Nick stood by the side of the bridge and watched the workmen. One man was lowering another over the side of it, and the man dangling on the end of the rope looked decidedly pale. He wore a hard hat, a suit and tie, and a high viz vest over the top, and Nick guessed he might be an engineer. Apparently, there had been a flock of them there over the past few days, supervising the removal of the tree and prodding at the increasingly exposed old stonework as the water returned to its former level. It was remarkable how quickly a river could rise, and just how swiftly it could fall again.

The brief inundation had caused some damage, mainly to the properties adjacent to the river itself, and now that it was safe to go back inside the residents of three of the five cottages had returned to deal with the mess. The fourth was still unoccupied and, as no one knew how to get hold of the owners, nothing could be done. The remaining cottage belonged to Betty Roberts who, Nick had been reliably informed, was still staying with Stevie.

He wanted to take a look inside, to assess what needed to be done. Which meant he'd have to go to the tea shop to ask Betty if she'd mind and to ask her to give him a key. Which also meant he'd probably bump into Stevie, considering she owned the place, and who he was determined not to think about. At least, not in the way he had been thinking about her.

He saw her before she saw him.

Lingering outside the shop, Nick watched her for a while, liking the way her hair was piled on top of her head, a bright beacon in the grey and overcast day, wisps of it curling around her face and neck like a cascading sunset.

Bloody hell, what was up with him?! Waxing all lyrical about a mop of ginger hair? Only, it wasn't ginger, it was more of an apricot or peach – strawberry blond, he thought they called it. And her eyes were a sort of smoky grey, not the green he would have expected with her colour hair. Not that he could clearly see her eyes from here, but he knew from memory how they changed colour slightly, depending on the light; or her mood. And those freckles, dusted across her nose and cheeks like the sprinkles of chocolate on a cappuccino.

He shook his head in exasperation, closed his eyes, and counted to ten.

He hadn't even made it to five when a tap on the shoulder made him jump. His eyes flew open and he looked straight into those grey eyes he'd been trying not to think about a few seconds earlier. He noticed they were a deeper hue today, like a storm-tossed sea, and—

'For Pete's sake, you nearly gave me a heart attack,' he said, wondering if he was coming down with something. The flu maybe, or at the very least, a nasty summer cold from getting soaked through the other day. It would certainly go some way to explaining the fuzziness and the silly thoughts he was having.

'What do you expect if you stand in the middle of the pavement with your eyes shut?' Stevie asked. 'Were you praying?'

Nick snorted. 'Yeah, praying you won't give me any more grief.' His tone was gruffer than he intended, but this girl kept popping into his mind and it was starting to annoy him that he couldn't stop thinking about her. Maybe it was because practically every time he came into contact with her, there was some kind of drama.

'When have I done that?' she wanted to know.

'Ever since you arrived. First, you nearly killed me in your car when you drove like an idiot around the horse I was riding, then—'

'Wait up there, cowboy, what do you mean, "I nearly killed you"?'

'You mightn't remember, but I do. Bloody idiot drivers. You've got to be careful around horses, especially if they are on public roads.'

Stevie sent him a sheepish look. 'I hadn't forgotten. I'm sorry, I was a bit distracted and I wasn't sure where I was going, and then this car beeped, and— Hang on, why were you riding it in the middle of the village if it was so dangerous?'

'He was doing fine until you appeared,' Nick argued.

'OK, I'll let that go, but I still think you shouldn't ride horses on a busy road.'

Nick glared at her, debating whether to keep arguing, but all he could think of was cradling her in his arms, and the way she had snuggled into his neck. He tried not to think about what he'd seen under the dressing gown, but it was hard not to when those lovely curves were standing right in front of him.

He dropped his gaze and kept his attention firmly on the pavement, hoping his discomfort wasn't showing too much.

'Are you coming in, or not?' she asked.

'Only to see Betty,' he said, grumpily. Stevie really was having a rather unfortunate effect on him – whenever he saw her he turned into a right surly git. What on earth must she think of him? Suddenly Stevie's opinion mattered very much indeed, and he got up the courage to look at her.

'How is Saul?' he asked, and could have kicked himself.

Damn it! He hadn't meant to say that and he had no idea where the question had come from. It had simply jumped out of his mouth without his brain having anything to do with it. He watched as Stevie's face closed up and he wished his mouth had stayed shut.

'Fine, I think,' she said, not looking at him.

'Did he stay and help clean up?' Nick really wished he'd offered to stay himself but seeing Saul there and the easy way he had with Stevie, and knowing she had spent the afternoon with him, made Nick feel like a spare wheel. He could tell Saul hadn't wanted him there too, especially when he had staked his claim by mentioning the date he had with her.

Which was the reason why he hadn't offered to stay and help, if he was honest.

'Is Betty here?' he asked, changing the subject with relief.

'Come in. She's in the kitchen whipping up some madeleines. She's a really good baker. Did you know? Her Victoria sponge is better than mine!'

He didn't. He knew very little about the old lady, apart from the fact she needed some help if she was to return to her own home.

He followed Stevie into the shop, trying not to look at the way her hips swayed or how well her bottom fitted into her tight jeans, and he was glad when she stood to the side to let him enter the kitchen on his own. Her nearness was rather off-putting. He felt a little hot and his stomach kept clenching. Maybe it was a sort of stomach upset he was coming down with, rather than the flu.

'Nick, my dear, what a nice surprise. Here, have a madeleine.' Betty picked up a shell-shaped cake and offered it to him.

He took it reluctantly. Eating was the last thing he wanted to do, although he could murder a cup of coffee.

Betty must have read his mind. 'You can't eat it without a coffee,' she announced. 'Sit yourself down and I'll fetch you one.'

He did as he was told, and as he waited for her return his eyes were drawn to the island in the middle of the room. What he saw there, wasn't racks of cooling cakes and pastries, nor was it bowls of buttercream, or compote, or jam; what he saw was a mound of clothes as they slowly sat up to reach for him.

The memory made him smile. He had acted like a right idiot, running out into the street as if the hounds of hell were after him. What a prat! Still, he'd had the guts to go back in, and he was glad he had (once more the image of a semi-naked Stevie nestling in his arms popped into his mind) because she'd needed warming up.

'Get your lips around this,' Betty said, scattering his thoughts. She plonked a cup of strong black coffee in front of him.

He was about to ask for milk, when Betty added. 'It's best to dip the madeleine in the coffee, then eat it. When you take a drink, the bitterness of the coffee will be offset by the sweetness of the cake.'

'Madeleine? I take it these are French? Is that how our cousins over the water eat them?'

'I don't know, but it's how *I* like to eat them. Now, you didn't come here just to eat cake, or to ogle Stevie,' Betty observed, astutely.

If he hadn't just had a mouthful of sweet, buttery goodness, he would have refuted the notion of him ogling anyone, especially Stevie, but the Madeleine was too good to rush, so he waited until he'd enjoyed every last bite before he said anything. Betty was right about the coffee, too.

'If you let me have the key to the cottage, I'll start cleaning up,' he suggested.

Was it his imagination, or did Betty suddenly look a bit deflated? Poor love, she'd probably managed to forget about her predicament for a while and now he'd gone and reminded her of her situation. But it had to be done, because she couldn't stay here forever.

'I don't know where they are,' she replied, her eyes darting about the kitchen as if she expected to see them hiding amongst the cake tins and spatulas.

'They're in your coat pocket,' Stevie said, catching the tail end of the conversation. 'At least, that's where I think they are. I heard a jangle when I hung it up last night. Let me go and check.'

Stevie darted up the stairs and was back down again in a trice, clutching the keys in her hand.

'Here they are,' she said, handing them to Nick.

An electric shock rushed up his arm and squeezed his chest when her fingers touched his. He inhaled sharply, and the scent of her flooded his nose – a faint hint of perfume mixed with something sweet. It made his mouth water.

Swallowing, he muttered his thanks and stood up.

Big mistake. Now he found himself almost nose to hair with her, their bodies nearly touching, and he took a quick step back, not trusting himself to be this close to her.

Disconcerted, he whirled on his heel and strode out of the shop, and as he stomped down the street towards the river, he wished he could rid himself of the sight of her beautiful smoky grey eyes.

Chapter 37

'William.' Nick gave a nod. He wasn't surprised to see him there – half of the village was out helping with the clean-up operation, in one way or another. Some were helping to strip out the damaged houses while others, like Tia, were on the phone organising alternative accommodation for the three families made homeless by the flood. At least they didn't have to worry about Betty, as she was being well looked after by Stevie.

'Nick.' William nodded back.

Nick wanted to say something to ease the tension but didn't know where to start. Tia loved William, William loved Tia – it should all be quite straightforward, but it wasn't. Maybe he'd have a quiet word with him later? But then again, what could he say when Tia was so adamant about the situation.

'The power's off,' Nick said, stating the obvious after a considerable pause.

'I thought it might be, so I've brought a genny,' William said. 'I'll need a hand to get it off the van.'

The two men worked in silence except for panting, grunting and the odd curse as they manoeuvred the gener-ator to the edge of the van's bed and lifted it off. A couple of other men stopped what they were doing and gave them a hand. Muscles straining, they gently lowered it to the ground and Nick straightened up, his back in bits already and he hadn't got started yet.

'Thanks, guys,' he said, as they returned to their own tasks. 'I've got a spare at the stables. Sorry, I didn't think to bring it, but I'll pop home later and fetch it, and I'll ask my sister to ring around a couple of the nearby farms and see if we can rustle up another two or three.'

'Geoff Green was bound to have a genny he could spare for a week or two,' Nick thought then frowned when the thought of Geoff's farm led to thoughts of Saul and his date with Stevie.

'Wait, there's a trolley in the back.' William hopped into the van and pushed the trolley to the edge. Thankful for the distraction, Nick turned his attention to the job in hand, and lifted it off as William jumped back down.

'I'll help you get it started,' William said, wrestling the generator onto the trolley and heading off down the path to Betty's house.

The cottage was a mess. The water had reached knee height and had left a disgusting tidemark to show how far up the walls it had come. The carpets were sodden and reeking, most of the furniture was beyond saving, especially the upholstered stuff, the electrics were probably shot (although they wouldn't know until they tried to switch the power back on) and the whole place stank. The smell was a mixture of mud, rotting vegetation and sewage, although as far as Nick knew, the sewerage system hadn't been affected.

William halted just inside the door and scratched his head. 'Oh boy, where do we start?'

'We take everything salvageable upstairs, the rest we take outside. I'll organise a skip. The other owners will need one anyway and we might be able to share the cost,' Nick said.

'Good idea. I'll get started in here.'

"Here" was the living room. Nick squelched his way past it to get to the kitchen and found the source of the smell – rotting food from the dead fridge-freezer, and an even deader pigeon.

Wishing he'd thought to bring thick rubber gloves, he gingerly picked the bird up by its tail feathers and deposited it outside. Operation clean-up was going to take longer than he'd anticipated.

By lunchtime, the two men had made a good start. Nothing could be done about the kitchen cupboards (they would have to be ripped out and replaced), but the living room was now empty, and William had got to work with a bucket and some hot soapy water (courtesy of the generator and a kettle) and was busy sponging the walls down.

Nick left William to it and was in the middle of pulling up the hall carpet to reveal a lovely Victorian tiled floor, when a familiar voice called out, 'Fancy a spot of lunch?'

Stevie. His heart flipped over – an odd sensation – and he paused for a second, trying to regain control of the thud in his chest. To give himself time, he rinsed his hands under the tap, found a clean tea towel and sauntered casually outside, feeling anything but casual.

William was already helping himself to a sandwich from a loaded tray which Stevie had balanced on the low wall which ran the full length of the cottages. She called to the other owners and volunteers to come and help themselves. 'There's plenty to go around and I can always pop back and get some more.'

He could see her trying not to look at the sorry pile of Betty's things which were stacked beside the path, and he watched as her eyes filled with tears.

'Poor Betty,' she said. 'She'll be devastated.'

Nick nodded, not trusting himself to speak. He and William were in the middle of throwing away memories as well as possessions, but there was simply nothing that could be done to save most of it.

'Can I see inside?' Stevie asked, and Nick gestured for William to carry on with his lunch. It was pointless both of them showing Stevie the mess. He could do that easily enough on his own. Besides, he wasn't particularly hungry, despite the morning of manual labour. He told himself it was because he was used to hard physical work, and had absolutely nothing to do with the fact his stomach knotted up every time he looked at her.

She stopped at the entrance to the living room and turned to face him, the tears he noticed earlier finally spilling down her cheeks.

Without thinking he stepped towards her, gathered her in his arms, and pressed her into his chest.

'I'm sorry,' she cried. 'I don't know what's come over me.'

'You're suffering from a healthy dose of compassion and kindness,' he said into her hair, his voice slightly muffled as he buried his face in it. It smelled of apples and icing sugar and she was warm and soft in his arms, and felt so *right* there, as if she belonged. He instinctively held her tighter, hating she was so upset. He wanted to hold her like this forever…

Nick drew back swiftly when he realised what he was doing, but as he tried to put some air between them by taking a step back and holding her at arm's length, he dipped his head at exactly the same time as she lifted her chin and their lips met.

Tentatively, feather-light at first, but with the taste of her invading his senses, Nick kissed her. He closed his eyes and revelled in the feel of her lips on his, trying not to tremble like a teenager, wanting to grab her and crush her to him. Instead, he gently wrapped his arms around her once more, and she melted into him, her body soft against his. Her lips parted and—

Oh Lord, what was he doing? he thought. He pulled away and released her. What must she think of me, taking advantage of her when she was so upset? he wondered.

'I'm sorry,' he said, his voice rough. 'I shouldn't have…'

Stevie put a hand to her lips. He saw how her fingers trembled and he hated himself for putting her in this position. If he'd just been able to control himself and keep her at a safe distance, then she wouldn't be looking at him now as if he'd just kicked a puppy.

Unable to stand her expression for a moment longer, he whirled on his heel and marched outside, leaving Stevie standing alone in the empty room.

He took a coffee off the tray, ignoring the food. There wasn't a great deal left, but any appetite he might have had, had fled in the wake of a much earthier one. Desire wracked him, his heart pounded, and he was as coiled as a snake ready to strike. No matter what his head said, his body had a different idea and he wanted her with every cell of it.

William kept shooting Nick little looks out of the corner of his eye, but refrained from saying anything and

Nick was glad William didn't suggest returning to work while Stevie was still inside the cottage.

He leaned against the wall, legs crossed at the ankle, trying to pretend nothing had taken place, trying vainly to look relaxed and unconcerned while feeling so tense he thought he might snap if anyone touched him. He held the cooling coffee cradled in his hand and waited for her to come out.

Stevie took an age to emerge from the cottage and when she did she carried a small suitcase. She'd obviously packed some essentials for Betty.

It hurt when she refused to look at him, her gaze turning to William instead, who was furthest away from the little wooden gate. 'When do you think Betty can move back in?' she asked.

'Want to get rid of her already?' Nick quipped, trying to lighten the mood, to pretend he hadn't been affected by what they'd just done. Unfortunately, as soon as the words were out of his mouth, he knew he'd said the wrong thing, especially since the light-hearted tone he was aiming for morphed into a gruff accusation the moment they left his lips.

Stevie still didn't look at him, but he saw her tense and she lifted her chin, her lips narrowing. 'Betty is welcome to stay as long as she likes,' she said to William. 'I'm only asking because I know how much she wants to return home.'

William wiped his hands on his filthy, wet jeans, and looked rather uncomfortable at being caught in the middle of something. 'It'll be some time yet. We've gotta set up the dehumidifiers to suck the moisture out of the walls, and that'll take a couple of weeks I expect, then she'll probably need new electrics and a new kitchen for definite. Then there's the furniture that'll need replacing...' he trailed off, then added, 'And the insurance won't be quick to come through either.'

'Thanks,' Stevie said. 'Betty got in touch with her insurance company this morning. She wasn't too keen, but I told her it had to be done, and sooner rather than later. They're going to send an assessor out, but who knows how long that's going to take.'

With her head held high, Stevie brushed past Nick and was out of the gate in a trice. He watched her go, noting the rigid set of her shoulders and felt like the biggest cad on the planet.

Chapter 38

Stevie walked up the street, somewhat shakily, her heart thumping and her head spinning. Every so often she put her fingers to her still-tingling lips.

What the hell had just happened?

She'd kissed Nick Saunders, that's what had just happened. And it had felt *good*. But then he'd pulled away and had told her he shouldn't have kissed her and Stevie had gone from euphoric bliss to embarrassed despondency in the space of a heartbeat.

Why had he done that – kissed her, then rebuffed her?

And more to the point, why had she let him? Kiss her that is; she could hardly do anything about the rebuffing bit. He was far too grumpy and withdrawn to have a relationship with, no matter how attractive she found him, or how much she kept thinking about him. He clearly had no interest in her, because if he had, he'd had plenty of opportunities to ask her out.

She pushed open the tea shop door and marched inside, determined to think no more about it.

'What the hell happened to you?' Cassandra demanded after taking one look at Stevie's face. 'You look like you've lost a tenner and found a pound.' Then she paused and her eyes widened. 'You know, don't you?'

Stevie blinked. 'Know what?' She slid Betty's case behind the counter; she'd take it upstairs later.

'Oh... er... nothing.' Cassandra pretended to be busy by wiping down the perfectly clean countertop.

'Clearly, there's something. What should I know, that I don't?' Stevie persisted.

Cassandra bit her lip and refused to meet Stevie's gaze.

'Spill,' Stevie demanded.

'Er... it's Allegra Johnson,' Cassandra began, still wiping. If she carried on at the rate she was going, Stevie anticipated she soon wouldn't have a countertop left.

'Allegra Johnson?' Stevie repeated.

'I've... er... been keeping track since she came in this morning.'

'Keeping track of what?' Stevie felt like a parrot. All she seemed able to do was to echo everything Cassandra said. For some reason, she felt like she had scrambled eggs for brains; she couldn't seem to think straight. Her fingers touched her lips again. She could almost still feel the pressure of his mouth on hers.

'TripAdvisor,' Cassandra said.

'Eh?'

'TripAdvisor.'

'I heard you the first time, but I haven't a clue what you're on about,' Stevie said.

'Allegra Johnson has posted a review on TripAdvisor.'

'So?'

'It's about us.'

'Us?' His lips had been incredibly soft, yet firm at the same time...

'Peggy's Tea Shoppe,' Cassandra said, patiently.

Stevie finally paid proper attention to what Cassandra was trying to tell her. 'Come again?'

'She's left a review. A really, really bad one,' Cassandra said.

The shop was practically empty, so Stevie pulled out a chair at the nearest table and sat down feeling sick, and tried to think about it logically.

OK, she reasoned, everyone gets a bad review now and again. Even Corky Middleton. He used to get them on a regular basis but they never seemed to do him any harm. In fact, he used to revel in them, celebrating each one with a scathing tweet and ridiculing the reviewer. Obviously, Stevie couldn't do that and neither would she want to (very unprofessional), but seriously, how much harm could one negative review do to her business?

'She's got all her cronies to post reviews too. Just like she did the last time.'

Stevie's ears pricked up. 'The last time?' She was doing the echoing thing again.

Then finally Stevie understood what Cassandra was getting at, and realised why her friend was so concerned. Everything was starting to fall into place.

'Why, exactly, did the previous owners sell up?' she asked slowly, her heart doing a slow plummet into her boots – but she feared she already knew the answer.

Cassandra, having finally stopped wiping, came over to the table, patted her on the arm, and sat down. 'Because they had so much bad publicity,' she said. 'I don't know the details, just that Allegra said some horrible things. Apparently, there was a rumour about food poisoning or something. Allegra claimed she'd eaten there and was really ill afterwards.'

'Did she eat there?' Stevie couldn't see Allegra eating *anything*, let alone eating in a *café*.

Cassandra sighed. 'I've no idea, but the next thing I heard was that the owners were selling up.'

'What was this place called before I bought it?' Stevie asked.

'The Coffee Pot.'

Stevie nodded. 'Thanks. I'll go and look it up.' She got out of her seat, feeling like she'd been run over by a bus (again), and made her way upstairs. With one foot on the bottom step, she turned to Cassandra and asked, 'Where's Betty?'

'She was here a minute ago,' Cassandra replied. 'Maybe she's gone upstairs.'

The living room was empty and Stevie was quite relieved to have it to herself. She needed a minute to think, to absorb Cassandra's revelation. She blamed herself in a way, although even if she had been more diligent and had looked into the history of the previous business, there was no way Stevie could have realised the significance of what she had just learned. She would simply have taken the news at face value and would have put it down to poor hygiene or food preparation on the part of the former owners, and she wouldn't have been at all concerned because she knew her own standards were very high indeed. Therefore, she believed she would never have had the same issue.

Sitting at her computer, Stevie read Allegra's review of Peggy's Tea Shoppe first.

"Disgusting". "Rats". "Big, black ones". "And it isn't just me who has seen them, my friends have, too".

Stevie frowned at the screen. *Rats?* What was the woman talking about?

She jumped, almost falling off her chair when a warm, furry body wound itself around her ankles.

'Peggy! You nearly gave me a heart att—' She stopped talking and stared at the cat.

Bugger. Peggy… Stevie slapped a hand to her forehead. Allegra must be referring to the cat.

'Oh, Peg,' Stevie whispered. 'What am I going to do with you?'

Despite her best efforts at keeping the feline out of the café, Stevie knew if Peggy was determined enough, the cat would find a way in. And those sills in the bay windows were simply pleading to be sprawled across. Stevie understood that.

Stevie also understood that if it wasn't the cat, it would have been something else Allegra Johnson would have found to complain about. And Stevie suspected if the woman hadn't anything vaguely concrete to run with, then she would have made something up. Allegra Johnson clearly had some kind of grudge against Stevie and her tea shop.

Turning back to the screen, Stevie typed in "The Coffee Pot" and waited for the page to load. When it did, it didn't make for very comfortable reading. Those poor people. The two ladies who had owned it had been hounded and harassed, and although the online news report (yes, the story had made it into the local newspaper) was relatively factual, Allegra's comments were quite inflammatory.

"…could have died…"

"…still feeling nauseous weeks later…"

"…bowels will never be the same again…"

'They went to live in France,' Betty said, right in Stevie's ear.

For the second time in ten minutes, Stevie nearly jumped out of her skin. Placing a hand over her poor thudding heart, she said, 'Don't creep up on me like that.'

'Pish. You could do with a bit of excitement,' Betty retorted, then her voice softened. 'But not this kind, eh?' she added, jerking her chin at the computer.

'You know about this?' How come everyone knew except her?

'Cassandra told me about Allegra's latest nonsense,' Betty said. She sat down. 'I don't think anyone actually believed her about The Coffee Pot, but what can you do? With the Environmental Health people called in, and with that woman walking around like she had the plague, those poor ladies didn't stand a chance. I hear they've got a guest house now. They just upped-sticks and left.'

'Did you used to come here when it was The Coffee Pot?' Stevie wanted to know.

'Sometimes, although it was more of a sandwich and snack place than a cake and pastry place. They did a mean fry-up, though.'

'I just don't understand why the woman has got it in for me? What has she got against The Coffee Pot and now Peggy's? It's not as though we're selling anything bad,' Stevie said.

'In her eyes, you are. She's a bit manic about healthy eating and doesn't approve of all-day breakfasts. I've heard on the grapevine she's now waging war on sugar,' Betty said. 'It's her kids I feel sorry for. Imagine going through life being denied a muffin. Everything in moderation, I say.'

'That explains her reaction when she caught her daughter in here today,' Stevie said. 'But it was a bit over the top.'

'It certainly was,' Betty agreed, getting to her feet. 'The issue now is, what are you going to do about it?'

Chapter 39

Saul picked Stevie up at 7pm. Stevie didn't really want to go and it was all Betty's fault. Mostly. Some of it. The old woman had done her best to put Stevie off Saul.

'He'll break your heart,' she had warned ominously. 'I know his type.'

'And what type is that?'

'Love 'em and leave 'em. You love *him*, and he'll leave *you*.'

'I'm not going to fall in love with him,' Stevie protested.

'Good. Because you want to save all your lovin' for someone who's lovin' you.'

'I think Gloria Gaynor said that,' Stevie pointed out. 'Only she did it better.'

'I can sing it, if you like.'

'No thanks, I'll pass.' Stevie smiled. She was really going to miss Betty when she returned to her own home.

'I'm being serious,' Betty said. 'I've seen the way Nick Saunders looks at you.'

Unconsciously, Stevie put her fingers to her lips before she realised what she was doing and hastily snatched them away.

'I've seen the way you look at him, too,' Betty carried on, oblivious to the scowls Stevie was sending in her direction.

'You're imagining things,' Stevie returned. 'I've got to go, Saul is here.'

With Betty's "hmmph" following her down the stairs, Stevie dragged a smile from somewhere and made sure it was firmly in place – Saul didn't want a miserable cow for a dinner companion and neither did he need to know about her problems. So with that in mind, she resolved to enjoy the evening. Or make the best of it, at least. It had been five days now since the awful reviews on TripAdvisor, and Stevie could have sworn there was a downturn in customers. Not her regulars, but tourists and visitors. Although, it might just as easily be explained by the continuing damp and drizzly weather. She'd just have to wait and see what happened when the weather improved. Karen, bless her, had been furious when Stevie had told her what had happened, and she'd left a glowing review, and had got quite a few of her friends to do the same, in an effort to counteract the poor ones.

'I hear you've got a problem,' Saul said, as soon as she opened the car door and slid into the seat.

'You could say that.' Stevie's miserable look was instantly back in place.

'Do you want to talk about it?' he asked, and she heard only sympathy in his voice.

'No thanks. I want to forget about it, for tonight at least.'

'Fair enough, but I'm here if you need a shoulder.'

A part of her thought "that's nice of him", but another part thought "does everyone know my business?" If she was in London the odds of some farmer (OK, maybe not a farmer – a media consultant, or a doctor, or a banker) knowing she'd had a series of one-star reviews on TripAdvisor was so slim it couldn't even squeeze through the gaps in the polished floorboards of the country pub Saul was taking her to.

It irked her a little that he knew, but in another way, she was actually relieved. At least she didn't have to explain to her date why she was a bit down.

'Mum said "Hi" and wants to know when you're coming to lunch again,' Saul said, and Stevie was grateful for the change of subject.

'I really did enjoy myself on Sunday,' she said. 'Your mum is a great cook.'

'My annoying family didn't put you off then?'

'No, it was nice, actually.' Seeing the warmth between them all, despite their teasing and bickering, had been lovely, and each one of them had made her welcome.

Since Sunday and the flood, Stevie felt she was finally starting to fit into the village. Even Mads wasn't so bad, once you got to know him – and although Stevie hadn't ventured into The Hen and Duck since, she'd bumped into him in the street now and again, and he always asked how she was and how she was settling in.

The rest of the short drive consisted of the pair of them discussing food and when the car pulled into the car park, Stevie was delighted to see that The Griffin was actually a pretty, old, converted farmhouse on the main road to Brecon. Ironically, she'd looked it up on TripAdvisor and had noted it had a good reputation, so she was really looking forward to her meal

She loved eating out. For her, there was nothing like analysing the balance of flavours, the ingredients, the textures, the choices, the cooking methods, the way the food was displayed on the plate and seeing if she could steal any ideas.

Tonight, though, Stevie found she had little or no idea what she was eating, because sitting at a table behind Saul was Allegra Johnson herself.

Thankfully the woman in question had her back to Stevie and hadn't noticed her, but Stevie could feel the woman's malevolence all the same. It lingered in the air like an expensive perfume, and although Stevie did her best to try to pretend AllegraJ83 (the woman's TripAdvisor name) wasn't there, Stevie couldn't prevent herself from glancing at her occasionally.

The man Allegra was with must be her husband, Stevie surmised. After all, only a man and woman who were in a long-term relationship could look so thoroughly disinterested in the person they were with.

Allegra didn't look too interested in her meal either, Stevie noticed, because she sent her plate back with almost as much on it as there had been when the waitress brought it to her table. He had more or less cleared his, Stevie saw. And she had no clue why the woman bothered to look at the dessert menu at all, because even from this distance, Stevie could hear the hard time Allegra was giving the waitress, quizzing her about what exactly was in each dish, then when she'd received an answer, dismissing the dessert in question and moving on to the next item.

In the end, her husband had what looked like a pavlova and Allegra had nothing except for a coffee.

'…and the hippo climbed out of the spaceship, wiped the dust from his visor and handed over a jar of Mars air,' Saul was saying, as Stevie dragged her attention back to him.

'You what?' She looked around as if expecting to see the hippo.

'You've not been listening to a word I've said, have you?' Saul asked, cheerfully.

'Um, no. Sorry.'

'Understandable. Although you should have said if you wanted to swap places.'

'Thanks, but I prefer to keep her where I can see her,' Stevie grimaced. 'I didn't realise you knew she was there.'

'I saw her the minute we arrived,' Saul admitted. 'I did think about walking straight back out, but it's Friday, and the nearest decent place is usually full and it's not half as nice as this, and—'

'It's OK.' Stevie smiled across the table at him. 'At least being here has given me the chance to see it's not just *my* place she gives a hard time to. She doesn't seem to like it here, either.'

'You did, though, thank goodness,' Saul pointed out, and Stevie was surprised to see she'd eaten every scrap of whatever had been on her plate, although she couldn't remember a single mouthful of it.

Stevie deliberately looked away when Allegra and her husband departed and she left it to Saul to tell her whether Allegra had spotted Stevie or not (she hadn't), but the whole experience, together with Stevie's rather lukewarm attraction to Saul, didn't make her want to share a kiss with him. So when Saul dropped her off at the tea shop, and leaned over the gearstick, Stevie gave him a swift peck on the cheek and scarpered, leaving Saul staring after her with a bemused expression on his face.

'I take it a coffee isn't on the cards then?' he called, as she went to shut the car door.

Stevie gave him a rueful smile and shook her head.

'Didn't think so,' he said, his own smile fairly cheerful, and Stevie wondered if anything actually got this man down.

She fished out her keys and opened the door, and as she turned to give him a quick wave Saul called through the open car window, 'Do yourself a favour and phone him,' he winked at her. 'You'll regret it if you don't.'

Stevie had no intention of doing any such thing, but it wasn't until she was through the door and locking it behind her that what Saul had said sank in and it occurred to her Saul must have known exactly how she felt about him.

And about Nick.

Chapter 40

Bristol was larger than Stevie expected and had loads more shops. There were the usual high street chains and department stores, but there were also smaller, independent shops, and it made for a nice mix.

Stevie was like an excited puppy on its first walk in the great outdoors – if she had a tail, she'd be wagging it. Boy had she missed this: the noise, the smells, the sights, the sheer busyness of a city, and she couldn't wait to get started on the shops.

Leanne dragged them into the nearest department store and headed for the lift and the second floor where the posh frocks (as Great Aunt Peggy used to call her nicest dresses) were located.

'What do you think of this one?' Leanne asked, holding up a fuchsia pink number.

It had so many frills and tassels Stevie grimaced and when she caught Tia's horrified expression she had to bite her lip to stop herself from laughing. 'Um, maybe a little too fussy?' she replied trying to be tactful.

Leanne held it at arm's length and stared at it, critically. 'Yeah, you're right. I love the colour though.'

It certainly was dramatic, Stevie conceded. She knew she wouldn't have the courage to wear something so bright, and anyway the colour would clash horribly with her hair, so she gazed around for a more sedate, subdued colour.

'How about this one,' Tia suggested, pointing to a gown cut so far down the front that the person who wore it would have to make sure their boobs didn't fall out. There was an equally revealing slit from floor to thigh, and Stevie pulled a face.

'Er…' she began, when Leanne and Tia burst out laughing.

'You should see your face!' Leanne cried, holding onto Tia's wheelchair for support. 'Although if you did buy it, Saul's eyes would be out on stalks. Saying that, so would every other man's. I dare you.'

'No thanks. If *you* want that kind of attention, *you* buy it,' Stevie retorted with a shudder.

'Talking about male attention, did my brother behave himself?' Leanne asked. 'He took Stevie on a date on Friday night,' she added to Tia.

'I heard they were dating,' Tia said.

'Can't a girl have any privacy?' Stevie asked and laughed when the other two chorused, 'No!'

'Well? You haven't answered my question,' Leanne persisted. 'Tell me about your date with Saul.'

Stevie rifled through a rack of evening gowns. 'It was OK. Ooh, look, this one is lovely.' She held up a silver, off-the-shoulder number.

'Why don't you try it on?' Leanne suggested. 'Tia, have you seen anything you like?'

'One or two.' She pointed to the ones she fancied and Leanne unhooked the hangers off the rails and draped the dresses over her arm, then she turned her attention back to Stevie. 'Just OK?'

Bugger, Stevie had hoped Leanne had dropped the subject. She shrugged. 'I guess…'

'No fireworks?'

'Nope.'

'That's a shame; I would have liked to have you as a sister-in-law.'

'Hang on, it was only one date,' Stevie protested. 'And even if I did feel like that about him, there would be quite a way to go before there could be any talk of wedding bells.'

An assistant showed them into the changing room and Stevie and Leanne crowded in behind Tia who frowned. Leanne said, 'You're gonna need some help getting in and out of that.' She jerked her head at the column of ivory silk with diamantes and beads sewn on the bodice.

'You've not got your eye on anyone else, then?' Tia asked as she wriggled her loose-fitting cotton dress over her head.

Stevie was very glad indeed the other two were concentrating on the task in hand and not looking at her face, because she felt a sudden blush heat her cheeks.

'No,' she said, but her response mustn't have been as convincing as she thought, as Tia's head popped out from underneath the hem of her discarded dress and she gave Stevie a hard look.

By the way she raised her eyebrows, Leanne wasn't fooled either, so Stevie decided to change the subject.

'I've got more important things to worry about,' she declared.

'I take it you're talking about the horrid reviews Allegra Johnson and her friends left?' Leanne asked.

Stevie nodded.

'The cow!' Tia exclaimed.

'Ooh, you look lovely. Doesn't she look fab?!' Leanne cried, straightening the hem of Tia's dress so it fell in a shimmering sheath around her lower legs. 'Now, imagine yourself with your hair up...' She gathered Tia's dark hair up with her hands and twisted it behind her head. 'Talk about sophisticated.'

'You look gorgeous,' Stevie said, meaning it. The other girl was very attractive, a delicate feminine version of her handsome brother.

'I need a hand taking this off and then it's your turn,' Tia said, nodding at the dresses Stevie had chosen. 'Can you unzip me?' she asked Leanne.

'Will it make much of a difference having a few bad reviews?' Leanne wanted to know, easing Tia's dress down her back as Tia hoisted herself up with her arms to raise her bottom off the seat of the wheelchair.

'I hope not.' Stevie crossed her fingers. 'But I've got a really bad feeling about it.'

'If there's anything we can do...?' Tia offered, and Stevie's heart melted.

The pair of them had such earnest expressions and so much love and sympathy radiated from both of them, Stevie felt like crying. She was grateful these two wonderful girls were her friends and she gave them each a heartfelt hug.

'Right, I've found mine,' Tia announced. 'It's your turn. And make it snappy, because I'm starving.'

'Tia...' Leanne sounded a bit odd and Stevie shot her a concerned look.

'What?'

'I'm going to miss you,' Leanne said. 'Do you have to leave Tanglewood?'

Tia froze and there was silence for a few moments, apart from the rustling of satin as Stevie struggled to free her curves from a slightly-too-clingy turquoise gown.

'Yes,' she said finally.

'But I don't understand, I thought you were happy here – you've got the stables, and your friends.'

'I'm going and I don't want to talk about it,' Tia said, her expression grim.

'I'll miss you, too,' Stevie added. She'd only just got to know the girl and she liked her immensely.

'And I'll miss you guys, but this is something I have to do. For—' Tia hesitated, then finished with, '—me.' But Stevie was almost sure she had been about to say something else entirely.

Tia added, 'It'll be good to live in a city again.'

Suddenly Stevie wanted nothing more than to go back to Tanglewood. To the peace, the serenity, the slower pace of life. She realised she actually didn't miss London at all.

She thought back to when she used to live there and how the crowds used to annoy her and how rude and disinterested people could be, and contrasted that with Tanglewood, where everyone knew her name, and where the villagers said hello to each other on the street (Try doing that in London and see how many people crossed the road to avoid you, Stevie thought). And the shops she used regularly often set aside the best cuts of meat or had her usual order ready for her. Suddenly life in the big city seemed so very impersonal and cold.

Tia would hate it.

Stevie had an inkling there was something bothering her friend. If only she could ask Nick what it was, so she could try to help. But Nick had made it perfectly clear he wanted nothing to do with her...

Chapter 41

'Crikey, but we're busy today,' Stevie declared. She pulled out the nearest chair and sank down into it with a weary groan. Her feet were killing her and her back ached. She guessed Cassandra felt the same when her friend sagged against the counter and blew her fringe off her face. And they had another hour or so to go before she could turn the "Open" sign to "Closed".

'We've run out of cake,' Cassandra announced.

'Again?'

'Again.'

'That's the third day in a row,' Betty added, coming out of the kitchen with flour up to her elbows.

'Have you noticed something?' Stevie asked, getting to her feet when yet another customer walked in. She watched Sid the butcher grab a seat and strolled over to his table, wishing her legs didn't feel so heavy.

'Hi, Sid, what can I get you?' She pulled her little order pad out of her back pocket and waited, pen poised.

'Can I have an iced latte with mango syrup, please?'

'Certainly. Anything to eat? Although I must warn you, we're out of cake. But we do have some scrumptious caramel and apple tarts, or how about a scone with crème fraiche and plum compote?'

'Both?'

'OK.' Stevie gave him a big smile, but it faded as she made her way back to the counter. She'd never seen Sid in her tea shop before and ordering two of her rather large portions was a bit excessive. Not only that, but when she placed his order on the table a short while later, she had barely turned away when she caught him with his phone in his hand taking a photo.

Sid the butcher didn't strike her as an Instagram kind of man, but what did she know? Maybe he took photos of his food all the time. It would kind of make sense, what with him being in the foodie business, as it were. It might be an idea to look into Instagram herself. Her cakes and pastries always looked gorgeous and taking photos of them would be a wonderful way to advertise her shop. At least those awful reviews hadn't seemed to have affected business. She was actually busier than she had ever been. It was a bit odd though, now she came to think about it, because she could have sworn that all of the people who had stepped through her door in the past few days had been locals. She knew most of them by sight now, and many of them to talk to, so—

'Your mum will have a fit if she sees you in here,' Cassandra said, pulling Stevie out of her reverie.

Oh, no. Stevie's heart fell. Please don't tell me Izzie and her friends intend to stay, she prayed. Her mother had caused enough trouble as it was. There was no imagining what she might do if she caught Izzie in here again.

'I don't care,' Izzie said. 'I like it here and she can't stop me.'

Yes, she can, Stevie thought, wondering how best to tackle this. There was no way she wanted to be in the middle of a mother and daughter showdown. If this was

Izzie making a stand against Allegra, then she wished the girl had chosen somewhere else to do it. Why here and why now? Just when things were starting to look up, too.

Stevie had the momentary thought of asking the girls to leave, but that wasn't fair on them either, so she did the only thing she could do under the circumstances – she served them.

She might have been tempted to give them a free sample of her latest veggie-laden cake, but thankfully it was all gone, so at least Allegra and her friends wouldn't be able to accuse her of trying to bribe their daughters. If the girls ordered and paid themselves, then the whole thing was above board and out in the open.

It was while she was making the next customer, Sally from the bank, a jasmine tea, that Stevie noticed the group of teenagers posing with their drinks, making those odd duck faces and peculiar pouts that all the kids seemed to do. Stevie had tried the pose once, but she'd ended up looking as though she was in pain, so she hadn't tried again.

'I hope that's not going to cause any more trouble for us,' Betty said, jerking her head at the teenagers.

'If it does, it does,' Cassandra said, philosophically. 'Allegra Johnson is going to have a fight on her hands if she expects to dictate what her daughter can and can't eat, not at her age. I bet she sneaks off to the chip shop at lunchtime, too. I used to, despite my mother packing me a school lunch. You can't beat the allure of a bag of salty, vinegary chips, and I actually had decent sandwiches. Imagine what Allegra puts in Izzie's lunch box.' Cassandra shuddered. 'There'll be fireworks in that family before long,' she added.

Stevie had to agree with her. She just hoped Izzie kicking over the traces wouldn't have even more of an adverse effect on Peggy's Tea Shoppe than it already had.

Chapter 42

'You look stunning, lassie' Betty said, watching Stevie put the finishing touches to her make-up. 'Turn around and let me look at you.' Stevie turned, and Betty let out a whistle.

'You don't look too bad yourself,' Stevie said.

The old lady was dressed from head to foot in crimson and white silk. On anyone else, the gown would have looked rather ridiculous, but it suited Betty perfectly. Stevie wondered if she'd found it in a vintage shop or whether Betty had bought it new at some time during the last century. She suspected the latter.

The red skirt was full, pleated and floor length, while the bodice was white with capped three-quarter sleeves and a modest neckline, which Betty had covered with several strings of gigantic pearls. She had draped a red silk scarf over her head, and she looked every inch an elegant Hollywood film star from the 1940s. Betty was even wearing a matching shade of lipstick.

The carpet slippers on her feet spoiled the effect a little, but Stevie hoped the dress was long enough so no one would notice.

Stevie was wearing a deep midnight sheath dress, with a halter neck and a ruffled skirt. It hugged her curves yet floated around her feet as though she was walking on air.

She'd fallen in love with it the minute she'd seen it but had been put off by the plunging back. After Leanne and Tia had urged her to try it on and had then convinced her the back wasn't as plunging as she thought it was, Stevie had given in and bought it. And a matching clutch bag. And shoes.

This damned ball had better be worth it, Stevie thought, turning back to the mirror and swiping the mascara wand across her lashes once more, her eyes and mouth both open wide.

'That colour really suits you,' Betty said. 'Black would have been too harsh with your skin tone and anyway, who wants to look like they're off to a funeral instead of a party. Woot, woot! Break out the bubbly.'

"The bubbly" was an inexpensive bottle of Prosecco, and Stevie did as she was asked with alacrity. She could do with a couple of fortifying glasses before they left. And no, the fortification had nothing to do with a certain man, she told herself.

'Nick Saunders is bound to be there,' Betty said, and Stevie sent her a sharp look. Did the old lady just read her mind?

'In fact, the whole village will probably be there,' Betty added. 'I've heard there's always a good turn out.'

'Don't you usually go?' Stevie asked, curiously. She'd assumed Betty attended the ball every year.

Betty picked up her glass with both hands and took a long drink. When she put it back on the table, Stevie noticed the old lady's hands were shaking.

'Haven't been for years. Not since...' Betty glanced down at her dress and stroked the fabric, frowning slightly. Then she blinked and heaved a big sigh. 'Never mind,' she said, but the too-bright smile which she now wore told Stevie that Betty did mind. Very much indeed.

'Tia's nice,' the old lady said, and Stevie guessed she was trying to change the subject.

'She is.' If Betty didn't want to talk about it, then Stevie respected her wishes, so she added, 'I told you she's going to live with her mum, didn't I? It's a pity, because we could have been good friends. She's really sweet when you get to know her.'

'I've known Tia since her and Nick came to live here,' Betty said.

Righto, back to Nick again. Great, Stevie thought.

'Did she tell you how she came to be in a wheelchair?' Betty asked.

'No, and I didn't like to mention it.'

'Horses. She used to ride and was almost as good as her brother. He was doing a training session with her and from what I gather, he put the bar thing up a notch and the horse she was riding refused to go over it. They fell and the animal rolled on her. Broke her back.'

Stevie's heart went out to Tia. 'Oh, that's awful.'

'The accident was bad enough, but now it's needlessly ruining four lives,' Betty said.

'Four?'

'Her brother has been blaming himself,' Betty stated, picking up her matching handbag and rooting inside for her lipstick. 'Nick Saunders needs to let go of his guilt. He's been kidding himself he is too busy and maybe he was in the beginning when his sister relied on him so much, but he's not got that excuse now. The second is Tia, but not because she's in a wheelchair, but because she's letting her disability get in the way of living. Tia's ruining her

297

own life and she's too bloody silly to see it.' Betty paused, dramatically.

Stevie's heart filled with sorrow for her new friend. Poor Tia – she just wished she could do something to help.

'The third is William Ferris,' Betty announced.

Stevie failed to see the connection, and she shook her head. 'You've lost me.'

'He loves her. She loves him.'

'Really? Oh my! She never said.'

'She wouldn't,' Betty said. 'She's far too private for her own good, that one.'

'Hang on, how do you know Tia and William Ferris are in love?'

'I didn't say, "they are in love". I said, they love each other. "In love" suggests a relationship when there isn't. She flatly refuses to have anything to do with him.'

'How do you know all this?'

Betty tapped the side of her nose. 'The same way I know Nick Saunders feels the same way about you as you do about him, but he's not going to do anything about it because he thinks you're dating Saul Green.'

'I'm not dating Saul!' Stevie said, then paused. 'Who is the fourth?' she asked, despite herself, because she had a feeling she already knew the answer.

'You are, my dear.'

Chapter 43

Nick wasn't deliberately loitering in the hall — it was just cooler out there than in the ballroom and less busy. If he told himself that for long enough, then he just might believe it, because the hall was neither cooler (the four sets of French doors in the ballroom were all open wide and he could have strolled onto the terrace if he'd wanted to) nor less busy, because the hall had a continuous stream of new arrivals.

Stevie wasn't one of them yet, but he had it on good authority she was planning to attend — new dress and new shoes, Tia had informed him. Tia had also informed him that Stevie's date with Saul hadn't been much of a success. The knowledge made his heart pound.

As for Tia, she looked marvellous, although she had huffed and puffed about looking like a sack of spuds dressed up in silk and she had continually fiddled with the long skirt until Nick had told her to stop, else she'd have nothing but dirty marks over it.

He smiled softly as he recalled her insistence he drive around the back to the family's more private parking area, so no one witnessed him lifting her out of the car and into her chair. He'd then spent a considerable amount of time making sure her hair was perfect and arranging her dress, before he accompanied her inside and into the air-kissing arms of the waiting Julia.

Actually, he didn't think his sister would come, despite buying a new dress. Since the accident, she hated being on show, and with her revelation she was in love with William Ferris, Nick had assumed Tia would want to remain as far away from The Manor as she could get.

Far away... that's exactly where his sister would be in a couple of months. Nick, not wanting her to leave, hadn't done anything to help with the forthcoming move, leaving it all up to Tia and their mother. He was slightly ashamed of his lack of support, but not ashamed enough to offer any assistance, so Tia had spoken with the people at the council and had sorted out things such as having a disabled bathroom installed and the doors widened enough to accommodate a wheelchair.

The work hadn't been done yet, which was why Tia was still living in The Furlongs. She intended paying for it herself, but the council wasn't exactly pulling its finger out to give the necessary permission. And they insisted on using their own approved contractors which slowed the whole process down. But even before that, Tia had hit a bit of a delay when the powers-that-be stated they had to send the work out to tender first. No wonder it took so long for anything to get done. If their mother had listened to him and had let him buy her somewhere nice, then all this could have been sorted out weeks ago. But for once, Nick was glad of their mother's stubbornness in refusing to leave the place she'd lived in for the past forty years, because it meant Tia wouldn't be able to move out for a while yet. He intended to use the time to convince her that she and William were perfect for each other. She deserved some happiness and running away from Tangle-wood was going to make her anything but happy.

'Penny for them?'

'What?' Nick jerked out of his reverie to see Betty standing in front of him, looking resplendent in bright red.

'You look as miserable as sin,' she said. 'Smile, it's a party.'

Nick smiled but he was aware of how false it must look – until he spotted Stevie walk into the hall, then he couldn't hold back the genuine beaming grin which spread across his face.

She looked wonderful. More than wonderful! The deep, almost navy blue dress suited her colouring perfectly, bringing out the red–gold in her hair and emphasising her smooth, pale skin. The fabric moulded itself to her curves, drawing in at her tiny waist before flaring out over her hips and dropping to a bubbling froth at her feet. Her hair was loose, tumbling down her back and (unlike Betty who was sporting scarlet lipstick), Stevie's make-up was so subtle Nick wondered if she was actually wearing any – although her mouth looked full and kissable and her eyes were all smoky and revealed depths he could drown in. She looked sophisticated and elegant, and utterly delectable. Her shoulders were bare and he had a sudden urge to kiss them.

He cleared his throat and leaned down to give Betty a peck on the cheek, hoping the brief interlude was enough to get his feelings under control. He had no idea how Stevie felt about him, whether she was interested at all, but the kiss they'd shared... oh, boy.

'You wanna get in there, my lad,' Betty said to Nick, giving him a punch on the arm.

Crikey, that hurt. The old woman was stronger than she appeared.

'Leanne, get over here and tell this stupid man what's what,' Betty called.

Nick glared at her, then at Leanne, who took absolutely no notice of his expression whatsoever, even going as far as to move in for a hug when she was close enough.

'What's up, Betty?' Leanne asked.

'Nick is in love with Stevie.'

'He is?' Leanne asked, her eyes wide as she stared at him.

'I am?' Nick asked.

'And she's in love with you,' Betty continued.

'She *is*?' Nick and Leanne chorused.

'She is.' Betty nodded vigorously. 'I can vouch for that.'

'Why? What's she said?' Nick asked.

'Nothing, but she doesn't need to,' Betty said. 'You can tell by the way she looks at you.'

'You can?' He coughed. 'I mean, can you? Really?'

'Look, lovey, take it from us,' Betty said. 'Stevie likes you. A lot. More than a lot. And you like her.'

'I do?' He was beginning to sound like a right idiot, but he didn't seem able to say anything more profound.

'You do.' Her voice brooked no argument. 'So, pull your finger out and get on with it. Time's a-wasting.'

It was indeed!

He'd only just taken a couple of steps towards the ballroom, when Edgar waylaid him. For a second, he debated ignoring the man, but his good manners wouldn't let him, so he sighed and followed the lord into his study.

'Well, have you had a chance to think about my offer?' Edgar demanded.

'We didn't really get much of a chance to go into details,' Nick pointed out. 'But I do think there are enough riding schools already. There's no need for another one.'

'You don't understand, my boy. It won't be any old riding school – this will be for disabled people.'

Nick's mouth dropped open but no words came out.

'It was William's idea. He felt disabled people shouldn't be prevented from doing things like riding, hiking, archery and stuff just because bits of them don't work too well. And I must say, I agree with him. It's a bloody brilliant idea.'

It was and even though Edgar was probably looking at it from a financial, advertising and marketing point of view, Nick could see the potential.

He only hoped his sister would too.

William Ferris, Nick thought, you'll make Tia a great husband.

Chapter 44

Grabbing a couple of glasses of sparkling wine from the nearest waiter, Leanne handed Stevie a drink which she gratefully accepted. Seeing Nick leaning up against the wall as she went into the grand hall had made her feel a little out of sorts. Of course, she'd expected him to be here, but she'd assumed he would be somewhere in the throng of the ballroom and not lurking about at the entrance, and she'd expected to have some time at least in which to collect herself, before coming face to face with the man she was falling head over heels in love with.

There was no sign of him now, so he hadn't come into the ballroom. Not that she'd been watching out for him, because she hadn't, but it would be nice to know his whereabouts, so she could avoid looking at him.

Stevie searched the room. No, she didn't think he was there, but it was hard to tell with so many people around. She suspected the whole village had indeed turned out, and what a wonderful sight they made, dressed in their finery. All the men wore bow ties and a tux (Nick had looked rather brooding and attractive in his), and the women sported gowns in an assortment of wonderful colours and styles.

She spotted Leanne's mum and dad, and Iris looked gorgeous in a dress of amber silk with beading all over the bodice. Geoff looked quite dapper too even though he kept pulling at his tie and making faces. Stevie laughed as Iris nudged him in the side with her elbow every so often, and for a while Geoff would stop playing with his bow tie but it wasn't long before he was tugging at it again.

'Ooh, look,' Stevie cried, as she noticed a live band in one corner of the room taking their instruments out.

She was enchanted by The Manor, what she had seen of it so far. She hadn't realised at the time, but when she'd taken the girls to Nick's stables (Just stop thinking about him, will you? she scolded herself.) The Manor was actually only a little further along the same lane. Tonight, as she'd driven through the huge gates (there was even a gatekeeper's cottage next to the entrance, although it didn't look as though it was lived in) and up the wide, sweeping gravel drive with a massive fountain dominating the centre, her eyes had been out on stalks.

She'd not been expecting anything as grand and had said as much as she was parking the car.

'Oh, it's grand, all right,' Betty had replied. 'But you should have seen it in its heyday – servants everywhere, no one allowed through the front door unless they had a title to their name. Except for on ball nights, when the hoi polloi were granted access to the house through the front door. I still recall the snooty look on old Lady Tonbridge's face as she saw the great unwashed traipsing across her pristine floor. I'm sure she would have stopped it, but Edgar's father was a stickler for tradition and he kept the ball going. I call her "old Lady Tonbridge" but she wasn't old then. She was nobbut a girl when she wed Percival.'

Stevie had looked at Betty out of the corner of her eye, because for a minute there she had sounded quite odd, but

Stevie couldn't put a finger on what it was, and then she'd forgotten all about it when she'd parked the car and they had made their way in through the Grecian columns of the porch and into the impressive hall.

Two staircases, one either side, dominated the space and sounds of laughter and music swirled out from the double doors which led to the enormous ballroom in which Stevie now stood. Julia Ferris was mingling, playing the hostess with a younger woman by her side who had her arm looped through that of a bloke, who kept squeezing her bottom.

'Who is that with Lady Tonbridge?' Stevie asked.

'Miranda and her fiancé. Everyone thought she had her sights set on Nick, but apparently not. I don't see William though, but I expect he's around here somewhere, because I can't see Julia letting her son get away with not attending the family ball.'

'I wonder where Tia is,' Stevie said, thoughts of William leading her to think of her new friend.

'I can't see her.' Leanne was craning her neck, but the crush of people on the dance floor made it difficult to see.

A male voice interrupted them. 'Would you do me the honour?' and Stevie turned to see a man holding his hand out to Leanne.

'Go ahead,' she said, when Leanne looked askance at her. 'I'm a big girl, I don't need babysitting.'

'If you're sure…?'

Stevie laughed. 'Just go, will you. I'm off to the terrace.' She watched Leanne half dance, half walk, her hips swaying in time to the music and she smiled. That girl certainly knew how to have a good time.

Stevie, however, wasn't in quite the same mood, and she'd meant it when she'd said she was going to explore the terrace. A bit of fresh air might perk her up and anyway, it was too lovely an evening to be cooped up inside, so she made her way around the dance floor, weaving between the tuxedoed men and the women in their glorious ball gowns. They reminded her of a flock of pretty birds, and she nodded at everyone, mouthing an occasional "hi there," or "love the dress" as she went.

Oh, this is gorgeous, she thought as she stepped out of one of the wide-open French doors which led to a large terrace dotted with tables and chairs, and strung with coloured fairy lights, and what looked to be hand-made bunting. With the setting sun dropping down over the Brecon Beacons, casting the mountain range into purpled shadows, and the fields below the terrace lit with an orangey glow, the view was breath-taking.

And if she tried hard enough, she could just make out the top of Nick's house.

She stared at it for some considerable time, lost in the memory of the kiss they had shared. Why had he done such a thing if he didn't like her? she wondered. And it had felt so good too, so right, as if she belonged in his arms. For a second she'd really thought they had a connection. Then he had let her go and apologised and she'd never felt so rejected in all her life.

Oh, for goodness' sake, stop it, she told herself. He doesn't want you, he's made that abundantly clear, so just move on. Put that one insignificant little kiss behind you and let it go.

Then she snorted. It was all right to tell her brain that, but what about her heart? That particular part of her didn't seem to be getting the message, because all it did was flutter whenever she thought about him.

'So, stop thinking about him,' she said aloud, then clapped her hands to her mouth. Lordy, she was beginning to turn into Aunt Peggy. She already had the cat – all she needed was a couple more and to start wearing some of Betty's cast offs.

Feeling rather out of sorts, Stevie decided to go for a stroll. She had no idea which parts of the house were out of bounds, but she'd wander as far as she could. She'd like to go for a walk in the gardens, but from where she was standing the steps leading down from the terrace were quite steep and the paths were uneven – these shoes were definitely not made for walking (and maybe not even for dancing, because her feet were killing her already), so instead, she returned to the ballroom and skirted around the edge again until she reached one of the doors on the opposite wall.

The first one she tried led into a sort of drawing room, with chairs set around tables, which were laid out with decks of cards or chess sets, or backgammon. Not that she played any of them, although she used to enjoy a game of Snap when she was little. There was even a big table with the most enormous jigsaw puzzle in the world spread out on it. The puzzle was half completed, and a handwritten sign saying, "give it a go, just don't lose any of the pieces" was next to it. Stevie let out a giggle – how awful if someone were to hide a piece.

The room was already half-full of people (elderly men, mostly) wanting a quieter spot away from the music, laughter, and dancing of the ballroom, but it wasn't quite quiet enough for Stevie. Seeing a door to the left of the fireplace, she headed towards it and found herself in a library.

'Ooh, I really could lose myself in here for a week!' she said to herself. Looking at the ceiling-high shelves crammed with books, 'and just look at those cute little ladders.' She squinted at them – they were on casters, and she had a vision of scooting from corner to corner on one of them. What fun!

All four walls had bookshelves on them, and there was another fireplace and another door opposite the one she had just come through. Was there any room in this huge house which wasn't connected to another one? Stevie wondered.

Thankfully, this room was empty and Stevie closed the door leading to the games room and sank carefully down into one of the wing-backed chairs near the fireplace, arranging her skirt at her feet. She wasn't really in the mood for reading (and it wouldn't look too good either, having been invited to the party of the year and hiding away with her nose in a book), so she took a minute or two to reflect on her turbulent feelings.

There was no doubt she had fallen for Nick, but the question was, what was she going to do about it? The feelings had crept up on her so slowly she hadn't realised until they'd ambushed her. The kiss had been the catalyst.

Oh, how she wished they hadn't done it. That one brief embrace had turned her world upside down and she didn't know how to right it again.

The sound of voices came from beyond the door near her chair and she wondered what room lay behind it? She'd already seen the ballroom, the games room, the library, and she had a suspicion there were loads more nooks and crannies to explore in this old house.

The voices grew a little louder and for a while she ignored them, until she heard Betty's unmistakeable tones.

'Grr, I could bang your heads together, I could! You're nobbut a pair of eejits.'

Stevie wondered who the "pair of eejits" were.

Ah, Betty was talking to Tia, Stevie guessed when she heard her friend's voice. It was muffled, so she couldn't hear exactly what Tia was saying, but whatever it was set Betty off a treat.

'Don't be so selfish!' the old lady cried. 'Can't you see he loves you, no matter what?'

Will was there too, Stevie realised when he said, 'If you move, I'm going to move, too.' His deeper voice carried better than Tia's.

'See?' Betty said loudly. 'You can't get rid of love so easily.'

Tia said something else and Stevie almost growled with frustration when she couldn't make out the words.

'No, you're not,' Betty cried. 'You're wallowing in self-pity and woe-is-me. You gotta grab love with both hands and not let it go. Take it from someone who knows.'

More low voices, then Betty said, 'I might be an old maid, but how do you think I got to be in this position, eh? Because I slunk away and didn't fight for the man I loved and he didn't fight for me, that's how. If you carry on, my girl, you'll end up just like me.'

Suddenly Will's voice became much clearer, as if he was standing right by the door and was about to walk through it. Stevie cringed back in her seat and tried to look as though she hadn't really been listening. There was a book on the side table next to her chair and she picked it up hastily, opening it at random.

'I'm not going to let you go, Tia,' William said. 'I love you too much for that. Please don't make me come with you.'

Then Tia said something and Will replied, 'I don't care. I love you and I want to marry you, and if I've got to follow you to the ends of the earth, then I will.'

More muffled words and Stevie held her breath again, willing Tia to see sense. She wished Nick loved her the way Will obviously loved Tia and her eyes filled with tears. Poor Will, she could hear the anguish in his voice and it tore at her heart.

Finally, just when she thought Betty's haranguing hadn't worked, there was a loud, 'Yes!' from William, followed by a shriek from Betty.

When the door was flung open, William shot through it, only to dart straight back through it again. Stevie craned her neck around the back of the chair and a huge grin spread across her face as she saw him bend down to kiss Tia soundly, then dash back out once more yelling, 'I've got to tell Dad!'

Stevie drank in Tia's ecstatic face, and she blinked away more tears. The girl looked happy and beautiful and radiant, Stevie was very happy for her.

She just wished she could be as happy. As Nick's handsome face popped into her mind, she let the treacherous tears fall.

Chapter 45

'I've got to find Nick,' Tia was saying. 'I want him to hear it from me, first.' But she'd no sooner spoken than Will was back yet again, kissing her once more before dashing around to the back of her chair and pushing her through the library and out the other side, towards the ballroom. His smile was so wide it threatened to split his face in two, Stevie observed.

Betty followed closely behind, dusting her hands together. 'Two down, two to go,' she muttered, letting the pair of them rush ahead. It was then she spotted Stevie trying to hide in her chair. 'Heard all that, did you?' she demanded.

Stevie gave her a sheepish grin. 'Erm, yes. Sorry.'

Betty shrugged. 'Doesn't matter. Everyone will know by the end of the night, anyway.'

There was a long pause as the two women stared at each other.

Stevie had a question and although it wasn't any of her business, she couldn't help saying, 'I don't think you're an old maid. My Aunt Peggy never married.'

'Did she want to?'

'I don't know.'

'I did. I would have given everything to get married – I did give everything, but it wasn't enough.' The sorrow in the elderly lady's voice cut Stevie to the quick. 'I just didn't want those two to go through what me and Percival went through. Such a waste…'

Percival? Stevie had heard that name before, and recently too. Tonight, in fact. And the name had come from Betty's own lips. That couldn't be a coincidence, could it?

'Percival? Not the same Percival who is Will's grandfather?' Stevie asked.

Betty walked to the chair next to Stevie and sat down heavily, the lines on her face more prominent than she had ever seen them. She worried at her bottom lip with her teeth and stared into the empty fireplace. 'The very same,' she confirmed.

'You and this Percival were in love?'

Betty shrugged her thin shoulders, then nodded slowly.

'What happened?' Stevie asked gently.

'It was different back in them days. I was a nobody and he was the heir to all this.' Betty waved a hand at the room. 'His father wanted him to marry some duchess or another; he wanted to marry me. We met when I was working in that hotel down south and I know this is corny, but it was love at first sight for both of us. But I wasn't rich enough and he wasn't strong enough. His father said no and Percy couldn't stand up to him.' She laughed sadly. 'Neither of us had any money, so even if we had married, we'd have had nothing to live on.'

'But Percival must have been rich,' Stevie exclaimed.

'Nah. None of them were. His father was land-rich and cash-poor, and Percy didn't have a bean to his name. All the money was tied up in land and property and none of it was his anyway. He was going to come into some funds eventually, but not until the ripe age of thirty, and when his father told him he would disown him, he caved.'

'That's so sad. But, couldn't you have managed somehow?'

Betty shook her head firmly. 'On what? He was a lord's son, and that hardly equipped any man for a life of proper work in those days. He had less chance of getting a job than a convict. At least a convict might have some skills, like safe-breaking, or sheep rustling. No,' she said. 'I was the one with the job, but what would happen when the babies came along? Who would keep a roof over our heads and food on the table then?'

Stevie's heart went out to her friend. 'How long ago was this?' Betty was making it sound as though it was in the dark ages. Betty was somewhere in her early eighties, wasn't she? Surely things couldn't have been so different then.

'In the late sixties,' Betty said. 'And I know what you're thinking, but the sixties didn't happen around here, and especially not to the aristocracy. They've stayed the same for generations.'

Surely Betty and Percival could have worked something out, for love? Love was worth it, wasn't it? Look at what Betty had done for Tia and William.

'I regret not fighting harder for him,' Betty said, as if she had read Stevie's mind. 'And for a while I hated him for not giving everything up for me, almost as much as I loved him.' Her old hands stroked her dress, her fingers sliding over the material, her expression wistful. 'I moved here to Tanglewood to be near to him,' she said. 'He never knew I was so close.'

'Oh, that's so sad.' Tears again brimmed in Stevie's eyes, threatening to spill over.

Betty continued to stare into the fire, her own eyes dry, lost in the past. 'I came to a summer ball once, hoping to see him. It was the year before Percival was married. He wasn't here. Apparently, he was in London with his new fiancée. His father announced the engagement during the ball. I haven't been to one since.'

'You wore the dress you have on now, didn't you?' Stevie asked, with sudden insight.

Betty's lips curled into a wry smile. 'I did. I've no idea why I kept it.'

'Thank you for coming to this one. It must be very hard for you, with all those memories.'

'It had to be done. I knew Tia was going to be here, and I hoped William would be too. He's a fine young man, and he loves her to bits. All it took was a push from me to make Tia see it doesn't matter to him whether she's in a wheelchair or not. He loves her, all of her, every part of her, exactly as she is.'

At this point, Stevie really did cry.

Chapter 46

Stevie didn't want to dance; her heart was too heavy. Although she was delighted for Tia and William, Betty's story was very sad. And Stevie was sad for herself as well. But one kiss did not a relationship make, and she really should man-up and get on with things. It wasn't as if she and Nick had even dated. Not once.

So why did she feel so bereft?

The ballroom was a swirling mass of dancing, music, and noise, but Stevie felt somewhat disconnected from it all. Everyone seemed happy, except for her, and she could hardly bear to see all those smiling, laughing faces, despite being privy to the fantastic news about Tia and William.

And to add insult to injury, Stevie spotted Allegra and her husband throwing some shapes on the dance-floor. She hadn't forgotten the awful reviews the damned woman and her cronies had left on TripAdvisor. In fact, there was one of those friends now, the one called Bev, standing a few feet away from her. Stevie stared at her, wondering what could possess someone to be so mean, especially when that person had clearly enjoyed the free samples she'd been given. The others had enjoyed them too, except for Allegra, who had refused to taste any of them.

When the vindictive woman caught Stevie's eye, she looked away quickly, a blush spreading up from her neck and onto her cheeks.

'Yeah, she should look sheepish after what she did,' Cassandra said, appearing at Stevie's side and giving her a squeeze. 'Don't let them get to you.'

'It's not me I'm worried about, it's the damage those reviews can do to the tea shop. Luckily the locals know better, but think of all the tourists and hikers who might fancy popping into Tanglewood for a spot of lunch or a cake and a coffee – if they check out the reviews…' Stevie bit her lip, trying not to cry again. She'd been looking forward to this evening, and now she was heartily wishing she hadn't stepped foot in the place.

She sighed and her gaze wandered towards the main doors, feeling more miserable than ever, when she spied Nick walk into the ballroom, his head turning, scanning the crowd. For a second, her heart lifted but it sank again just as fast when she realised it probably wasn't her he was searching for.

Stevie's gaze dropped to the floor and she wondered how soon she could leave and whether she could persuade Betty to come with her – otherwise she would be obliged to stay, because she didn't want to leave the old lady on her own when Lord and Lady Tonbridge announced their son's engagement. The comparison between the two announcements so many years apart, made Stevie feel like crying all over again. With the first, Betty had her heart broken, and here was the old lady, decades later, part of yet another engagement announcement at another ball. It must be bitter-sweet for her, Stevie thought.

She looked around for Betty but couldn't spot her in the crowd and she vowed to go and find her as soon as the announcement was made.

'I know you've been encouraging my daughter to eat that rubbish you sell,' a voice shouted in her ear, making Stevie jump.

Bloody hell, it was Allegra. Wonderful, just wonderful. As if Stevie didn't have enough on her mind tonight…

She took a deep breath, not wanting to get into an argument.

Cassandra had other ideas, though, and Stevie let her breath out in a whoosh when her friend waded in. 'You're not going to close Stevie down, not like you did The Coffee Pot. We won't let you.'

'We? Who is we?' Allegra's tone was scornful. 'You and that old biddy who now work there? You would say that, wouldn't you? You're both as bad as her, selling food laden with fat and sugar. Huh, that stuff shouldn't be called food at all.'

Stevie stood rooted to the spot, wishing the ground would open up and swallow her whole. She was mortified and furious at the same time.

'Not everyone agrees with you,' Cassandra retorted. She tapped the arm of the person standing next to her. 'Mrs Evans, do you think Peggy's Tea Shoppe serves unhealthy food?'

'No, I do not!' came the emphatic reply. 'Something nice now and again does you the world of good.'

'See?' Cassandra said. 'Alfie Powell comes in every morning for a slice of cake to take to work with him. Avril Edwards,' she nodded at a woman standing a few feet away, who shuffled close enough to join in the conversation.

318

'Do you want to see Stevie closed down?' Cassandra asked her.

'Definitely not. I loves Stevie's cakes, I do. Where else would I get such yummy gluten-free chocolate cake?'

'What about the rats?' Allegra demanded her arms folded across her narrow chest and a defiant look on her face.

'There are no rats,' Cassandra replied, promptly.

'There most certainly are!' Allegra retorted. 'I know what I saw and it was definitely a rat.'

'What did it look like?' Cassandra asked.

Allegra held her hands out, about a foot apart. 'It was this big, as black as night and it had a long tail—'

'Furry?' Cassandra interjected.

Allegra huffed. 'Of course, it was furry. I don't think you get many bald rats.'

'I meant the tail.'

'Um, yes, I suppose it was. And thick, too. Nasty it was!' Allegra shuddered dramatically.

'Then I can categorically say you didn't see a rat. You saw Peggy, Stevie's cat.' Cassandra was triumphant.

Allegra opened and closed her mouth, but nothing came out.

'So, Allegra, are you going to remove those ridiculous reviews or not?' Cassandra wanted to know.

'Well, are you?' Leanne asked from behind Stevie, and Stevie turned to give her friend a grateful smile.

'Stevie is a big part of this village and I, for one, am not going to stand by and watch her business go down the pan because you've got a thing about healthy eating,' Leanne ploughed on. 'Anyway, your measly review doesn't make the slightest bit of difference.' She held up her phone, turning it so Allegra could see the screen. 'Ninety-six five-star ratings!'

Allegra screwed her mouth up until it resembled a cat's bottom, and turned to walk away.

'And another thing,' Cassandra called after her. 'Your review and those of your friends have been reported to TripAdvisor and taken down. So, stick that in your celery stick and smoke it!'

Stevie watched her nemesis stalk out of the door, lost for words. Had she just imagined it, or had Allegra Johnson been well and truly trumped.

'Let me see that,' Stevie demanded, grabbing Cassandra's phone. She scrolled, her eyes wide as she recognised some of the photos. 'That's what they were doing!' she exclaimed. 'Did you put my customers up to this?'

'All I did was tell them what had happened and that if they didn't do something, Peggy's Tea Shoppe was in danger of closing down.'

'You did this for me?' Tears welled in Stevie's eyes, and she blinked hard.

'We can't let our favourite baker go bust, now can we?' Cassandra said. 'You're one of us now and we stick up for our own.'

For the third time that evening, Stevie let her tears fall, but this time they were happy ones. More or less. Now, if only she could get Nick Saunders to notice her…

She had to find Betty and tell her the good news. Stevie hadn't spotted her in the crowded ballroom, so she made her way through the dancers and out into the hall.

She spied Betty talking to a gaggle of elderly ladies.

'Betty, Betty, you'll never guess—' she exclaimed as she reached her friend's side.

'Nick Saunders has admitted he loves you?' Betty asked, hopefully.

'*What?* No!'

'But you wish he had?'

'Yes, but…'

'And you love him?'

'Yes. Er… no. Bugger!' Stevie stamped her foot. 'Look, stop it, that's not what I want to tell you.'

'Do you love him?' Betty persisted.

'Yes, but—'

Betty glanced over Stevie's shoulder and smiled. Stevie stopped talking, her eyes widened, and she turned around, snail-slow. Damn Betty.

Nick was standing right behind her, as she had guessed he would be. Her face flamed as she realised he'd probably overheard her admitting she wanted him to say he loved her and that she was in love with him, because his jaw hardened and his eyes narrowed. Great.

She turned her attention back to Betty, lifted her chin, and said, 'Thanks to Cassandra, Allegra Johnson's nasty review has been taken down.'

Betty whooped and gave her a high five. Stevie risked a quick glance at Nick, who was grinning at her.

'What did she do?' Betty asked Stevie. 'Threaten her with a sugar cube?'

'She only went and got the whole village to come into the café to try our cakes, and asked them to post a good review if they enjoyed it,' Stevie said.

'That explains why we've been so busy these last few days,' Betty said, then turned to Nick. 'What do you think of Tia and William's news?'

'Pardon?'

Stevie nudged Betty hard with her elbow and almost pushed the old lady over. Betty bit her lip and looked guiltily at the floor.

'What's going on?' Nick asked, his gaze going from one to the other and back again.

'Nothing,' Stevie and Betty chanted in unison.

'There you are!' William appeared out of the crowd and dashed up to Nick. 'I've been looking everywhere for you. Tia wants you. We've got some news.' William was positively hopping with excitement and happiness. He was bouncing on the balls of his feet and his grin was wide enough to steer a canal boat through sideways.

'What news?' Nick's expression was wary.

'Tia wants to tell you herself,' William said, practically jogging on the spot.

Nick turned to Stevie and Betty. 'You know what this is about, don't you?'

Stevie nodded, not trusting herself to speak in case she let the cat out of the bag.

A slow smile started to spread across his face. 'Is it what I think it is?' he asked.

'Tia doesn't want anyone else to tell you that we're getting marr— oops!' William grimaced and gave the women an apologetic smile.

'You'd better go with him,' Stevie advised Nick, 'before he gets himself into any more trouble.'

She watched a bemused Nick being led away, but before he'd taken more than a couple of steps, he stopped and turned to look at her. 'Wait for me?' he mouthed, his eyes full of promise, and her heart did a slow flip.

She nodded. She would wait for him forever if she had to.

Chapter 47

Stevie and Betty were sitting on the terrace a short while later, the soft, warm night illuminated by the fairy lights and a low-hanging full moon. It glowed a yellow-orange, and Stevie thought it was probably one of the most romantic sights she had ever seen.

They had the terrace to themselves – everyone else was in the ballroom, drinking the champagne that had been brought out on silver platters when Tia and William's engagement was announced. Stevie and Betty had stayed to toast the happy couple, but Stevie was acutely aware of Betty standing at her side with tears in her eyes. So, as soon as it was polite, she suggested they sit on the terrace for a while to get some fresh air. Stevie had also been acutely conscious of Nick, standing behind his sister and wearing a stunned expression. He did look incredibly happy, though, just a bit shocked.

'It's been a fairly successful evening,' Stevie said. 'What with Tia and William, and Allegra's awful review removed.' Stevie had checked, and confirmed that the others had been taken down, too.

'You'll be keeping me on, then,' Betty said.

Stevie bit back a smile. 'I am, am I?'

'You'll have to.'

'How do you work that out?' She was totally planning on Betty continuing to work in the café for as long as the old lady wanted to and felt up to it, but she was having fun, gently teasing her friend. 'Because of all the new customers?'

'Because Cassandra is pregnant,' Betty announced.

'She never said!' Stevie's mouth dropped open for about the twentieth time that evening.

'That's because she doesn't know yet.'

Stevie darted her a swift look. 'And you do? How?'

'I just know these things.'

'Like you just knew Tia and William were in love?'

'Exactly! Cassandra will have to stop work to have the baby at some point, so are you going to give me a proper job, or what?'

Stevie reached out to pat Betty's hand. 'It's yours if you want it, for as long as you want it. You're a damned fine baker.'

'I know.' Betty smirked.

Stevie let out a laugh. The old woman was incorrigible and she opened her mouth to tell her so, when her attention was caught by a figure leaning against one of the French doors. He was studying her with such intensity it stole her breath. Betty followed Stevie's gaze.

'Righto, I think that's my cue to leave,' the old woman said, levering herself out of the chair with a grunt.

Stevie nodded absently, unable to take her eyes off Nick. To be fair, he seemed unable to stop staring at her, either.

They stayed that way for several long seconds, then slowly, oh, so slowly, Nick straightened up and ambled across the terrace. He seemed to be in no hurry. It was as if he had all the time in the world, but Stevie wished he would get a move on. She was desperate to hear why he had wanted her to wait.

She got to her feet and waited nervously for him to approach, butterflies doing somersaults in her stomach and her heart thumping so fast and so loudly she felt certain he must be able to hear it.

'Are you pleased?' she asked, when he reached her. He was standing so close she could smell his cologne and the heady masculine scent of him.

'Very.'

He took hold of her hands and pulled her closer, until she came up against his muscular chest.

'Me, too. They make a lovely couple. Have they decided on a date? I expect they'll have the wedding here, it's really lovely, and a perfect venue, and—'

Stevie stopped talking. She had no choice, because Nick had gathered her into his arms, and his lips were on hers and he was kissing her soundly.

She melted into him, letting the kiss sweep her along, until she was almost faint and giddy with it. At some point, he tore himself away long enough to murmur, 'I love you,' before he claimed her lips once more.

He loves me, her heart sang, and she found herself with tears of pure joy trickling down her face. He loves me!

When they finally pulled apart, Nick gazed down into her eyes, the emotion shining in his stealing her breath. Gently, he stroked one damp cheek, then the other, and smiled down at her.

'I love you, too,' she whispered. She had never felt more certain about anything in her life. Being in his arms, being held by him, felt right, it was as though they had been made for each other.

He continued to gaze into her eyes, his lips inches from her own, and asked, 'Can I take you out to dinner?'

'I'd love you to,' she replied and before she could say any more, his mouth was on hers again, his kiss tasting of love and the future.

Their love and their future, *together.*